Tell Me How You Really Feel

Tell Me How You Really Feel

Aminah Mae Safi

Feiwel and Friends

New York

A FEIWEL AND FRIENDS BOOK
An Imprint of Macmillan Publishing Group, LLC
175 Fifth Avenue, New York, NY 10010.

TELL ME HOW YOU REALLY FEEL. Copyright © 2019 by Aminah Mae Safi.
All rights reserved. Printed in the United States of America.

Our books may be purchased in bulk for promotional, educational, or business use.
Please contact your local bookseller or the Macmillan Corporate and Premium
Sales Department at (800) 221-7945 ext. 5442 or by email at
MacmillanSpecialMarkets@macmillan.com.

Library of Congress Control Number: 2018955766

ISBN 978-1-250-29948-2 (hardcover) / ISBN 978-1-250-29949-9 (ebook)

Book design by Liz Dresner
Feiwel and Friends logo designed by Filomena Tuosto
First Edition, 2019
10 9 8 7 6 5 4 3 2 1
Fiercereads.com

For Amy Sherman-Palladino. Thank you for never giving Rory Gilmore a decent boyfriend. She's always had Paris.

Princeton University: Admission Office
P.O. Box 430
110 West College
Princeton, New Jersey, 08544-0430

March 15, 2019

Dear Sana:

Once again, congratulations. We are thrilled to be offering you admission for the Class of 2023. As you applied early admission, we know you are as excited as we are about this splendid news.

As we wrote earlier, you and your parents or guardians are invited to join us for our April hosting program to learn more about Princeton. An invitation is enclosed with our earlier mailing. Our faculty members are interested in meeting you and we hope you can join us.

We are still waiting on your response card, which you need to fill out and return to us with a May 1 postmark.

Sincerely,
Irene McAndrew Malloy
Dean of Admissions

Re: Congratulations!

April 1

30 Days Until Deadline

1

Establishing Shots

—— *Sana* ——

"And, finally, *why you?*"

Sana watched the interviewer. The woman had on a dark, boxy suit and had her hair fixed in a sleek, long bob. She was dressed to blend, to be forgettable. But Sana saw the interviewer's sharp eyes.

Sana smiled—a calculated half smile. "Why me? As opposed to someone else? Look, I know you've got thousands of applicants for this position. Who doesn't want to add *working at a research genetics hospital in rapidly industrializing India* to their future med school application?"

The interviewer nodded. Patient, but unimpressed.

"I've wanted to be a surgeon my whole life. I've practiced stitching with cross-stitch and embroidery since I was ten. I've been playing video games for longer than that. My hand-eye coordination is off the charts, frankly. I've taken every premed class you can take while you're still in high school. I elected to take organic chemistry in my senior year. I've shadowed doctors. I've done internships. I'm, like, a poster child for *doing the most*. My whole life has built up to being a doctor. My whole life."

Sana paused so the woman could give another noncommittal nod.

The walls of this room were a faded slate gray. An intentionally neutral room. A space for evaluating fairly. Aside from the interviews Sana did for summer jobs, every interview room she had ever been in had been similarly painted. Similarly outfitted with beautiful, institutional mahogany furniture.

"But that doesn't make me different. I'm sure all your other applicants feel the same. Have done the same."

The woman nodded again, her sharp eyes a little narrowed, waiting.

Sana had practiced this part alone in her room. Having to admit to herself what she was about to say had been terrifying enough the first time. But in front of another person was something else altogether.

She took a deep breath, ready as she would ever be. "The thing is, I don't know. I don't know what it is to wake up every day and go into a hospital. To actually help people in this way. We didn't have the money growing up for me to take any of those medical mission trips. And even those, they aren't everyday conditions, are they? They're an exceptional week in the life. I want to know what it's like to go into work every day and treat patients. I want to know that the past ten years of my life will be worth the next forty. I guess that makes me kind of bananas. Train to be a doctor, take the big paycheck, kid. That's what my dadu would say. My father, too."

Sana didn't like bringing up her father, but for some reason, he seemed pertinent here. He'd focused on career so much that she only saw him when he came back for birthdays and holidays. And sometimes not even then. Mom was the one who had worked because she'd had to, because she'd had no other options. Her father had thrown himself into his work because he'd wanted to find an honest means to stay away. The interviewer was so focused now that it was nearly impossible to hold eye contact.

But Sana didn't break. "So why me? You know I speak Urdu and Hindi and Bengali. And Farsi, if that matters at all. You know I've got the grades. You probably even know I got into Princeton, even though I turned in my application with you before I'd heard back from them. But honestly, why me? Because I need to know that the future I'm banking on isn't just good in theory. I need to know it's not just good on paper." Sana might have fudged that a little. Urdu *was* Hindi after all. But the interviewer didn't need to know that.

The interviewer bit the inside of her cheek—but Sana wasn't sure if that was to bite back a smile or a grimace. It didn't matter anymore, anyhow. She'd told someone. She'd told the truth, and the truth was the one thing she'd never confessed to anyone. Not to Dadu or Mom. Not to Mamani or even her father.

Sana swallowed. One more hard thing left to say. "I know I'm good at becoming a doctor—the tests and the classes and the science. But I don't know if being a doctor would be a good thing—for me or for my patients. I'd like to figure that out."

"That is, without a doubt, the most selfish answer I have ever heard." But there was no malice in the interviewer's voice. She remained neutral—her tone, her expressions, her manners. She'd clearly been doing this for a long time.

"I know." Sana nodded. "But I thought I'd tell the truth."

The interviewer leaned in, over the clipboard she'd been writing on. "And why on earth would you do that?"

Sana shrugged. "Everything I've gotten in life has been because of hard work and talent and some luck, but mostly this one assumption—that I would be a doctor. I don't want the position on those terms. I want the position knowing I got it, even if I've got doubts."

"And that's your final answer?" The woman looked at her clipboard, then back at Sana. Still unreadable, still inscrutable.

"That's my final answer."

Rachel

Shit. Shit, shit, and double shit. Rachel knew not to say it out loud. Not while the film advisor and photography teacher, Ms. Douga—who everybody just called Douga, even to the teacher's face—was in the room. But she thought it all the same. And the look, Rachel knew, was written all over her face. An open book—that was what her mother had always said. *I can read your face like it was an open book, Rachel.*

It hadn't been a compliment.

A freshman had knocked into the props table, causing a Magic 8 Ball to go toppling off of it. That should have been the end of it, since Magic 8 Balls aren't actually round enough to go rolling around on set. But this one managed a good 270-degree turn before knocking into a light fixture. That should have been steady, too, but one of the crew members must have forgotten to sandbag the base down after Rachel had set the diffuser. The lamp tilted, then wobbled, then went crashing down sideways.

It was like a Rube Goldberg machine from Rachel's own personal hellscape.

"Are you going to help, peabrain, or are you going to sit on your behind all day waiting for me to solve it?" Rachel shrieked. She rushed over, picking the light back up. But it was too late; the soft-focus light she'd balanced with was done for. Her diffuser now had a solid rip down one side.

The freshman she'd addressed startled, then froze. *Wonderful,* thought Rachel. *Another incompetent sent my way.*

"I guess I have to do it myself, just like everything else around here." Rachel was constantly doing things for herself. She couldn't rely on anyone else to actually do a good job.

The freshman—Ryan, she remembered his name was Ryan Ayoub— finally set himself in motion.

"Too late," said Rachel. "You had your chance and you choked. Don't ever mistake me for a patient person, Ryan."

She supposed some people would have just said "freshman" and been done with it. But Rachel knew the importance of names. She knew that it would spur Ryan into better action the next time. Because knowing your name—that was like the Mafia don knowing your family, knowing where you lived. You weren't a faceless screwup. You were an *individual* screwup. You would be remembered the next time.

"Rachel," said Douga. "This isn't boot camp. You don't get to test if everyone's tough enough to handle working with you. Leave the poor kid alone." The tone behind Douga's words—the "Rachel, you should already feel lucky enough to be admitted into these hallowed halls" speech—was familiar enough.

Rachel didn't even flinch when she heard *that* anymore.

"Not if he can't do his job properly." But Rachel wasn't trying to scare Ryan—or anyone—away, not really. He needed to learn, the way she'd had to learn. The way they'd throw you into the deep end on a real set. Rachel couldn't make anyone unhirable. The worst she could do was yell at someone. This was an industry where people lost jobs over not stapling paper at the correct forty-five-degree angle.

Rachel was being positively gentle.

She was shooting the film in color, for God's sake. There had to be continuity. This wasn't some accidentally satirical Ed Wood kind of feature. Rachel would bet cold hard cash that nobody ever gave Tarantino this kind of shit on set. Rachel hated Tarantino, but at least he got respect from the people he worked with. Rachel knew she was supposed to calm down; knew she'd been told to calm down on many an occasion. But she wasn't blowing a fuse over something minor. She didn't actually care where the props table was set up or how much people talked between takes. This was about the colors that the camera was picking up. This was about lighting continuity.

White balancing was *important*.

"The white balance isn't *that* off." Douga wasn't just the photography teacher and the cinematic advisor for the Royce School. She was a natural-born peacemaker. A smooth talker. That's what the head of a department had to be, when they dealt with the kinds of parents and administrators that Douga dealt with.

Douga's tone gave Rachel the sensation that she only got Douga's attention as much as she did because she'd become a real pain in the ass. Rachel watched the faces of her crew as Douga's words landed. Rachel was losing them. Maybe she'd already lost them. She'd probably never had them.

"It's off." Rachel found the balancing board, then she shoved it in Ryan's hand. "Do you think you can manage holding this still?"

He nodded meekly. Better than she'd expected out of him, honestly. Rachel adjusted the camera efficiently. The soft, muted tones she wanted for the piece were what people might call seventies inspired, or Wes Anderson–esque. But to Rachel, they were an homage to Sofia Coppola. Her viewers were going to be haunted, à la *The Virgin Suicides*. But she couldn't do that if the balance was off from the start. She couldn't do that if the lighting changed within a scene *for no reason*. Postproduction could only correct so much. One more adjustment, one more twisting knob. Perfect. The balance was perfect.

The scene, on the other hand, was far from it. The sophomore she'd cast as Helen of Troy wasn't performing half as strong as she had been in auditions back in September. The props looked ridiculous, and the entire premise, Rachel realized, was falling apart because of it. Not that Rachel was blaming the props master, per se.

As the director, the burden of the credit—and failure—of a production fell to her. But these details were taking the scene from raw and honest to camp. And not the good kind of camp, not the intentional kind. The shitty kind that led to the creation of shows like *Mystery Science Theater 3000*. Rachel would not make a cinematic production that belonged on *Mystery Science Theater 3000*. Rachel was going to make art, goddammit.

Allison Heron—the girl playing Helen—called out "line" for the fifth time that day; Rachel had enough.

"Cut," she said. Mostly for herself. Mostly to calm her frayed patience, which, as she had informed Ryan, was thin on its best days. "That's a wrap. Everyone, go home. I need to do some massive rewrites. Don't bother coming back, Allison."

Allison looked like she was about to cry. Douga put her head in her hands. This was not, as everyone new to the set could tell, an unusual occurrence for Rachel.

Rachel instructed Ryan on how to pack up the lighting and sound equipment. She herself took apart the camera, piece by piece. She wound the cords efficiently, neatly. It was sacrosanct, this ritual. Nobody else could be entrusted with the equipment. It was too valuable, too precious. The money was one part of it—Royce had shelled out a good deal of it for the camera alone. But it was more than that. Directors should understand how to handle their own equipment. They shouldn't just let their lackeys and crew members on set do all the labor. Directors ought to understand all the jobs they were effectively managing. They ought to respect that they were captains of a ship and needed to be able to do even the smallest tasks.

Douga stopped about a foot away. "Rachel."

"It's just wrong," said Rachel—cutting Douga off—with her signature whine in her voice. She hated that whine. Made her sound like Mickey Rooney, complaining that the newfangled movies had gone to the dogs. But Rachel could never keep the tone out of her voice. Acting had never been her forte. Everything she was feeling came out and came through, in whatever she was doing. "I know it's wrong. I thought this would be believable but it's far from it."

"You don't know that from one hour of shoots, Rachel," said Douga. "You haven't even seen the dailies."

Rachel didn't need dailies, not on this one. She could see it in her mind—the shoot was already totally derailed. Again. Between the lighting and her piss-poor lead, she'd have to reshoot it all. True, she'd already gotten her application materials in, so none of this counted toward college admissions or scholarships. But Rachel had chosen to do an independent study as her final send-off from school.

Her last semester.

Rachel looked her advisor dead in the eye. "I know what makes a good film. I know when it's right. And this, all of this. It's just wrong. None of it works. None of it's believable. None of it makes you want to take that leap of faith. It's just bad." Rachel picked up what was supposed to be a light diffuser but was actually just a cheap paper lantern and threw it on the floor. Not in a rage. Not in a tantrum. Just to show how easily the illusion shattered.

"Nothing on set is built to last, Rachel," said Douga, and then, even lower, so only Rachel could hear, "We need to talk."

Before Rachel could argue, Douga turned to the room at large. "Good job, everyone. When you're done, I want to have everyone meet in the film lab."

Douga shot Rachel a pointed look. She was probably regretting putting Rachel in charge, even if Rachel was a second-semester senior. Probably thinking about what a control freak Rachel was. Probably thinking what a waste it had been, giving this shoot to her, giving this spot to a kid with a chip on her shoulder.

Except they both knew Rachel was good. Honestly, she was better than good. She was going to go to NYU—as long as the scholarship money came through—and she was going to be a filmmaker, damn them all and their horrible nicknames for her. Rachel was bossy, it was true. She was controlling. But she was good. She was so fucking good. And even if she made them hate working for her, they had to acknowledge that. That she had talent and a drive that couldn't be matched. She had a vision, goddammit. She wouldn't let Ryan or Allison or even Douga get in the way of that.

Douga turned her attention back toward Rachel now that everyone had left set. "I gave you the benefit of the doubt last winter when you said you needed an extension on your project. You said you wanted to make a full ninety-minute pilot that you could workshop around. I believed you were capable of it."

Douga paused, and it was the worst pause of Rachel's life because she knew it was a giant, unsaid "but" to everything that had come before it.

"Now it's April. You've got no pilot. No movie. Not even a five-minute short to turn in. You've got two semesters' worth of credits that you *need to graduate*. If you cannot produce something, *literally anything*, by the end of this month, I'm going to have to report you to NYU."

Rachel sputtered. "What?"

"I'm sorry, Rachel. It's my job. I can't in good conscience tell them you finished an amazing project I wrote you *a letter of recommendation for* if you can't get it across the finish line. You've gotten so many opportunities. More than one second chance on this alone. Do something with it. You've got until your showcase on May first."

Rachel watched as Douga walked away, carrying the promise of Rachel's dreams, her scholarship money, her college admissions in her wake.

Rachel packed away the camera and she slung her messenger bag over her shoulder. She could deal with this project. She could deal with lugging this equipment across campus all by herself. She could deal with being called into the principal's office to have a discussion about morals and values and upholding the Royce model of behavior again and again at a school she certainly never belonged at—because that's what the Royce School was, a school Rachel attended but didn't belong at—and be lectured on what an opportunity was, and not burning bridges down when she got them. She'd learned to nod meekly and apologize. It was the only time Rachel could find any meekness inside of herself. But she'd learned to do it. To bite her tongue then, to bide her time.

She could even deal with another lecture from Douga.

What she couldn't deal with, what she refused to deal with, was this final project being anything less than spectacular. It was going to be better than good. It was going to be the best. Her work and her passion and her obsessive control were going to take her places, the way it took boys places. She wasn't going to end up stuck editing local TV for the rest of her life.

No, Rachel Consuela Recht was getting out, and she'd claw her way there if she had to.

2

Never Let Go

Sana

Sana slipped out of the interview room. She was on the far end of the Royce School's campus, and she'd scheduled herself for the last interview of the day on purpose. There was nobody to run into her, nobody to see her leave.

Nobody who knew she was considering deferring from Princeton for a year. Nobody who knew that she hadn't put down her deposit yet.

Sana hunched her shoulders slightly. She could hear the way her grandmother, Mamani, would fuss at her about posture. She could practically feel Mamani's fingers pinching her shoulder blades. Only Mamani could manage to convincingly nag someone when she wasn't even around. But Sana persisted in her slump. Once she got farther away from the room, she'd relax her shoulders and straighten her back.

Sana made her way out of the building, out into the early spring sunshine. It was the kind of day Los Angeles was famous for—sunny, but not hot. Blue skies and a small breeze. Sana inhaled—dust and smog and the faintest hint of eucalyptus. She dropped her shoulders, repositioned her backpack.

She'd done it.

She'd interviewed for a year abroad and nobody had found out. She probably wouldn't get it. The competition to work in a genetics hospital—actually work, not just file paperwork or shadow a doctor— was fierce. But she'd done it all the same. Without anyone being the wiser.

Including Mom. Including Princeton.

Sana had taken a few more steps when she caught sight of a figure moving across the lawn, weighted down with several cases and bags. Sana froze for a moment, watching.

Rachel Recht.

She must have been carrying camera equipment. That's what all those bags and cases were. Sana squinted, just to be sure; it really was her. Rachel Recht, a film student so extraordinary that she was granted a scholarship plus special filming privileges within the high-walled hedges of the Royce School. Rachel Recht, who was the kind of girl who vibrated *going places* and *doing things* and *get out of my way already*.

Rachel Recht, who had hated Sana with every fiber of her being since they had met in October of their freshman year.

Sana knew she needed to unstick herself from this position before Rachel noticed her staring. She'd learned to turn away, to not look at Rachel for as long as she wanted to, over the years. Learned that Rachel sneered at her whenever she caught Sana looking. So Sana tried her best to ignore Rachel. Ignore her own urge to look. Ignore the way her heartbeat kicked up a notch. That was just the leftover thrill from having finished her interview, anyway. Sana grabbed both of her backpack straps and pulled, willing herself to turn away and keep moving.

And that's when everything went haywire.

Sana watched in slow motion as Rachel tripped over something. A sprinkler head popping out from the field. Rachel began to stumble, all that equipment still in her hands. She was either going to land on the equipment and do some serious damage to some expensive cameras, or the cameras were going to land on Rachel and do some serious—

and likely as expensive—damage to her. Somehow, Rachel missed both as she came crashing down onto the ground.

But Sana was in motion and halfway to Rachel before she realized she was running. And by the time she realized what she was doing, realized she was running, it was too late to second-guess herself. She slammed chest first into Rachel, just as Rachel had recovered and was standing back up again.

Sana tried to catch Rachel, she honestly did. But Rachel clawed the entire way down and the two went tumbling over each other. Sana landed on top of Rachel, her arms on either side of the girl's head, their skulls millimeters from cracking into each other. Sana breathed heavily, her legs tangled in between Rachel's.

Holy Hades.

Sana ignored the jolt she felt at the touch. She buried the thrill down deep, easily covered by the choreographed stiffness with which Sana had to hold her body in that moment. Rachel was all softness, her years spent behind a camera rather than on any athletic field. Sana supposed Rachel's arms had muscle from her time spent hauling all of that camera equipment. But everything pressed up against Sana right now was so, so soft.

It was dizzying. And it was terrible. Sana had never wanted to know that Rachel's hair smelled like pineapple shampoo or that she had faint freckles across her tan cheeks. Didn't need the knowledge that Rachel didn't have pierced ears—they were small and unmarked. That would just make all those daydreams Sana had to tamp down on so much more *vivid.*

"Get off of me," said Rachel, her tone at once righteous and imperious and every one of the worst kinds of -ouses that Rachel could probably muster.

Sana reeled backward. She should have been used to it by now, but she wasn't. She lifted herself off of Rachel—efficiently enough so that Rachel wouldn't have further cause to yell at her for lack of speed, but not so quickly as to possibly jostle Rachel in the process. Rachel got up immediately. And then, without warning, Rachel shrieked. Sana rushed forward, to see if Rachel had hurt her leg and needed support standing. She held her arms out to Rachel's, but the girl slapped Sana's arms away. The sting in her forearms chased away any lingering heat left in Sana's limbs.

It was probably better that way. *Remember this sting, not the pineapple shampoo.*

"Stay away from me, you incompetent purveyor of benevolent sexism!" Rachel shoved her, then she ran toward where her camera case had fallen.

That's when Sana saw it. The latch to the pelican case must not have been secured. The camera had come tumbling out of it. She covered her mouth with her hand.

Oh no. "I'm so sorry. Do you need help?"

"Stay. Back." This, Sana knew, was Rachel's most authoritarian tone. There was probably only one tiny thread of control left to keep Rachel from a full-blown meltdown.

The lens in Rachel's hand looked fine, but Sana saw the body of the camera. A huge crack ran down the front, on the right-hand side. It was probably cosmetic. Hopefully. Sana stayed still and quiet.

Rachel placed the lens into the pelican case. Then she caught sight of the camera. She whimpered, picking up the camera body gently. She looked up to sneer directly at Sana. "Look what you did. Oh my God, just look."

Sana took a step backward. *This was all her fault.* "I'm really sorry."

Rachel was scrambling with equipment and taking stock of the damage Sana had unwittingly caused. "Oh, good. So long as you're sorry. Jesus. You nearly destroyed the camera. You're lucky this is just a crack in the plastic that hopefully doesn't affect any of the actual mechanism or mounting functions. You're lucky you don't have to explain this damage to the head of the photography department, like I do."

"I'll go explain what happened." Sana didn't want to have to do it—resented that she'd listened to her own instincts and tried to help Rachel in the first place—but she wouldn't run away from the consequences of her own stupidity. This was why Sana made plans and to-do lists and action items. She had to counter bad instincts. Instincts that had her running over to Rachel. Instincts that were trouble.

"Don't bother." Rachel snorted.

But, despite the meanness and the tension flying between them, Sana acted on instinct again. She reached out and touched Rachel's arm. It was almost like she couldn't help it.

Rachel wrenched her arm away from Sana's touch. "In your dreams, Khan."

The two girls stood there, locked in that moment, by bitterness and memory and, for Sana, no small amount of longing. Then the grass rustled—and around the corner stepped Nashville Harrison, his hair still wet from the pool. He took in the tension between Sana and Rachel and he froze.

Everyone called the boy Diesel and had been doing it for so long that few people ever thought to ask why anymore. Diesel was a water polo player and the kind of guy people jokingly called a golden god, because between the athletics and the bleached-out hair and the deep tan, that's what the dude looked like. But he was Sana's friend and had been since the beginning. Though even Sana didn't know why he went by Diesel, especially since Nash ought to have been a perfectly good nickname for "Nashville."

"We're just over a month into second semester and you're already picking fights with the cheerleaders. That's got to be a new record, even for you. Leave them be, man. You know they don't have the ego to handle you." Diesel winked.

Rachel sighed and rolled her eyes, like Diesel was too stupid to even be worth the time of her insulting him properly. Except the only thing Diesel had ever been stupid about was thinking that staring longingly at a girl for years would do anything to further his romantic interests. Sana and Diesel were, unfortunately, alike in this way.

"Do you need any other help?" Sana knew she would be rebuffed. She asked anyway. She was a one-woman masochism parade today.

"You've done plenty already, thanks," said Rachel, still hunched over her gear.

Diesel had already started to help Rachel get the camera and lenses and equipment back into the pelican case. His movements were quick and efficient. "There we go. Easy solve. You'll be all right." Diesel clicked the latch to the case shut.

"No thanks to her." It was the first time Rachel hadn't ignored something the water polo player had said, even if it was an indirect kind of statement that mostly took aim at Sana.

"I said I was sorry," said Sana.

"That's not good enough," said Rachel.

"Was there any other damage to your equipment?" Against her better judgment, Sana stared into Rachel's eyes. They were a deep golden brown that reminded Sana of the best kind of bitter tea.

"Luckily, no. You just made the camera look awful, not work awful. And it's not my equipment. It's the school's. I can't afford a camera like this. I don't go out and buy everything I need for my activities. There's not some vending machine of technical equipment that I've got unlimited access to. There's a reason I'm aiming for a scholarship for college." Rachel looked Sana up and down.

Sana wished it had been a different kind of elevator glance, rather than this cutting one. But disdain was the only thing she'd ever gotten from Rachel, and probably would be the only thing she would ever get from her. She'd somehow become the girl's nemesis, and all she'd been trying to do was ask for her phone number that one time.

It had gone horribly sideways. Everything where Rachel Recht was concerned went horribly sideways.

"I'm glad you're not injured," said Sana, knowing she shouldn't say anything but needing to say something. "And I'm glad your camera equipment is still working, despite the crack."

"Yeah, thanks, Khan, for nearly damaging thousands of dollars of school property."

Sana nodded at Diesel. "That's my cue."

Diesel gave a slight, sad nod. Like he remembered that once upon a time, Sana had tried asking out a girl on her own for the first time. And that that first girl had been Rachel Recht. Because what Diesel didn't know, what he probably did not suspect, was her crush wasn't firmly rooted in the past tense.

As Sana walked away, she willed herself to take deep breaths again. It was a trick Sana had learned a long time ago. Breathe in, breathe out. The more deep breaths she took, the more she envisioned the tension leaving her shoulders.

It stung to know that Rachel was clever and ambitious and pretty, that Rachel created whole worlds and put them onto film, even with a shoestring student budget, and she thought Sana was lower than dirt. But Sana knew better than to expect anything anymore. Even if moments like this—where Sana could smell Rachel's hair or look directly into Rachel's bright brown eyes—made Sana forget she wasn't supposed to have a crush on Rachel at all. And anyway, the feeling was *mostly* in the past.

Sana certainly wasn't about to tell anybody the truth, not even herself.

——————— *Rachel* ———————

Fucking Sana.

"It's not her fault," said the water polo player. Like he could read Rachel's thoughts.

Rachel's eyes snapped toward him. She hadn't realized he was still here, hadn't realized he hadn't gone with Sana. He had a stupid name, like Chet, or Chip, or Colt, or Petrol. *Diesel*. Rachel snorted. *Who names their kid Diesel?*

Rachel put her hand on her hip. "What isn't her fault?"

"Any of it." Diesel watched her, like he was trying to pick up clues for some kind of mystery that only he knew about. "Even if she knocked you over, I know Sana. I'm sure she was trying to help."

"Look, meathead," said Rachel, resenting his close inspection. "I get you think you're helping. But some jock saying the cheerleader is really nice underneath it all doesn't mean shit to a girl like me."

Rachel had learned that when it came to pretty girls, people would bend the rules—even laws—for them. Nobody had ever bent the rules for Rachel. Much less laws. Rachel waited for his response. But instead he just shook his head. He handed her the pelican case wordlessly and walked off the field. *Great.* She'd just been deemed less than by a guy named Diesel.

Fucking Sana.

It had always been like that between them. Sana was one of those perfect, delicate, tiny girly girls. Her shirts were never wrinkled and her skirts—the girl only ever wore pants when practicing her stupid, idiotic cheers—were never stained. Her ponytail was always sleek and in order, despite humidity from the marine layer or sweltering heat or even spring breezes. She was like a South Asian Elizabeth Taylor.

More Maggie the Cat than Martha, though.

Even from the start, Sana had looked like that—like a leading lady who'd stepped off the silver screen. Back during freshman year, Rachel had walked by Sana several times, having noticed her on campus pretty immediately, without knowing who she was. It was hard not to notice Sana. And Sana, she'd been watching Rachel the whole time too, of that much Rachel had been sure. *Did Rachel look that out of place among these people? Could this perfect cheerleader notice the difference so immediately so as to always stare in her direction?* It had been impossible to say.

But one October morning in that fateful first year, Sana had come right up to Rachel with her prim, swishy ponytail and had said, "Hi," in a way that was all smiles.

Rachel had known just by looking at Sana to mistrust that girl's intentions from the start. "What?"

Sana's smile had faltered then, slightly. But she'd pressed on regardless. "I've seen you around. But only after school. Are you new?"

It had been a perfectly normal question, as far as they went. But it was one Rachel hated. It was why, up till then, she'd mostly hung around the film labs, the darkrooms, and the film lab, trying to hide away.

Rachel's work had caught Douga's eye during a summer arts program that she'd applied to on scholarship. Douga had thought that Rachel showed promise, so the instructor had gone to the Royce administration with Rachel's final film project to show them the exact nature of that promise. They'd offered Rachel a spot then and there, but Rachel initially had turned it down. She didn't know anybody with forty-five grand to blow every year on her college education, much less for high school. The Royce School had amended their offer, telling her that *of course* she would be there with financial assistance.

That's how they had phrased it, "financial assistance." Rachel was being given a specific kind of training for her specific kind of talents that the Royce School thought worth investing in. They had a whole fund for this kind of human investment. In this world, *new* and *outsider* seemed to mean about the same thing.

Rachel had shrugged, trying to play it cool. Her mother had just left and Rachel spent most of her waking hours back then either making films or trying to pretend everything was okay, was fine, was totally and completely all right. "Kind of."

Sana had tilted her head, her ponytail swishing along with the move. "Cool."

Rachel had stared, mesmerized by Sana's hair. It had reminded her of one of those desk toys, what were they called? Perpetual motion machines. Sana's hair was like that. A perpetual motion machine.

"Do you wanna grab a coffee sometime?" Sana had asked, breaking Rachel's reverie.

"What?" Rachel shook her head out, like she'd left on monitor headphones and someone had been trying to talk to her through them.

"Coffee? Or like if you don't drink coffee, tea. We could swap numbers." Sana's eyes had been so wide, so hopeful, that they were a punch to Rachel's gut.

"Are you fucking with me?"

Sana had gasped; her glossy mouth had dropped open. Sana's expression had turned raw and naked; it had confirmed every one of Rachel's worst fears.

"You are. I can see it. You're totally messing with me." There was no way the girl wasn't. Rachel had seen *Carrie*, for Christ's sake. And that scene from that godawful movie *Never Been Kissed*. All anyone had to do was watch a teen movie for about ten minutes to get the message: Never trust beautiful people bearing invitations.

It wasn't a question of whether or not Sana liked girls. It was that Sana was so secure in her position. She came from the right kind of family and she had the right kind of pedigree. Her mom worked in the movies and her dad was some kind of big-deal TV reporter.

Rachel was so wrong that even at this point, she still hadn't figured out the right kind of sneakers to wear so that nobody noticed how out of place she was. Rachel's hair had been short and she'd spent as much time as she could covering it up with a beanie. Her curls were too coily to wave in a tousled way—the way that girls with short hair had looked in her feed—and not quite curly enough to make a nice halo around her face. The haircut had been a disaster. Rachel had been a disaster.

Rachel had felt her voice shaking. She wasn't going to cry. Wasn't going to let some rich, entitled cheerleader get to her. She belonged here. She wasn't just an outsider muscling her way in. Wasn't just *new*. She had talent. Just because this girl thought she looked like an easy target, that wouldn't stop her. No. It would *fuel her*. She'd show Sana. She'd show them all. "Stay away from me. I'm not a joke. Asking me out is *not* a joke."

"No—" Sana had said, like she could apologize for this kind of cruelty. "I meant—"

But Rachel had already whirled off.

Fucking Sana. Fucking cheerleaders. Stupid fucking water polo players with hearts of fucking gold.

Rachel shook her head. She was sick of the lot of them. She hauled up all her equipment, squaring her shoulders and balancing the weight of the bags and cases and cameras. She had footage to review and she couldn't waste her time worrying about Sana or Diesel or even Douga. Rachel had to focus.

She had to find a new lead for her final project.

Again.

3

Your Big Dumb Combat Boots

——— Rachel ———

Tip tip tip. Tiptiptip. Tip.

Rachel watched as the back of her pen hit the counter.

"Will you stop that racket." Jeanie held a pitcher in one hand and a platter of food in the other. Jeanie Silber was anywhere between forty and sixty, though she liked to tell everyone she was still thirty-eight. Her hair was pulled back into a long, poofy ponytail and her orthotic shoes squeaked along the linoleum of the deli floor. "And table six is ready to order."

Rachel stopped tapping her pen. She pulled out her notebook and went over and took table six's order. They were one of those couples that kept waffling with their order, each one depending on the other to be able to finalize a decision. Neither one willing to bear the brunt of being wrong.

They finally settled on a matzo ball soup and a Reuben with turkey. A Rachel, ironically enough. Because of all the sandwiches in the world, Rachel had to be named for the one that took something delicious and made it weird and healthy. Which—what even was the point of a Reuben without the pastrami?

Rachel put her order in back at the counter and waited. She pulled her hair back off her neck and away from her face. She'd contemplated cutting it again, but for now, she slicked as much gel in it as she could. At least with it to her shoulders, Rachel could pull her hair back when she needed.

"What are you just standing around for?" Jeanie managed to be everywhere and nowhere at once.

"I've got one table. It's five thirty on a Tuesday." Rachel huffed.

"So go help bus."

Rachel sighed. Nobody else would dare sigh at Jeanie, but Rachel knew she could. Jeanie pointed toward the uncleared tables. Rachel went and grabbed a rag to wipe up.

Because Rachel would do what Jeanie told her to. When Rachel's mom had left and it had just been Rachel and her dad—everyone in the Jewish Mexican community had reached out to see if she'd wanted help. If she and her father had *needed* help.

¿Necesitas ayuda? they had asked.

And she had needed help. But instead she had recoiled. Papa had been drinking then and Rachel hadn't known what to do. She'd run from the people who had reached out. Run from her usual—though only attended on High Holy Days—synagogue. Run from everything that had been familiar and known.

She and her mother had been alike in that way.

And in all her running, Rachel and her dad had run out of money. There ought to have been a safety net, a cushion to fall back on, but there hadn't been. Faith wasn't something Rachel had in a religious way. To her, faith was community. It was the safety net she had rejected, had run from. But despite running from help when everything had gone wrong at home, that community—that safety net—had only been lying dormant. All she had to do was pick it back up again. Two years ago, Rachel had marched straight into Factor's and right up to Jeanie and asked for a job busing tables. Jeanie had taken one look at Rachel and immediately taken her in. Trained her on the spot to wait tables so she could earn more in tips.

Papa had gotten back on his feet again soon after, which had helped. Had kept them out of real dire straits.

But Rachel couldn't forget how Jeanie had let her start over. Jeanie wouldn't let Rachel forget that she'd been the only person Rachel had let in. So Rachel would huff and sigh but ultimately do what Jeanie told her. And Jeanie, for her part, wouldn't ever force Rachel to do anything unpleasant. She was a believer in hard work, but never for its own sake.

Jeanie was worth a thousand perfect tracking shots.

Rachel finished wiping down the table. The order for table number six was ready and she served that without a smile. Jeanie never made Rachel smile.

Rachel refilled water glasses and double-checked soda orders and waited for the dinner crowd to pick up a bit. The rush was typically at lunch. Weekday dinner was a pretty mellow situation. Jeanie fussed over a couple of tables, so Rachel went back and cleaned them again. Did the setup nice and exact.

Rachel worked part-time. She only cared about her grades that involved writing or film work. Her math and science grades weren't bad, they just weren't anything to particularly brag about. She didn't see how biology would affect whether or not she'd make a solid film. Though she had enjoyed using trig to construct triangulated shots and line up imaginary rigs on paper.

The rest of the evening was slow, which was less than ideal from a tipping perspective but more than ideal from a needing-to-think-about-how-to-recast-her-film-lead perspective.

Rachel was all out of ideas, though.

Then Rachel had the joy of checking her email and getting a particularly fun message in her inbox.

Subject: Equipment Checkout

Rachel,

The camera you checked out has been returned with a
GINORMOUS CRACK IN IT. Please come to my office
first thing in the morning to sort out.

—Douga

Rachel was not one to take criticism lying down. Or standing still.
She sent her response right away.

Douga,

Had a run-in with a cheerleader. Double-checked the
equipment and no damage done to the camera. Purely
cosmetic.

R

There. That would show Douga. Until a ping sounded, letting
Rachel know she'd gotten a quick response.

Rachel,

Bring the cheerleader.

—Douga

Rachel clicked the lock button so hard she was surprised she didn't
do any lasting damage to her phone. She was not going to meet up with
Sana. She was not going to take her to Douga's office. That was Rachel's
space. Her domain. She wasn't about to have it invaded by some preten-
tious cheerleader who thought asking out an outcast and a film nerd
as a prank was some kind of hilarious joke for everyone to enjoy.

Except Rachel didn't have any leeway in this. She was already hanging on with Douga by a thread. And now she'd returned damaged
equipment back to the film lab. She'd have to explain herself. And

unfortunately, Rachel had to explain herself with the one person she truly hated in the world right by her side.

Rachel would rather watch a Tarantino movie double feature than face what she had to tomorrow morning.

Sana

Sana and her mother lived in a one-story bungalow in Studio City, which they had bought back before Studio City had become the place to buy for young and upwardly mobile professionals in the film industry. Sana's mom had bought the place when the neighborhood was filled with all the cinematic support staff—studio lot workers, crew members, craft services, and the other countless invisible jobs of the movie industry. Back when Sana's mom was just a carpenter on set and too young and too determined to fail.

Sana had apparently lived in some crappy apartments in the Valley and North Hollywood, but she'd been too young to remember anything but this place as home.

A bang sounded from the front of the house.

"Sana-joon, I'm home!" shouted Sana's mom into the void of the house. Farrah Akhtar was many things—punctual, diligent, and a real pain in the butt to anyone in her way—but quiet, formal, and home at a reasonable dinnertime were never any of them. She made up for this by bringing free food home from the set whenever she could. "I've got dinner!"

"Coming." Sana hoped her mom had brought home Chinese. After two hours of cheerleading practice, all Sana wanted was endless piles of noodles and salty, tangy chicken.

"You would not believe"—Mom kissed both of Sana's cheeks—"the day I've had."

"Oh, really?" asked Sana.

"Yes, really. We couldn't get the electric department in, so the grips had all the lights set up and in place, but nobody to plug them in." Sana's mother sighed. The grip department could position lights, but not plug them in. The electrical department dealt with anything with plugs. For real. "That's six hours wasted on set, and we were going to have to go to time and a half if I kept them, because of course the delay happened after the lunch break. Ida needs to take control of the set again. She's losing them. It's not her fault, but she's losing them. And I'm losing the production's money in the process."

Ida Begum was the director of Mom's current project. Sana knew her mother sympathized with female directors. As a woman who had clawed her way up from carpenter to art director to production designer, Sana's mother couldn't help but understand what it was to be a woman in a largely male space. But Mom tended to say that the leeway was millimeters for women where the male directors got miles.

"You're not in charge of budgets anymore, though," said Sana.

That had been her mother's job as an art director. All of those daily tasks, all of that system administration, all of the coordination between costume and set and FX and the director. But now Farrah was a production designer. Mom had climbed and carved her way to the top of her field.

"Of course it's my job. It's all my job. The buck stops with me on this one. Even if I don't spend my day in the details, it all reflects on me." Farrah waved Sana's hand away with a swat. She set the reusable grocery tote that she carried over one shoulder on the kitchen counter. "Luckily crafty was amazing today. And there were tons of leftovers that Rebecca couldn't reuse tomorrow. So we've got a total feast on our hands."

Mom started pulling out containers from her bag. One had egg rolls, another had little sandwiches filled with roast beef or tuna fish. She had one with salad in it and another with mozzarella sticks.

Sana pointed at the cold, rubbery cheese, trying to figure out how anyone thought *that* was a good idea to have on a table on set for several hours. "Really?"

"The lead on this production. You wouldn't believe his contract requests. There's no end of the shit he pulls. He's the one causing all the disruption with the crew, too. Trying to undermine the director while she's working. Pissing off the electric department and in turn causing them to piss off the grips, which of course pissed off crafty, makeup, and me. Some men just can't take direction from women."

"He sounds like the worst."

Sana's mother grabbed a plate of food, then moved into the living room and collapsed onto the couch. "Tell me about it. But, and I quote, *he pulls in the theater.* Heaven forbid you give a woman the directorial keys to a large production without a leading man to bring in box office numbers."

Sana put several sandwiches, two egg rolls, and a heap of pasta salad onto her plate. She took her plate into the living room and sat beside her mother on the couch. "That's unfair."

Farrah shrugged, like she was used to how unfair the world was. "Nobody likes to take a risk with fifty million dollars. Particularly not the good old boys in charge of the studio money."

"Gross. Oh! This girl picked a fight with me at school today," said Sana through a mouthful of food.

"That cow! What did she do?"

"You don't even know her. Or what she did. I could have deserved it."

"I'll call her as many names as I want," said her mother. "And I doubt you deserved it; you are my most perfect child."

"I'm your only child. Which probably makes me your *least* perfect child as well. And I saw her trip over a sprinkler or something, which was going to knock her video equipment out of her hand. Of course I try to help and end up knocking her video equipment out of her hand. And breaking it. She says I'm going to pay for what I did."

"That's tough. I guess I'll just have to see you in the next life, then.

32

When you've got that kind of money. I am assuming you're talking Royce School levels of camera of equipment here. Maybe after you've gone to Princeton and have become a world-famous surgeon."

Sana felt her eyes go tight and her jaw clench as she forced out a laugh. Sana's mother didn't notice the tension, though. She got up and went back into the kitchen. She grabbed several of the containers of food, all balanced perfectly along her arms, like she was used to bearing a heavy burden with ease and grace. She set the containers on the coffee table.

Once that was done, she snapped on the TV. "There. Much better. We can have as much as we want without having to get off of our butts. I don't want to have to leave this couch again. Not after the day we've both had. I live here now."

"Cheers," she said, lifting her plate toward Sana's like it was a glass of champagne. "To the end of a lousy day."

"Cheers!" Sana returned the gesture with more enthusiasm than she had. An extra tilt of the head. A brighter smile than normal. It was hard to find the right expression anymore. Harder to figure out what her face should look like. But Sana knew she had to find the right expression; otherwise, her mom would start asking questions.

Sana grabbed a container of noodles that she had missed before off the coffee table. She piled some on her plate and then slurped them down with greedy noise. Everything was salty and tangy and perfection. It was delicious. That, at least, she didn't have to fake.

April 2

29 Days Until Deadline

4

Alright, Alright, Alright

—————— *Rachel* ——————

It had taken Rachel three years to get the niggling sensation that she was an intruder out of her head as she passed through the Royce hallways. The precise sort of person who was meant to be kept out by the wrought iron gates and the high, manicured—but of course, sustainably planted—hedges. Somehow along the way, she went from feeling like she violated every sacred code this school held dear to sailing through its shitstorm. Not as though she belonged, but more like she knew the treacherous waters. Here there be dragons and monsters and coral and shoals and Rachel knew where they all lay now.

Rachel had to find Sana and convince her to go to Douga's office. *Tell her*, more like.

Besides, Sana was a cheerleader—she must, on some level, *like* to follow orders. Rachel had it all mapped out. She was just going to walk right up to her and tell her they had to go into Douga's office because of the broken camera. There was no way Sana was going to stay no. Rachel was going to get to her in the early morning hours, before either of their homerooms started. And Rachel knew from the couple of times she had done early morning shoots that Sana was the sort of girl who arrived early to school, well before the first bell. And not because Sana was scrambling to do her homework at the last minute.

Sana clearly *liked* school.

Rachel shuddered. School was a means to an end. A way to get to where she wanted to go. Sure, she could start working on a crew at any time. But she *needed* the pedigree, the legitimacy that a degree would provide. Men could climb their way up the blue-collar work of the film world in a way women couldn't. And even the women who did—they went up through the stunt-coordination route more often than not. And Rachel was not what anyone would term stuntwoman material. Or even stunt coordination material.

Rachel was decidedly sits-in-the-editing-bay-with-snacks material.

Lost in thought, Rachel didn't realize she'd come up on the senior locker area. She startled as a small, shadowy form stepped into her path.

"Hello." Sana had stopped a foot away. Her eyes were a beam of spotlight that refused to let go.

"Sana." Somehow the rest of Rachel's planned speech went flying out of her head.

Sana didn't break eye contact. And Rachel wouldn't. They would be stuck in this state, eyes locked, staring each other down, possibly until the end of time. Rachel was unable to speak. She just watched the way light played across Sana's face.

Real people should not look like an incredibly tanned Hedy Lamarr.

Sana tilted her head. "Is this about the camera equipment? Have you come with an itemized bill?"

Rachel felt her heartbeat pick up a kick. As Sana's ponytail swished, Rachel visualized her plan crack in half, then fizzle and pop as it drained neatly out of her mind.

"I need you in the film lab."

Whatever Sana had been expecting, it clearly wasn't for Rachel to say *that*. She stood there, blinking repeatedly. Rachel noticed a cup of coffee in the other girl's hands. Much like Sana, the cup looked like it would photograph well. Made to be in a staged picture even more than it was made for real life.

Leave it to Sana to blow six dollars every morning on a cup of coffee.

"I'm sorry. I must be hallucinating this morning. There's no way you asked for my help in the film lab." Sana turned, as though to get back to her business at her locker.

It was a dismissal. Rachel refused to bow to it. "You're not hallucinating. You, me—Douga's office. Right now."

Sana turned, her hand still absently on the lock. Her eyebrows drew together. They were full and straight eyebrows, not bushy ones. Though on anyone else they would have been bushy or at least overpowering. On Sana, the eyebrows and their expression were simply striking. "Why?"

"Douga asked for us both." Rachel shrugged.

Sana leaned into her locker. The action brushed her shoulder and that damned swishy, shiny ponytail up against Rachel's arm. "I see."

Rachel held her breath, waiting to see what Sana would do. She'd probably abandon Rachel to her fate. Leave her to be yelled at alone by Douga.

But Sana turned and shut her locker door. "Lead the way."

Douga's office was a glassed-in side room off of the film labs. She had a big slab of a desk with papers strewn all across it and seemingly little to no method to her madness. She had bookshelves in her office, but they were empty. All the paperwork was either on the table or on the floor.

It was the camera equipment in the film lab itself that pulled the focus off any of Douga's organization efforts. There her organization system shone. Everything was filed on a shelf and tagged in a pelican case and placed in order by type, by model, by function. Her office, by contrast, was mostly a place for her to put stuff that she would prefer to never do. And Rachel had seen Douga's inbox over the teacher's shoulder. She was one of those psychopaths with two thousand unread messages.

Douga saw Rachel and Sana approach and waved them in. Rachel sat down opposite Douga. Sana took the seat farthest from the door.

Douga pulled out the camera and placed it on top of some papers on her desk. "Explain."

"It's a purely cosmetic crack on a camera," said Rachel. "The overall functionality is undiminished."

"Rachel," said Douga. "You cannot return damaged equipment."

"But it's not real damage!"

Douga made a silencing motion with her hand. She looked over at Sana. "Your turn. Answer carefully."

"It was an accident. I ran into Rachel by the practice field." Sana looked Douga in the eye and everything.

Rachel snorted. *Accident my ass.*

"It was, even if you don't believe me."

"You know I don't."

"There's a shocker."

"Almost as shocking as being tackled while innocently crossing a lawn."

"You were carrying too much equipment! You nearly fell over all by yourself! I was trying to help." Sana folded her arms across her chest.

"So you decided to sprint tackle me and finish the job? I know you're a cheerleader, but where was the logic in that if it *wasn't* to take me out?"

"You are so dramatic. I have never nor will I ever aim to take you out."

Rachel raised an eyebrow. She had just the retort for that.

"GIRLS."

Rachel and Sana both turned to Douga. Rachel had almost forgotten that the teacher was sitting there.

"Do you honestly think I want to sit here, listening to you two whinge, as I try and figure out if there was a responsible party to this destruction?"

Rachel and Sana answered with a grumbling and simultaneous, "No."

Douga looked over at Sana. "I don't think you did this on purpose, but just because you look innocent—well, looks can be deceiving."

Rachel felt a smirk coming on.

Then Douga turned her focus onto Rachel. "And you. You should have help putting away the equipment. You should be delegating some of this to your crew members. *You should not be firing your lead again and derailing your final project right now.*"

The smugness that had been enveloping Rachel was destroyed—like a well-coordinated flash bang effect across her mood.

Douga pinched the bridge of her nose. "Here's what we're going to do. You, Rachel, are going to cast Sana as your lead because I have no time left to deal with your casting shenanigans. And you, Sana, will take time to film in Rachel's project as a show of goodwill that you meant no harm."

"But you don't even know if she can act?!" Rachel would *not* be casting Sana. She couldn't.

"How do you know I *can't*?" Sana crossed her arms and glared.

"Enough." Douga held her hands up in the air. "You two will work together. There will be no more damaged equipment. If I don't hear that things on set are improving, I am going to be very disappointed. Neither of you want me disappointed right now, got it?" But Douga didn't wait for their assent. "That's all. Get to class."

And with a wave, Douga shooed them out of her office.

Rachel's palms had begun sweating. She ought to make a quick retreat and live to fight another day. Right in front of her was the heartless girl Rachel knew. She stared at Sana for a long moment.

This is a terrible idea. One of Douga's worst.

"Well, Khan. What do you think?" Rachel waited for Sana to destroy all of her dreams with a swift and vicious *no.*

Sana swallowed hard. "I can help. I mean, I can at least try. I have cheer practice until five most days. I can't do anything until then, obviously. And I usually have organic chemistry lab during lunch."

"Right. Organic chemistry," said Rachel.

Sana took more advanced science than she did. She was probably nice to children, too. A regular Mary Fucking Poppins. Minus the button nose. A strange kind of misery began to well in Rachel's chest. There had to be a catch. There was always a catch. A moment where the angle of the camera changed and what had once looked like a dream transformed into a fearscape from hell.

Sana put her hand on her hip. This caused her head to tilt again, which invariably caused her ponytail to swing back and forth like a goddamn pendulum. "Look, do you want my help or not?"

"Not." *Not not not. An infinite loop of nots.* "But I need it. My film project needs it."

Sana nodded, short, perfunctory, and full of an understanding of doing unpleasant things for a higher purpose. "Then meet me in the gym tomorrow after five."

"No. *You* meet *me* in the film lab after five." Rachel sure as shit wasn't ceding home court advantage. The stakes were too high.

Sana sighed. "Fine."

"Good." Rachel gave a tense nod in Sana's direction. Some piece of her brain began to scream about all of the setup she'd have to do after school to get an audition room ready by five that evening. She was definitely going to have to skip last period. Maybe she could get Douga to send a note and get her excused.

Unfuckinglikely.

"Great," said Sana. "The bell's about to ring."

Rachel readjusted her messenger bag across her shoulder. She wasn't going to be dismissed, she didn't care who Sana thought she was. Rachel wasn't done relaying the most essential pieces of information. "No need to bring a monologue. I'll provide the lines. You're just going to read and I'll see if you've got it. I mean, I doubt you do, but I'd be stupid not to check. Come straight after practice. Don't be late."

Sana must have seen something in Rachel's expression because her next move was to salute Rachel, full of sarcasm, and say, "Aye aye, captain."

And before Rachel had time to retort, Sana swished her way out of the hallway. Rachel had just sacrificed her dignity on the altar of cinematic production.

When looked at from a logical perspective, Sana shouldn't have loved cheerleading as much as she did.

First there was the obvious, which were the uniforms: scarlet and gold, long sleeves and short skirts, a combination that was practical neither for the weather nor for modesty. There was also the ribbon that went in her hair with her name in puffy paint: SANA in neat, bright, bold block print. There was something deeply impractical about a hair ribbon that was meant to be read while she was being thrown up and down in the air or bouncing or shouting or cheering.

But of course, Sana tied hers tight with a square knot and then a double bow so that her name always faced out on the ribbon just so. She had a secret, small rebellion—she refused to put a curl in her hair. She smoothed and pressed her waves flat. But otherwise, her hair was tied up just like Coach K had taught them: a sleek, tight ponytail and a neatly bowed ribbon.

Then there was the fact that Sana spent every Friday night in the fall—and Wednesdays, Thursdays, and Saturdays in the spring—cheering on a bunch of boys she felt lukewarm at best about as they played a sport she couldn't have cared much less for. Oh, Sana knew when to cheer. Cheering for four years gave her knowledge of the rules, gave her some sense of play in the game, whatever the game was.

But there was a good joke there—in a girl who liked other girls spending her free time cheering for boys and fawning over their lockers with homemade decorations and baked goods.

Purveyor of benevolent sexism, indeed. Sana held in a snort at the thought.

Then there was the fact that this was LA and cheerleading didn't really make a girl popular anymore. Not in a school where people were connected to moviemakers and Hollywood legacies and the real, serious money of global entertainment empires. Sana had enough industry connections that cheerleading didn't affect her social standing, one way or the other.

But Sana didn't cheer for the popularity. Or the uniforms. Or, clearly, the boys. Or the love of some game.

Sana cheered because she loved to.

There were very few times in Sana's life that she didn't care what everyone else thought about her. But cheerleading was one of them. She didn't care if anyone else liked her or for flow and parallel structure didn't because of it. And so she put up with the sweaty, entitled boys and the skepticism of her grandparents and the friendly derision of her mother. The casually sexist uniforms and the immense amounts of hairspray and the particular hierarchy of the cheerleading world itself. She waved them all away for the chance to be basket tossed in the air after standing on one foot and holding her other beside her ear.

She liked the impossibility of it—she made shapes flying through the air that required flexibility and strength and no small amount of nerve.

It was the only way that Sana could forget herself. Forget that she'd agreed to help Rachel Recht make a movie. Forget that she'd gone behind her whole family's back and applied for a medical fellowship. Forget that Rachel's hair smelled like pineapple. Forget that Rachel could dream up movie after movie, but couldn't imagine a world where Sana wasn't her enemy.

Sure, learning to do a horizontal split in under a second after being thrown upward had been difficult. Not to mention the first time she'd put on her cheerleading uniform and realized she would be flashing an entire crowd with an underwear cover that was basically just underwear with her name monogrammed on the butt. Thank goodness the uniform had sleeves, or she'd never have been able to convince her grandparents she was doing a legitimate athletic activity.

But the sensation of her muscles flexing while her body launched skyward—if only for a few seconds without any other support or protection—was a high Sana had no name for, in any language. It was probably the only space in her life Sana could be untethered. Up here, in this fraction of a second, she wasn't cheer captain or honor student or only daughter. Wasn't a future surgeon. Wasn't even Sana Khan. She was just a mass, momentarily in defiance of gravity.

It couldn't last, though.

Gravity did the inevitable, pulling Sana back to earth.

Sana jackknifed so that her body was caught in a cradle—two girls at the bottom who locked their arms to create a human net—and her arms were caught under the shoulders by a back spot.

"Excellent," said Coach K. "Really excellent, girls. Everybody follow Khan's lead here. She's a second-semester senior and she's still not slacking. You hear?"

Sana cringed a bit, but said, "Yes, Coach," in unison with everyone else.

Everybody knew Sana had gotten into Princeton. That she'd applied there early action. That she'd pulled all her other college applications. That she'd given her nonbinding commitment. That she was perfect. That's what they always said. That was the way they looked at her. *Too good* and *too perfect*. It was nauseating, but Sana had cultivated the image on purpose. She supposed she had to live with it now.

What they didn't know, what they couldn't guess, what they'd never suspected was this—Sana hadn't put down her deposit. It had sat on her desk, hidden under her books and her school folders. She hadn't secured her spot. Instead, she'd been working on her application material for a fellowship that would probably come to nothing.

Instead, she'd been dreaming of a future that didn't have clear, delineated lines. Instead she'd been wondering what life looked like without getting on a path at eighteen and never getting off until she retired or died.

Then the drill was setting up again and she was up, up, up in the air. Sana let out a breath she didn't know she'd been holding in. *Whoosh*, she was flying. *Snap*, she'd been caught again. She didn't have to think midair. She just had to act. It was one of the only places Sana could trust her instincts. Trust that she'd catch herself.

"All right, girls. That's it for practice today. I'm really proud of all the work you've all put in this year." Coach K scanned the small crowd of girls. Because even though cheerleading was open to all, benevolent sexism really hadn't changed all that much.

"We've just got the tail end of basketball left. The next pep rally is only ten days away. We're still going to decorate all the players' lockers before the game, which means some late nights after practice this next week to get all the decorations together. I will remind you that cheering is the heart of our school spirit and pride. I know you'll all live up to this."

Coach went on—about the responsibility and the visibility of the cheerleaders, about the kind of character and reputation expected of young ladies at the Royce School. Sana could practically deliver the speech verbatim herself. The squad members were ambassadors to their school—on the field and off. Nobody was more visible than a cheerleader. Except maybe a water polo player or a lacrosse player. But they were boys and they weren't expected to behave like ladies. They were allowed to roughhouse and blow off a little steam.

But cheerleading *was* how Sana blew off steam. She didn't drink, she didn't smoke. She didn't particularly like to swear.

What she wanted was to be thrown high into the air and not have to come down for a long while. What she wanted was for time to stop and for May first to just never arrive. If she could cheer and work on new stunts, Sana wouldn't have time to think about her deadline for Princeton or her pending fellowship application or being in a movie directed by Rachel Recht. Besides, the deadline was basically a whole month away. She didn't have to think about the future right now. She'd be fine for a little bit longer.

Coach K wrapped up the last of her regular pep talk. "If you have any requests for lockers that you want to decorate, remember to get those in to your captain by the end of tomorrow."

Sana pasted on a big smile. She didn't even try to act surprised that Coach had passed the responsibility onto her. She wasn't, and she didn't need the squad to think she had been. Everybody trusted Sana to get things done.

That was the problem.

Sana was trustworthy and reliable. She didn't get stage fright or performance anxiety. She already had the locker decoration assignments done for all the girls on the squad. She had written down their preferences at the beginning of the year. Getting things done had never been an issue until she'd gotten a form from Princeton asking for her dorm selections. Her mind had gone in circles until she'd tucked the papers out of sight. Like that helped and like email notifications weren't also a thing that Princeton was sending her.

Sana had a lot of unread messages these days.

She went over to her bag and pulled out the sheets she'd printed with everyone's locker decoration assignments. That was something easy that she could do. Achievable. Get papers out of bag. Pass out sheets. Nod and smile at the squad. Generally act like she knew what was going on, like everything was fine.

Like she wasn't stalling on her future. Like she wasn't making a bet on a fellowship that would never come through.

Sana was more of a planner than a visionary. She saw a goal and she broke it down until it was in actionable, completable tasks. But she'd completed all her tasks, save for the most obvious, looming one from Princeton. And she'd cleared her mind in the last hour of cheerleading practice. As she got together her gym bag, all she had left was how on earth she was going to spend the next month helping Rachel Recht make a movie.

She had to get out of it. There was no other option.

5

Basket Toss

—————— *Rachel* ——————

Rachel didn't like to admit that Douga was right about anything, but sitting there in the film lab, she had to recognize that she had *a lot* of footage.

She'd started the project the summer after her junior year. It was supposed to be a grand epic, in the vein of *The Odyssey*. She was making it modern so she didn't have to worry about costumes. Rachel had already learned that lesson, the hard way, in her second film. Now, this, she was making about the women—the ones inside the walls of Troy—rather than the men battling it out in the war zone beyond the city. It was a familiar plot and it should have been simple.

It also should have been finished by now. It should have been done in November. December at the latest. But instead she had all this footage and not a single coherent film to show for it. Instead she'd had reshoot after reshoot.

Rachel had about a hundred hours of footage and absolutely no direction.

The problem was, she couldn't get her vision right. The film needed to be perfect. Rachel could think of only one solution—reshoots. Again.

This time with Sana—Rachel's unfairly gorgeous mortal enemy—as the lead.

The universe could be cruel sometimes.

Rachel got up and began calibrating the camera she'd set up in front of one of the room's desk chairs.

Sana was late.

Rachel should have anticipated that. Should have seen that Sana wouldn't show. That she'd try to back out somehow.

But Rachel hadn't.

She kept fiddling with her stupid camera in this stupid room hoping that the worst person on the planet would show up and do Rachel a solid. Nobody ever seemed to be able to show up when Rachel needed it the most. They just gave her verbal commitments that never went anywhere. Nods that meant basically nothing.

What had made Rachel think Sana would be any different from anyone else?

Rachel dialed the focus back in, despite knowing that she was tuning the camera for nothing. At least she had something to fiddle with, something to do with her hands while she waited.

Then the door swung open and a sweaty but somehow not disheveled Sana rushed through it. "So sorry, Coach K called me into her office because we've got to cheer for the JV game tonight even though that was not on the schedule at all. I mean, JV cheerleaders are supposed to cheer for JV games but they all got the same stomach flu or something and now we're all up a creek unless the varsity squad takes over but those girls are probably all halfway home in five o'clock traffic as we speak," she said, all in one breath.

Rachel stared. Holy hell did Sana pick up light well. They were both standing under fluorescents and Rachel knew only one of them had all of her expressions cleanly lit by the overheads. This must be what other directors felt like watching Diane Lane.

"Is something wrong?" Sana tilted her head.

Rachel ducked behind the camera, pretending to look through the viewfinder. "I skipped class in order to book this room and get my equipment set up, just to make sure I had everything ready in time, and now here you are. Late."

"Oh." Sana's eyes dimmed a little.

Rachel tried to find a tone that was all business, all command. She shuffled through some papers, trying to regain her composure, then she handed Sana the page from the top. "Sit. Read this."

"All right." Sana grabbed the office chair and slid into it. Her eyes scanned back and forth, reading the pages.

"Out loud." Rachel went back behind the camera so she could tape the reading and see what needed improvement on Sana's end.

Sana coughed. "Should I start, or . . . ?"

"Whenever you're ready." Rachel expected a complaint about the camera, but instead Sana opened her mouth and read the words loud and clear.

Rachel hadn't noticed the resonant quality to Sana's voice before. Of course, she'd have to have that, from cheering. But it surprised Rachel all the same. It was a voice you leaned in toward, a voice that made you listen. Sana was reading the Cassandra role. She was the tie that bound the story together. The narrative wasn't a direct translation, but Cassandra was the same—the girl nobody listened to, just because she was a girl. The unheard prophet. The harbinger of what was to come. Sana saw to the heart of her—the core conflict of vengeance and pain. The darkness—that Rachel assumed Sana would have glossed over with her sweetness and light and a flick of that long, long ponytail— was beautifully highlighted by the timbral quality of Sana's voice.

And then something glinted off of Sana's nose as she tilted her head. Sana's tiny gold nose ring. And rather than looking punk rock or vicious, the detail somehow made her look daintier, smaller, even more feminine. More vulnerable to the whims of the world. Especially through the lens of the camera. Sana tilted her head back, straightening, and the glint was gone. But Rachel couldn't erase it from her mind.

Sana finished the monologue and looked up. Her eyes went wide and she looked suddenly self-conscious about what she'd done, about the camera on her, about being in the room alone with Rachel.

"Good. That was good." Rachel shuffled through her stack of papers again. "Here, try this one."

Sana took the offered pages that contained the other monologue. *"The Odyssey?* Really?"

Rachel stood up from behind the camera. She leveled her best glare. "What? I can't make a movie about myths and the classics? That's only for bros who wanna make epic, ridiculous battle sequences?"

Sana rolled back in the chair, making space between herself and Rachel's hostility. "That's not what I meant at all."

"If only you could communicate what you meant." Rachel snorted.

"I just—*I* hated *The Odyssey.* I guess I assumed you did, too." Sana stretched her toe out and pulled herself slightly closer, back toward the camera.

"Because we're so alike, you and I." All Rachel could do was roll her eyes at that idea.

Sana cleared her throat, clearly unable to give in and admit she'd lost the argument. "Well, we're both women and *The Odyssey* is overall pretty terrible to women."

Oh. "That's true. But there's this great hidden story inside of so many Greek myths. I chose Cassandra. To tell the story from her point of view."

Sana hummed noncommittally at that.

Fucking snob. Leave it to Sana to not see the brilliance of Rachel's art. Rachel pointed back at the page. "That's a different character, so don't mistake them as the same. Read it to yourself. Then do the lines." It had worked so well the first time, Rachel just gave her the exact same direction. She didn't want to overly explain what was happening. Rachel wanted, for some reason, to know if Sana would get it, if Sana would see what was happening. She watched as Sana read, her eyes still scanning the page.

Sana's mouth stopped moving for a moment to quirk upward. Rachel's breath caught. Sana must have seen it, must have understood. Sana looked up and Rachel felt as though she'd been caught with her hand halfway into a cookie jar. Like she hadn't gotten hold of the cookie, but she'd been caught wanting it all the same.

"Why do you hate Helen?" Sana wasn't doing the dialogue.

Sana waited for Rachel to answer.

But in that moment Rachel couldn't. She felt raw and exposed. More so than when she'd described what had made her so excited about the project.

After a moment, Sana shrugged and began reading. Her voice took on a scratchy and tense quality. The threat of her was evident. Sana was one of those people with annoyingly good posture. Probably the years of cheerleading and dance, now that Rachel thought about it. Dancers always stood up straight and never slouched in chairs. But reading these lines, Sana looked as though she sat straighter, somehow.

Before she'd read these lines, Rachel would have said Sana always had the look of someone with a stick up their ass. But she didn't. Rachel could see that now. Sana had found the difference between good posture and ramrod straight. She'd found the difference between confidence and threat. Sometimes, when Sana went swishing through the hallways wearing her cheerleading uniform, Rachel forgot that there was a sharp, clever girl under all the hairspray and school spirit. A girl who took organic chemistry and taught underclassmen in labs after school.

Sana finished and Rachel quickly shut off the camera.

"That was good." Rachel couldn't think of anything else to say. *Good* didn't quite cover what she'd just seen.

"You never answered my question." Sana stared, so still and unmoving. "Why do you hate Helen? You've made her the villain."

That awful tension was rising in Rachel's chest again. "*Isn't* she the villain of the whole war?"

"To the men she is. The *bros*."

Rachel didn't know why Sana wasn't letting this go. "Whatever."

"Whatever?" Sana's eyes bugged out of her skull. "I'm the purveyor of benevolent sexism but hate for Helen of Troy is *whatever*?"

"Of course you'd take the pretty girl's side." Rachel folded her arms across her chest.

"Are you kidding me right now?" Sana took a deep inhale, then an audible exhale. Then she stood up, smoothed out her workout pants. "Pardon me."

"Who the hell says 'pardon me' anymore?" Rachel watched as Sana tensed at the use of *hell*.

"Could you please try not to constantly wield curse words at me like a weapon?" Sana nodded.

"Excuse me." It was the primness of that nod that was Rachel's undoing. Rachel felt her ears were ringing. "Who *the fuck* says 'pardon me' anymore?"

Sana didn't bristle this time. No, instead her eyes turned to molten earth. Like she could melt the floor beneath her. "I don't know why I even bothered. I knew I should have quit when I came in, instead of reading. Instead of giving this a chance. I knew it."

Sana got up and grabbed her gym bag. The glare she gave Rachel could have sliced out a heart. "I'm not doing your stupid movie. Leave me alone or go back to yelling at me in the hallways. But don't ask for my help."

The door clicked shut behind Sana. It should have slammed. Doors were always slamming in Rachel's face. But the door as Sana quit just swished gently and clicked in place. It was probably designed to do that, to prevent students from slamming doors through the hallways all day long. But it felt like Sana could do that—could shut a door in Rachel's face in the most ladylike and insulting way possible. As though she wasn't even worth a proper slam. She wasn't even worth the appropriate amount of rage with the gesture.

For a moment, all Rachel could do was stare at the door in wonder and disbelief.

"Fuck," said Rachel to nobody in particular, including herself.

Maybe the footage wasn't as good as it looked on her monitor. Maybe it was her imagination, a trick of the light in the room, the glint in Sana's eye as she approached. Maybe Sana didn't understand her story better than anyone had before. Maybe Douga wouldn't follow through on her threat and completely tank Rachel's chances at NYU and scholarship money.

Rachel unhooked the camera and plugged the data card into a nearby computer. It took a moment for the footage to upload and render, but once she had it open in Final Cut, she watched it over again.

"Fuck," she said, most particularly to herself.

Sana

Sana flexed her arms as she went through the motions of the cheer. She had to keep her arm ramrod straight. No bend, no curve. Just a clean fist pump in a line. *Perfect*, like usual.

Perfect Sana. Just like every perfect girl that she was supposed to be. That everyone was also meant to hate. Just like Perfect Helen of Troy. An ideal and a villain all at once.

Sana shook her head out. She had to focus. She had a cheer to get through.

The cheer started like this—*clap, stomp, clap, stomp, pause*. The rhythm of it built until the pace was frenetic, then the squad would move in unison, doing a bounce—shifting from left to right on the balls of their feet. As the chant built to a crescendo, Sana gave the rest of the squad a nod. They were going into formation, with Sana at the center. She was going to do a standard liberty, no more or less than she'd ever done for years. The girls on her base—Alexis and T—boosted her up, with another girl—Maddie—standing behind her, her arms around Sana's waist, ready and willing to spot.

The first part of the trick went like clockwork—

boosted up *one, two*—
up in the air *three, four.*

Sana stood firm, holding her base leg straight as she took her free leg in hand. Everything was perfect because everything had to be perfect in order to stay safe. The movement was smooth, it had to be smooth. This smoothness never looked fast, but it was. In a moment she had her left foot at her ear, her smile wide, and her ponytail with its perfect ribbon still as can be. Sana's ankle wobbled. She let go of the tautness in her body for less than half a second. She let go of the perfection for once in her life.

It was the snap when something started to go wrong.

The snap went *one, two*—

boost Sana into the air from a force applied at her ankles.

For less than a beat, Sana was weightless and untethered. Free.

Three, four—
Sana piked her body,
ready to be caught in a cradle made of arms.

Maddie's arms locked underneath her armpits as Sana performed her controlled fall. But something went sideways at the base—it had to be the base, because even with wobbly ankles Sana could do this stunt in her sleep—because instead of them catching her in a cradle, she went down hard on her right ankle.

The fans on the benches gasped—parents, students, faculty alike. That's how Sana knew it was bad. Not from the throbbing in her ankle. Not from the weakening, light-headed sensation pulsing through her mind. No, it was that gasp. She'd come down hard enough that everyone had stopped paying attention to the boys and instead had noticed the girls. Sana heard Maddie swear under her breath.

"I heard that," said Sana.

"Come on," said Maddie, shooting daggers out of her eyes at Alexis and T. Maddie must have decided it was their fault. "Loop your arm around my neck. They're all still watching."

Alexis was making apologies that Sana couldn't hear over the ringing in her ears. T had her hand over her mouth. And as Sana looped her arm around Maddie's neck and began to limp off, she heard the faint clapping of hands echo around the gym. She'd walked it off. She hadn't passed out. She'd made it to the bench, and this provided at least the crowd in the bleachers with some level of comfort, though it was hardly any at all for Sana.

"How are you doing?" Maddie didn't keep her hair back with a ponytail. Instead she braided the front of her hair off of her face, with the rest of her curls let loose in a crowning halo around her face. It gave her the look of a rescuing brown angel right now.

"Ice," said Sana. "Just get me some ice, please."

Maddie set Sana down on the bench, next to a couple of the boys who were either helping out with water or were perennial benchwarmers, before rushing off to grab some ice. The other girls had managed to get back in formation and do some cheers. But they were all eyeing her as she sat on the bench. All warily waiting to see what the damage would be.

"That can't be good," said a rumbling voice beside her. Diesel stood, his hand reaching out casually as he leaned against the bench. There was a touch of concern in his voice. Something about Diesel reminded Sana of an overgrown golden retriever, all limbs and eagerness.

"I'm hoping it's just a sprain." She hadn't heard a snap, so she was praying it wasn't a break. But she'd never had an injury pulse like this. Sana strained her neck, looking up at his towering figure.

"Here's to hoping." Diesel snagged a water bottle and handed it to her. "If you've broken it, there's no way you'll win a fight with Rachel Recht next time you knock her over. I'd put all my money on her. What's going on with you and her, anyway?"

"Same as always." Sana gritted her teeth through the throbbing. She didn't want to think about Rachel when her defenses were down. She'd already spent the past three days thinking too much about Rachel. She could feel her foot in the temples of her head. She needed some ice or she might actually swoon.

Sana did *not* swoon. She was going to be a surgeon, for heaven's sake. She'd watched medical videos in her feed countess times. But apparently what she could take visually was different from what she could take in her own body.

"No, it's not the same. I can tell." Diesel couldn't let up once he'd gotten hold of an idea. "Do you owe her money?"

"No." Sana never wanted to think about Rachel Recht and her stupid movie ever again. She wanted Diesel to shut up and stand still, if he wasn't going to go help Maddie get some ice.

"Does *she* owe *you* money?" Diesel raised his eyebrows like he really had it this time. Like he *knew* what was up.

Diesel had to have been the only person on planet Earth who had ever guessed without being told first that Sana liked girls. Everyone else had had to be told, and half the time they never brought it back up again. Diesel was different from most people, though. That's why Sana wanted him to drop the subject immediately and back away from it forever and ever. Diesel wasn't stupid, the way people thought—the

58

way he wanted people to think. He wasn't *only* an affable lug of meat. He could read people better than anyone Sana knew.

Sana tried to get down a swig of water, but tilting her head back made the throbbing sensation develop an unfortunate spinning quality. She set the bottle onto the bench. "No. She does not owe me money."

"Wait. You two didn't . . ." Diesel made a flapping hand gesture that ought to have been beyond human comprehension.

Sana understood what he meant pretty immediately.

"No. No no no no no. Definitely not. No." *Nope, nope, nope.* Sana blocked out every image that was flashing in front of her because thinking about Rachel in that way only made Sana's brain short circuit. It was like a bug in a video game, where once she jump-started the glitch, her mind would loop images over and over again until she would go out and do something incredibly stupid, like buy her own bottle of pineapple shampoo. Not safe for any situation. Particularly not school.

Diesel raised an eyebrow. "So that's a no, then? I definitely don't need to meet her or check out if she's cool behind your back or anything?"

Sana hissed. She was in too much pain to process her responses properly. "Yes. No. Please do not try to check up on her behind my back. Accept whatever answer that means that we've never had beef the way you have with half the theater girls."

Not for any lack of trying.

"Definitely not *half of them*." Diesel shrugged. "Anyway. Those girls are particularly theatrical."

Sana closed her eyes. "I'm in too much pain for your awful sense of humor. No dates. No back seats of cars. No jealous exes in the chorus line. Just the same grudge since freshman year. It's that simple."

Minus the fact that Sana was seriously considering ordering some pineapple conditioner once she got ahold of her phone. Conditioner was totally different from shampoo. Right?

"First of all, that was one chorus line, and I didn't know that those two girls were seeing each other." Diesel put up a hand in his own defense.

Sana raised an eyebrow. There was no way he hadn't known that.

Diesel shook his head. "Fine. Whatever you say."

Sana was saved the effort of having to respond to that by Maddie's return with a bag full of ice. Diesel stood immediately, like he was some kind of nineteenth-century dude who always vacated his chair in the presence of ladies.

"I grabbed your phone, too." Maddie held a bag of ice in one hand and Sana's phone in the other. She handed the bag of ice over to Sana first. She set the phone down on the bench beside her.

Sana took the ice and yelped as cool plastic surrounded her tender joint.

"Good luck icing that injury to your foot," said Diesel, clearly trying to impart some kind of farewell but unable to remember how to do so like an actual human.

Maddie finally looked up at Diesel. She blinked at him repeatedly. Diesel blinked back, trying to somehow employ a secret code beyond his understanding. It looked like Morse code with eyelashes.

Sana coughed. "Go watch after the squad for me, would you? Tell Coach K to stay with them. I'm good."

Maddie stared for a moment. "You don't need anything?"

"I'm fine." Sana didn't mean to sound as dismissive as she did. She was just in so much pain and the ice wasn't working fast enough and Maddie was looking at Sana with a mix of concern—her eyebrows were puckered—and hurt—her eyes had gone wide and had that awful wounded look. And soon Coach K would head over here and poke and prod and crowd and Sana would like to just avoid all of that.

Had the accident been Sana's fault? Sana couldn't be sure. If she had wobbled or if Alexis had missed her cradle or if Maddie had simply missed her catch. It had all happened too fast.

Sana's instinct was to look away, to flinch. But instead she kept her face placid, kept her gaze unwavering. Maddie nodded. She looked over at Diesel and narrowed her eyes suspiciously. Then she turned, and Sana watched as Maddie's puff of hair retreated into the distance. Maddie talked to Coach K for a moment, then clapped the other girls into formation, starting a couple of cheers.

Diesel, thank heavens, stopped blinking as soon as Maddie left. "You know, she already doesn't like me. You don't need to make it worse by being a jerk to her when I'm around. She'll just associate the behavior with me."

Sana nestled the bag of ice against her ankle. It had blessedly gone totally numb by this point. Another few minutes and she could take the bag off, though she'd probably have to get fresh ice again to give the joint a couple of solid rounds of numbing. "You'll live. And if you think Maddie's disdain has anything to do with me, well, you're the lug of meat that everyone thinks you are."

"I am not a lug of meat." Diesel jutted his lip out and pouted like he was the bearer of a great injustice.

"So quit acting like one. Maddie dislikes you on your own merits." The game was a blowout for the other team and Sana couldn't bear to watch the cheers right now. She got out her phone.

That got a laugh out of Diesel. "Fair enough. I assume you need a ride home."

Sana nodded. She clicked through her phone. First Sana sent a message to her mom. *Had a bit of an accident at the game. Diesel bringing me home. I'm OKAY. PROMISE* 💚 💚 💚 💚

Then she checked her missed messages. One from her grandfather. *My dear Sana, Looking forward to seeing you tomorrow. Love, Dadu.*

Another from Mamani. *Make sure your mother wears something appropriate to lunch. Just because it's not dinner! She cannot wear jeans! I raised her not wolves!!*

Then a new message popped up from Mom. *Okay. Explain when you get home* 😣

Sana locked her phone. She checked the game clock. Nine minutes left. Nine minutes to figure out what she was going to do with all of the free time she was about to have on her hands. Nine minutes to figure out how she was going to make it to May first without cheerleading to fill her time and to exhaust her body.

Suddenly, working on a movie with Rachel Recht didn't seem like the worst thing in the world.

April 7

24 Days Until Deadline

6

Lost in Transition

—— *Sana* ——

Sana looked over at her mom as she got into the car. She'd already thrown her crutches into the back seat. "Are you sure about those pants?"

Mom smiled. She was wearing high-waisted, floral-and-striped flare pants that she had hemmed so they stopped at the top of her flat sandals. "They're not jeans."

"You know that's not what Mamani meant by not wearing jeans." Sana sighed—Mom would prod and Mamani would likely rise to the bait.

Mom shrugged and slid into the driver's seat, closing the door behind her. "Then she should have been more specific."

"Your funeral." Except it wouldn't be, not really. It would be Sana's funeral, because Sana was the one who had to smooth out Mamani's mood whenever Mom went around intentionally ruffling her feathers.

Mom started the engine and began backing out. "She's going to flip her lid when she sees you on those crutches. I've got to have something to enjoy myself with, or I'll feel beaten. I'm already anticipating a repeat of the pink ombré hair debacle."

Sana refused to entertain that idea. She cracked the window and let the cool spring breeze blow into the car.

Sana's grandparents had one of those large, open-plan hacienda-style houses in an Orange County gated community with a fancy name. Orange Grove. Beach Grove. Orange Grove Beach. The Beach by the Orange Grove.

Whatever.

Sana didn't need to know the proper name to get there, so she never remembered it. Even though her mother did all the driving down from LA, Sana could have gotten to the house on sight memory alone. Down the 405 South, off the exit by the odd grove of trees. Left at the gas station. Up the winding but wide road into the hills. Take a right before you hit the first cul-de-sac. Then stop at the far end of the other cul-de-sac. *Boom.* There stood a stately house that was large and white and nearly identical to all the other neighbors' stately houses.

Sana's mom rang the bell when they arrived. Sana had a key. Her mom had a key. Her mom never used her key. Sana had been instructed—by her mother—never to use her key. Her mom was fierce when guarding her independence from her own parents. In retaliation, Sana's grandmother, Mamani, would send a maid to fetch them from the door.

Sometimes just ringing a doorbell could be exhausting.

Leni led Sana and her mother through the foyer into the parlor. Thank God Mamani had stopped requesting her maids wear uniforms and instead asked for "a dress code," so that Leni could wear slacks now. Leni didn't say anything, but she made a face at Sana's crutches, like Sana needed to be warned that she and her mom were in for it.

"It's a sprain," said Sana as she crutched toward where Mamani sat. Sana was taking charge of this situation before it ran away from her. Though technically, in her state, anything could run away from her.

Mamani, sitting on the impeccably white linen couch in a silk print shirt and white capris, said nothing. She didn't have to. She had looks for everything, particularly for all the varieties of displeasure that went beyond words. Her spine was perfectly straight and her eyes were filled with the kinds of flames that could reignite a dying sun.

Sana went on, sure she could keep a firm grip on the situation. It was exhausting, but she was going to get through this. "And it's temporary. The trainer only had an air cast. But he said I could go to the doctor to get a boot so I wouldn't have to crutch. So I'm only borrowing the crutches until I can get to the doctor."

Sana sighed, a little breathless. The crutches winded her in a way that running regularly and being tossed into the air never did. They also made strange, tender spots under her armpits. Right where her base would typically catch her. It was an unwelcome reminder of how much she had lost.

"And you let her do this, Farrah?" Mamani was shooting death glares at Mom. "You let your own flesh and your own blood do this activity that can hurt her? What kind of a mother are you?"

This was so much worse than the time Mom had decided to try the pink ombré hair trend. Sana felt the need to slump from the weight of it all. Instead she stood up straighter, trying to dig into her years of dance training. She would be perfect at this and then they would stop fighting and they would have a lovely lunch. She'd wished that she and Mom had been able to go to dinner. At dinner, Mom's siblings—Farhad Mama, Zain Mama, and Athena Mashi—would have been able to provide another buffer.

For now the buffer was Sana and Sana alone.

"I don't let her or not let her; she needed an activity for Princeton and she picked cheerleading." Sana's mother slumped onto the formal blue settee with a flop and a sigh. She'd had late-night shoots all week, which didn't put her in a good state. And trips to her parents' house weren't the thing to improve her mood, even on the best of days.

Sana felt a twinge of jealousy that her mom could slide into a chair so satisfactorily while she couldn't let herself entertain the idea of slumping for more than half a second. But that was quickly washed away by the heart-hammering guilt of Princeton being brought up.

Mamani made a disgusted sound between a sneeze and a shushing. "Science fair is an activity. *This* is ridiculous."

"Mamani, Mom, can we please not fight about this? It's like any injury I could get from any sport. I'll be back on my feet again in six weeks. Maybe less. It's a sprain." Sana crutched pathetically over toward the blue settee, hoping to garner sympathy points from her grandmother. But it was the wrong tactic.

Mamani's mouth formed a disapproving line across her face. "It's uncivilized."

"You're uncivilized." Mom was usually quicker on the draw, but the sleep deprivation must have been taking a toll on more than her posture.

That's when Dadu held up his hand—the universal sign that he'd adopted from his courtroom for "I am going to render a judgment now." He was lounging in his rattan chair with his back slanted and his legs wide. It was a powerful position, this large and imposing sprawl. "Enough, beti. Apologize to your mother."

Mom's face went extra sullen. Her lips pouted out and her eyebrows puckered forward. "Sorry, Maman."

Mamani turned and sniffed the air. She hadn't been made for forgiveness. She'd been made to survive a world that was harder on her than on many. To her, forgiveness was like mercy—a kind of weakness that others would take advantage of. Mom sighed and slumped farther in relief.

Dadu kept his focus on Sana, though. He leaned forward. "Are you practicing your stitches?"

Sana nodded. She was still covering all her bases. Except for the part where she didn't follow through on her college acceptance and put down a deposit. "Of course."

Dadu smiled, his pride evident. Sana's stomach somersaulted with guilt and nerves. Could he see right through her? Know she wasn't following through on her plan? Did he say this because he knew he'd expose her in some way?

Despite the better respectability of her aunties and uncles and their children, despite all of them still living in Orange County, rather than having hightailed it out to Los Angeles like her mother had—Sana was the favorite. To say that Sana had, since the moment of her birth, become a future piece of redemption to her grandparents—a do-over for the daughter whose life they had not successfully molded into the shape they had demanded on their first go—would be an overstep, a glossing over of the truth. They had another daughter. Dadu and Mamani each had their own pursuits beyond family.

But Sana had Dadu's eyes.

"Good, poti. Good." Dadu's lips twitched with the edge of a joke they always shared—the two of them keeping the peace while Mom and Mamani swiped at each other's throats.

Sana looked away, avoiding the moment and the camaraderie. Right now, Mom and Mamani were taking turns glaring and avoiding each other's glares. It was too nonverbal for either of them to last for long.

"Mom, you look like a gremlin. Spit it out." Sana's mom crossed her arms over her chest.

Sana snuck a glance at the expression on Mamani's face. It *was* like a gremlin. If gremlins could be beautifully polished, with sun-kissed golden hair, pearly white teeth, and impossibly clear skin, that is. An elegant Persian gremlin. Sana tried to remember the last time she'd seen such unmitigated triumph on her grandmother's face.

"That is a terrible thing to say. I'm not a gremlin. I am your madar." Mamani pulled herself up to her full seated height. "You apologize right now."

Off of the look she got, Sana's mother simply averted her eyes. "Sorry, Maman."

Mamani took a deep, cleansing inhale through her nose. The smile resurfaced, more dazzling and more terrifying than before. "I've got some good news for you both."

"What is it, Mamani?" Sana had meant to sound bright and excited—the tone she used to gloss over any tension between her mother and her grandmother—but some deep, primal instinct had placed a note of caution in her voice. Something was headed her way, she just didn't know what. She didn't know if it was a small breeze lifting off of the ocean or a tsunami headed straight for her home.

"Your father is here!" said Mamani triumphantly.

A tsunami, then.

And then, as if the news alone were not enough, in walked Sana's father, just as handsome as every photograph he ever posted, as every broadcast he ever did. He was dark and lean, like her grandfather, but with none of the middle-aged paunch. He had a full head of black hair with a few silver streaks. His eyes were dark in color while staying bright in expression. He said nothing at first, and Sana, though rarely a girl of many words, was left temporarily speechless at his presence.

Note to self: Mamani's gremlin face is reserved for when Massoud is in town.

When Sana's parents had gotten divorced, her father had gone back to school. He had been so desperate to prove himself—to his family, his peers, and even himself—that he had accelerated through his degrees. Now Massoud Khan was a bigwig national correspondent and occasional anchor, earning the money American dreams are made of. The kind of money that enabled him to do stories that had a conscience attached to them now.

He was insufferable.

"What are you doing here?" said Sana as soon as her mouth began working again.

Mamani's eyes went wide with shock. Sana was normally so controlled, so composed. Their best-behaved daughter.

But Dadu laughed like he'd heard a good joke. "I told you this

would not go well. You have to warn her. She is not one to like sur-
prises. Remember her eighth birthday party?"

Her father stood in the archway of the room, like a hyperreal
photograph rather than a person. Sana was unsure of whether to bolt
from the room or to go out and shake his hand. Her mom had sat up
from her slump, like her entire fight-or-flight response had been lit up.
Then she settled for glaring directly at Mamani.

The crutches now seemed nothing in comparison to this bomb-
shell.

Dadu rose from his seat. His body faced his erstwhile son-in-law,
but he stopped where Sana stood. He frowned and placed his hand on
Sana's shoulder. "I am sorry, poti. I knew you would have our head for
this. But it was not an argument I could win with your mamani."

"It's okay," Sana said automatically. Maybe if she said it out loud
she would believe it herself. She buried the panic clawing up her chest.
She checked the anger at the back of her throat. The desire to shout
was so strong it was drowning out all the other noise in the room. But
maybe Sana was imagining things because there was no other noise
in the room. Just the slow thud of Dadu's shoes as he crossed the space
of the room until he reached Massoud, stretching out his hand and
taking the other man's in this own. They shook hands and kissed each
other on the cheek.

"Sit." Dadu was all command.

Massoud entered the room without further question and sat on the
cushions of the high-backed rattan sofa opposite the white linen one.
He took his time, arranging his pants and his dress shirt before turning his eyes on Sana and saying, "To answer your question, I am here
to see you."

"Sure you are."

"Sana," Massoud said in a measured tone. He dipped down low for
the low *u* sound at the front of her name and gave a nice clip to the
long vowel at the end.

That was a warning.

"You must have some business. You've never come into town without a story to take you here before." Sana watched him warily. She'd have to be on her guard. She was not a child to be tricked by foolish language or missing words.

Massoud's jaw dropped. Mamani gasped. Dadu coughed uncomfortably.

"Thank you, Sana-joon. For sticking up for me. That's enough." Mom got up, walked over, and held out her hand to her ex-husband. "Good to see you."

"No, it isn't. You've always been a rotten liar, Az." Sana watched her father take her mother's hand to shake, like they did this all the time. Like it was normal. Like he still had a right to call her by her childhood nickname. And then he leaned in to plant a kiss on her cheek.

Mom pulled away then. "True."

Mamani tsked—a noise that had equal parts *t*'s and *ch*'s. Perhaps Mamani thought this was rude—another intentional jab in Mom and Mamani's struggle for one-upmanship. But Sana saw no rudeness. All she saw was her mother flinching away from the hurt. It was a protective move, a reflex rather than an attack.

And because her mother was in that kind of defensive pain, Sana did the only thing she could think to do. She defused, as she must. "You're here now. I think Mamani made tahdig."

Massoud put his hand over his heart. "Now aren't I lucky?"

Mamani blushed. She honest-to-God blushed with pleasure. Which was what Sana had been counting on.

"I remembered how much you like it, Massoud-joon."

"Now I really have been spoiled," said Massoud with a wink.

Sana did her best to suppress a snort.

Mamani rose elegantly from her couch and led them all into lunch, with Sana's father beside her, Sana's mother behind, and Sana and her grandfather leading up the rear. Lunch was a tense affair, with globs of polished, polite conversation pouring forth from all quarters, excepting Sana's mother, who sat still and slightly mute, trying to process this new development in her life.

Mom left her parents' house with barely a goodbye, packing Sana away in the car and driving off in near silence.

Rachel

Tap, tap, tap.

Rachel bounced her fingers on the keys of her laptop. Not so hard as to press them, but loud enough to carry a sound.

Even her fancy computer was by grace of the Royce School. It never helped, remembering that when she was already in a mood. It was like when she'd get stuck in LA traffic on the way to Royce, then remember she had a car all because they bought her a computer and she could use the cash she earned at Factor's Famous Deli on a beat-ass Lincoln Continental that was so retro it was making a nineties comeback.

Rachel kept reading her script. Kept seeing the holes and the gaps. It was the only thing she could see now—the pitfalls in her project. Easier to think about the gaps in her plotting than the giant crack in the camera she was using. Easier to think about the holes and the gaps than the fact that Sana made a perfect lead and Rachel has destroyed her project's future with a few choice words. Douga would probably fail her for this.

Fucking Sana.

Rachel had to think of somebody better than Sana. Somebody a little less Liz Taylor. Somebody so good that Douga wouldn't care that Rachel had ignored the teacher's express mandate. Rachel looked around her room. There were movie posters all over the walls—she'd learned that she could get tons of great posters after a movie went out of theaters. Employees usually just threw the posters out. Rachel asked for whatever a theater had in stock when she went to go and see a film. Her prize possession was an old poster for *Marie Antoinette* that one of the old independent theaters in LA hadn't managed to throw out. Even though *Somewhere* was Rachel's favorite Coppola film, the *Marie* poster was almost as old as Rachel and that made it feel more authentic and real than any of the other ones she'd snagged.

Rachel went to the lone bookshelf in her room—she cataloged all of her films by year made along the shelves. She'd spent the time burning them onto discs and then putting those discs into cases. She had hard drives with storage, but for Rachel, materializing her films, making them a tangible, finished thing, gave her a sense of accomplishment. On top of the shelf, were a couple of battered old library sale books on cinematography, a screenwriter's bible, and one of the yearbooks her father had sprung for last year. Rachel reached up and pulled down her yearbook and started circling and crossing through potentials.

Rachel felt a little guilty, defacing with a red permanent marker the yearbook her father had paid for. But she had work to do, and work was more important than preserving memories she didn't much give a damn about.

Sana managed to look good in a yearbook photo. The light from the flash of the camera somehow picked up all of her angles and not a single flaw. Rachel wanted to scratch Sana's entire face away with the permanent marker, but stopped. Sana didn't just look good on film. She looked wholesome and angular, all at once. Rachel couldn't quite tell if Sana was smiling or smirking in the photo. Or maybe that was just Sana's face, resting naturally. It was unnerving.

She'd be perfect. The thought was instinctive and unwelcome. *A villain and a hero all at once. Helen of Troy.*

Rachel flipped away. She drew a deep gash against a random photo of some unsuspecting, unpromising sophomore girl.

She slammed the book shut. She'd never get any work done, not with the image of Sana's face floating around her mind. Rachel had to end this. She needed to find another picture of Sana and see how inappropriate she would be as a choice for the lead. Sana wasn't mysterious or complicated. She was devastatingly simple. Rachel got out her phone and went down a well-worn rabbit hole.

Fucking saved searches.

There she was. Sana in her cheerleading uniform, her ponytail frozen by the camera along with her perfectly straight, white teeth in a perfect smile. But Rachel stopped to look at it for a moment and she suddenly saw what she had already glimpsed in the yearbook photo— there was a determined set to Sana's eyebrows, along with that innocent, Disney-like quality to her eyes. Maybe it was the nose ring. Maybe it was the way her smile crinkled around her eyes but didn't change her strong, linear jawline.

Sana would be perfect. Rachel could see it so clearly now. The visualization of it all had made it so much worse. Just a few reshoots and Rachel could get the last of this production rolling all the way to the finish line.

Rachel didn't want anything to do with Sana. She tried to open the yearbook again, to flip through the pages and find someone, anyone else. But she kept reaching back for her phone, against her own will. And Rachel had a pretty considerable will. She kept seeing the angles. Kept envisioning how Sana's face would film. Kept seeing the light as it might strike across the girl's face.

Rachel needed advice, feedback. But her first reader and best confidant was her father, and he wasn't home. Probably wouldn't be home for hours. He was driving on the night shift, which he often did on weekends.

Rachel was used to being alone. That's how she'd gotten behind a camera in the first place. All that time spent alone—when her father was out, before he'd turned the corner after her mom left—she'd started shooting videos on her phone, until she'd had enough material to make a narrative, a story. Enough material to apply to that summer program all those years ago.

Rachel decided to call her father rather than continue scrolling through Sana's feed.

"What did you do this time?" asked her dad when he answered. Because they never had to say hello to each other. Because she didn't have to censor herself with him. It was more like one continuous, drawn-out conversation throughout the course of their lives. Because Papa would always pick up for Rachel.

But that didn't mean Rachel didn't ask if he had time. "Can you talk?"

When he was driving, sometimes he could talk, and other times, he had passengers who would definitely ding his rating. Other times he was recruiting drivers, because that paid better than driving did.

"For you, mija? Anytime." Papa had started calling Rachel *mija* instead of *habibti* after her mom had left. Mama had always called her habibti. For all her running, Rachel's mother remembered the old ways—remembered that her people had come from somewhere before they'd arrived in Mexico. Papa had stopped using the old terms of endearments when he'd stopped drinking. A clean break from an unnecessarily painful reminder. Habibti was *before* and mija was *after*. As though having another tradition to draw on helped heal both of their wounds. And maybe it had.

Papa's voice was warm and scratchy at the same time, like his stubble-flecked face. Papa didn't have an accent—his parents had come from Mexico but he had been born here. Still, when he was tired, the rhythm of his speech lilted through English like it ought to have been Spanish. "So what's the problem?"

"Douga cast the cheerleader who cracked my camera in my movie for me. Says she'll fail me if I don't use her. I mean, that's not the problem. She's perfect for it."

"And?"

After a long pause in which Rachel tried to phrase several versions of what had happened, she settled on, "And she doesn't like swearing."

And then Papa laughed, a low belly laugh that started with a rumble and finished at a high peak. Papa was laughing *at* her. And he was thoroughly enjoying it. Papa took a deep inhale, as though he were trying to fill his lungs with enough oxygen to calm himself down. "She doesn't like swearing?"

"She asked me not to say 'hell.'"

"And what did you do?"

"I replaced it with another word that she found even more offensive."

Papa let out a low whistle. "You *are* screwed."

"Not. Helpful."

"I mean, you're not screwed if you're actually willing to grovel come Monday morning. But we both know you don't grovel. You're going to have to get back that terrible actress, what's her name?"

"Allison." Rachel felt numb and purposeless. She had wanted to submit it to festivals this summer. Probably wouldn't have come to anything, but she needed to get in the habit, go through the practice. Now this film was what would blow her ride to NYU and stop her from graduating on time. "I know how to grovel."

"Oh really? How's it done, then?"

"You say you're sorry and then the person forgives you."

Papa made a noise like a buzzer running out. "Wrong. You apologize profusely, assuming the other person won't forgive you and that you will do anything to get them back on your side. And you have to mean it. Anything."

Rachel shuddered. "I don't have anything that she wants. What the hell do I have to offer other than rage and a shitty car?"

It wasn't a question. It was a definitive statement of all of her hopes going up in flames, like an old school film storage house that had caught alight by someone stupid enough to smoke there.

"Mija. Find out what she likes. Then give that to her. While you apologize."

Rachel thought about that for a long beat. She'd do anything to make an all-important piece of history-making cinema. There wasn't much she wouldn't sacrifice. Granted, her dignity and her pride would be the last thing on the list, but she'd still do it. If it meant getting the footage she'd need. She'd do it fifty times over, no matter how much it felt like eating dirt.

Rachel remembered the overpriced coffee in Sana's hand that morning by the lockers. "And it'll work?"

"I dunno. But it sure will work better than doing nothing." He paused. "Picking up a new rider and they look. Well. Particular. I'll see you when I get home. Don't use up all your time on something that won't pay off."

And with that Papa clicked the phone off. Rachel pocketed her cell phone. She apparently had some groveling to plan.

7

Overhead Boom Box

Rachel stood next to Sana's locker. The bell would ring soon to let them all out from last period, and Rachel had to be ready to grovel. Really, really grovel. She'd skipped seventh to make sure the coffee was still warm when she gave it to Sana. She hoped that would help Sana get through cheerleading practice and help her out again. She wasn't used to this feeling, nerves tingling, her senses firing on all pistons. Rachel was used to getting out of her body and into her head. Now all she could do was feel the overly warm cup of coffee in her hands and smell the nutty, roasted steam wafting toward her face.

What Rachel hadn't been expecting was Sana walking toward her locker with a hard black boot on her right foot, half limping and half rolling through the motions as she walked.

Rachel's jaw dropped. "What the hell happened to you?"

"Do you have to swear all the time?" said Sana with a sniff. She actually *sniffed*. It was horrible.

"Look, if you're going to work with me you're going to have to take a few swear words now and then." That, Rachel realized, was the understatement of the century.

"Who says I'm going to work with you?" Sana folded her arms across her chest.

Dammit. Hell. Shit. Fuck. Best to get them all out of her head for right now. "No one. But I was going to ask if you'd come back after cheerleading practice today."

This was apparently exactly the wrong thing to say. Sana's mouth formed a disapproving line across her face. Sana narrowed her eyes at Rachel. "Har, har. Very funny."

"I'm not trying to be funny."

"Do you think I can go to practice like this?" Sana waved her arms toward her boot.

"I mean," said Rachel. "Maybe? Don't you have things you do other than cheerleading? Like decorating shit and making all those boys feel like gods?"

"Seriously? Did you really come here to apologize or what?"

"I mean, I did, but 'or what' is feeling a lot more accurate right now." Rachel slumped against the nearest locker.

And that's when Sana caught sight of the coffee. Her whole attitude shifted. She leaned toward the coffee like a kid pressing her face up against the bakery counter loaded up with cookies and pan dulces. "Is that Demitasse?"

"Yeah," said Rachel, shoving the cup in Sana's direction. Rachel couldn't keep the disapproval out of her voice. *Who had the cash for a six-and-a-half-dollar-a-day latte habit?* Only spoiled princesses, that's who. "It's for you. A latte. A really expensive latte, by the way."

Sana popped the eco-friendly travel lid off the cup and took a deep inhale of the coffee. She sipped it like it was something sacred or precious and stayed quiet for a long moment. "You should have led with the coffee."

"I *tried*," said Rachel, knowing she sounded disgruntled. She couldn't keep the peevishness out of her voice. "But I couldn't not ask. About the foot."

"Curiosity killed the cat, etc."

"Luckily I'm still alive to finish this groveling."

Sana raised an eyebrow. "This is you groveling?"

"Yes," said Rachel through gritted teeth.

Sana laughed. It was a clear-as-a-bell laugh. It was a laugh that Victorian ladies probably would have envied, if Victorian ladies were allowed to laugh in public, which Rachel was pretty sure they weren't.

"I'd hate to see you on a bad day," Sana said.

"You already have."

Sana sighed. "This isn't going to work."

There were so many ways that Rachel could answer that. But for some reason, the truth fell out of her mouth. "If you don't, I'll fail."

Sana shook her head. "That isn't fair. You can't put that on me."

"I know it isn't, but I didn't make the rules." That was probably the realest thing Rachel had ever said. "Douga did. Now we have to live with them."

Sana nodded. Like she got it—the world was unfair and now they were stuck with the rules they would never have written had they had the chance themselves. "All right. I'll do your film."

"Excellent."

"I've got one condition." Sana leveled an even stare.

"Of course you do." And Rachel had felt so hopeful for that brief, shining moment.

"I'll only play Helen of Troy if you don't make her the villain."

"You're joking, right?"

"Nope."

"Rad. Anything else her majesty would like to deign to offer?" *Deign* was such a good word. Rachel patted herself on the back for that one.

Granted, Sana was a private school cheerleader, so odds of it going over her head were low. But using such a big, powerful word made Rachel feel expensive and worthy. Made her feel like nobody could look their nose down at her. Even if said nose was an elegant, sloping nose with a gleaming piece of gold in it.

Sana's mouth twitched, like she sensed the implicit *screw you* in Rachel's words and she couldn't think of anything funnier than Rachel trying to get the best of her. "Now that you mention it, I do. I'd like to help make the film. Not only be in it. Think of me as helping with your wandering creative direction. And on that note—maybe don't just lead with the coffee next time. Maybe stick to the coffee and the request. I think you're gonna do better with straight bribery rather than groveling. I don't think groveling is really in your repertoire."

Just when Rachel was feeling good and solid about *deign*, the cheerleader had to come in with *repertoire* and completely ruin everything.

"Fine." Because Rachel didn't have a choice on this one. It was Sana or fail. And Sana knew it.

Sana took a sip of her coffee. "You have a time I should meet you or are you just gonna give me this coffee and stare?"

"Tomorrow. After school." Rachel definitely hadn't been staring. At least she hadn't meant to be staring. Rachel had just gotten so used to ducking behind a camera and getting to observe people that she wasn't used to being noticed or observed herself. "In the film lab again."

"Cool," said Sana.

"Cool," repeated Rachel. But she needn't have bothered. By that point Sana had turned with her stack of books in hand and walked off to whatever class required eight billion textbooks the size of the Torah and the Talmud put together.

Sana checked her phone. She'd be able to catch Diesel at the tail end of water polo practice and grab a ride home if she headed to the gym without stopping.

"Sorry about your foot," said Diesel as he saw Sana approach.

"S'okay." Sana shrugged. "Coach shouldn't have had any of us catching such an elaborate stunt."

Diesel's face had gone blank. Unreadable. And Diesel had an amazingly expressive face. All the muscles of the face could be studied, watching the amazing contortions he could make to express his displeasure. "My dude. Is there something you forgot to mention?"

Outside was dry and hot, but Sana went cold all over. She wasn't one for premonitions. She was built for logic, for analysis, for solid methodology, and for science. But she knew if she turned around, she'd see her father. Sana stopped walking, keeping her back to the parking lot that they had been heading toward not a moment before. "My dad's in town?"

"Wow, can you hold out on information." Diesel was mad. But not the permanent kind of mad. The kind that bristles and rushes through, like a vacuum-sealed explosion.

Sana winced, but she didn't say anything about it. "I so do not want to turn around right now."

"If you don't, I think he's gonna head over here." Then Diesel did the impossible—he raised his arm into a light wave. The irony coating his face was unmistakable.

"Are you crazy?" Sana yanked his arm down.

"He's waving. Seriously. You've got probably forty-five seconds until he walks over and starts to chat with me. I assume you don't want him to chat with me?"

"I don't want him to chat with *anyone*." Sana straightened her bag on her shoulder again. She set her spine straight, with her shoulders down. Her ponytail was still slicked down; she didn't need to worry about that. She wiped the edges of her mouth with her finger, lest there was errant lip balm around them. She smoothed her eyebrows.

"You better tell me about this later." Diesel gave a nod and walked off to his own car.

And then Sana turned, with a perfectly placid expression on her face. She tilted her head when she caught her father's eye. He stood in front of an impossibly obscene sports car. Give-me-a-ticket red. With rims that gleamed in the last of the day's remaining sunlight. Sana refused to eye the badge. That would only encourage him.

She walked toward him briskly, and with purpose. "Hello."

He must have sensed her formality, because he said with some contrition, "I asked your mom when you got off. She said you had cheerleading practice until now. Sorry, kid. I thought she would have told you I was coming."

"She didn't." Sana was going to leave it at that, but somehow he'd made this whole situation her mother's fault and that wouldn't do at all. "Did *you* tell *her* you were coming today?"

"No," he said. "I assumed she'd figure it out."

Sana raised an eyebrow and said nothing. She opened the red door on the passenger's side and slid into the shining black bucket seat. It must have never spent a day unpolished. Sana wondered who her father paid to have *that* chore done.

Sana's father opened the door and peeked his head in. "Your friend need a ride?"

"He *was* my ride."

"Right," he said, hopping into the driver's side seat. "I'll never understand how a kid of mine ended up hating driving."

Sana said nothing to that. After a beat, the engine purred to life, a whooshing, throaty noise that set Sana's teeth on edge. Sana sat upright, her scapulae lightly resting on the back of the passenger's seat. She stared straight ahead, watching as the road lined with cars and palm trees wound through the city.

Sana normally loved the drive home from school. Something about watching the dusty yet green roads by school give way to the wide boulevards of Hollywood, then farther east as the businesses grew shadier and grimier. Like LA wouldn't let the gleaming, moneyed hills forget its roots as the Wild West. Los Angeles was a city with grit, with dirt underneath its manicured sheen. And for a moment, after she had left school grounds and before she'd reached the increasingly polished suburbs of Studio City, Sana could see all the dust that lay underneath. Like a secret that only the worthy could see, could discover, would appreciate to the fullest measure. The AC was on full blast in the car, but all she wanted was to roll down the windows, let in the dry air of sunset and smog. Sana didn't touch the window button, though. She tried her best not to touch anything that she didn't have to in Massoud's car.

"How are you doing?" he asked, glancing over quickly as he curved the car around a winding section of road.

Sana turned, staring Massoud directly in the eye. "Same as always."

The car jolted. They'd hit a particularly nasty pothole. "Yikes."

"Yeah," said Sana. "Not the best city for this car. There are potholes everywhere now."

He looked over at her, catching her expression. For a moment, Massoud looked like he wasn't sure how to respond to that. "They don't look so bad."

"They're nasty." Sana didn't flinch.

"I see," he said, putting his eyes back to focusing on the road. "Well. I asked about how you are since I've heard all your good news from your grandmother. Getting into Princeton? Congrats."

"Thanks." Sana felt her stomach slowly form a knot.

"Funny, too," he said carefully, so carefully that it checked the next sarcastic comment that had come to Sana's mind. "Because I checked in with a buddy of mine after you got in. He works admissions—no, don't worry, I waited until all the applications were through like you asked—and it turns out the school still hasn't gotten your deposit."

"So?" Sana turned to face her father. She could tell he was about to say something important. It was the way he focused so casually on the road, the way his tense shoulders belied his otherwise easy posture. Sana braced herself.

"So didn't you have to pull your other applications since you went in early action?" Massoud hadn't meant it as a sucker punch, but Sana had felt it all the same.

"I did."

Her father looked over. He let out whatever breath he had been holding. "Christ. Sana-jaan. If you don't put down that deposit, you're not going to college at all next year."

I know. "I'll get it done."

"When?"

The car rolled to a stop. She should have noticed that the rocketing sensation had lulled long ago. They'd pulled off the wide, main boulevard onto the narrow streets of her neighborhood a little while back. She looked over at her father. He really was handsome. Whatever everyone else said, Sana knew her good looks and the trouble they brought with them didn't just come from her mother's side.

"Soon. Tomorrow." Sana wasn't going to tell him about the fellowship. She wasn't going to tell him about a future that had less structure, that had more space. He wouldn't understand. Not the way he had turned out.

"Sana. I really am here for you."

The gray streak that was forming through the front of her father's hair should have aged him, but what it really did was lend him some distinction. A sense of gravity that he hadn't had before. He was aging like a dream. And with a teenage daughter and salt-and-pepper hair in his mid-thirties, he looked the part of debonair and worldly journalist, long before he had any right to the title. That was Sana's father for you.

Sana nodded, because it was easier than telling him she didn't believe him. Easier than getting into an argument with him. She opened the door and swung her legs out. She pulled her schoolbag out of the car without looking up. She closed the car door without slamming it, and also without looking back.

When she got into the room of her empty house, she closed her door. Then she dropped her bag, curled up on her bed, and began to cry.

8

Tumbling

Sana

It was the worst pep rally in the history of pep rallies.

First, with Sana in a boot, the squad had to do cheers with none of the stunts. The sophomore they'd pulled up from JV still wasn't ready. Now, this didn't have to be horrendous. Enough spirit, enough pep in your step, enough crowd-favorite cheers and the squad could overcome this one. But Alexis and T were making the whole situation so much worse. Alexis, who felt responsible for dropping Sana in the first place, kept stepping out of Sana's way.

And—as if the entire squad going in and out of formation in order to avoid Sana and not having the star flyer weren't bad enough—half the squad had lost their voices practically overnight from some kind of a cold that was going around.

Sana spent the majority of the rally trying not to put her head in her hands. So much for leading the squad with dignity and grace. So much for finishing out her senior year strong.

After the squad finished to mild applause, Sana should have gone to the nurse's station and gotten some kind of painkiller. Should have gone somewhere she could sit alone, calm and quiet.

Instead she headed toward the film lab. It was a strange impulse.

But Sana had stopped thinking too much about sudden impulses. She had at least kept herself from ordering pineapple shampoo or conditioner, so far. She'd take that as a clear win right about now.

Rachel looked stunned as Sana walked in. "You're here."

Sana shrugged. "I said I would be."

"Yeah. After school. You're like three hours early."

"I can go." Except Sana felt arrested to the spot. She ought to go. Come back later, when they'd decided to work on this insane project together. But instead, Sana stood there, staring. That's how life had felt since January. Frozen, waiting. For something to happen. For someone to shake Sana out of her stupor.

She'd applied to her fellowship. And for a while that had helped. But now she was waiting to hear back. And waiting to decide about Princeton. And waiting as she watched everyone else cheer and do stunts.

Sana was sick of waiting. She wanted the space to *do* something. Anything.

"Here." Rachel reached into a stack of papers on the desk where she worked. "This is your script. Read through and let me know if you've got any comments or notes. Tell me what you really think."

Sana was in motion again, grabbing the papers. They were three-hole punched and had metal brads in the top and bottom holes. "You take notes?"

"Not really. But you elbowed your way into this and now you've got to put in the work."

Sana took a seat next to Rachel. She grabbed a pen off of the desk. "You have a plan?"

Rachel nodded. The nod was knowing, confident. Full of the kind of self-assurance that Sana could only dream of in a situation like this. Rachel created worlds, built stories. She took nothing and turned it into tales with scope and brilliance. "The classics."

"Of what?" Sana wasn't sure. The movie itself was based on the classics, in the literary sense of the word. The kind English teachers talked about—the thousands-of-years-of-the-written-word kind of classics. Sana sensed that Rachel meant another kind of classics altogether here.

"The classics of cinema." Rachel said *cinema* like *cinemahh*, like she ought to be smoking a hand-rolled cigarette out of a long holder and wearing all black.

Sana resisted the urge to laugh. She crossed her arms over her chest. "I know those. My mom *does* work in the industry."

Rachel ignored this. She had clearly planned a whole speech out and no fact that Sana could include was going to interrupt Rachel and her already formulated procedure. "The classics are always changing. They're the ideal. The heart of movies. They're supposed to be stable. And sometimes they are. But they're also subject to whims. Like. *Breakfast at Tiffany's*. That's a classic. But it's gonna be dead in twenty years, because it's got Mickey Rooney in yellowface. And eventually that's gonna make people uncomfortable. Maybe not today. Maybe not tomorrow. But one day, it's gonna fade out. It'll be too distasteful to be a real classic, beyond the halls of film school."

"You mean, it's like scientific research."

"*Scientific research?* How is my version of the classics like scientific research?"

"You know. Peer-reviewed papers. New science replacing the old. But some stuff, well, it lasts. Like gravity and laws of motion." Sana shrugged. It was the simplest thing in the world.

"Then, yes. Except with feelings and aesthetic rather than data." Rachel paused, scrunched up her face, examined Sana for a long moment. "If you wanna help make a movie, I'm going to need you to watch movies."

Sana stared for a moment. She loved watching movies. Cheesy movies, artistic movies. Action to romance back to Oscar bait. Her mother had given her a love of the movies, and years in LA had only honed that love. "Okay."

"Okay?" Rachel's voice sounded like she believed Sana all of about ten percent. Maybe less.

"Okay." Sana nodded. She wondered if Rachel knew that Sana had seen all of her movies, had loved watching her artistry change and grow. "I mean, I need to have a sense of definitive time. I do have some practices to go to and lots of male athletes to make feel like gods. Plus schoolwork and labs. So how many hours per week? One movie? Two?"

"We're going to have to watch at least a movie a week together. Maybe two. So make time for that," said Rachel. "Plus filming and working on scripts. I'll handle shooting schedules, because I know how to do that efficiently now."

For a moment, Sana fiddled with the hoop on her nose ring. It was thin and small and sometimes she needed to check that it was still in place. Needed to ground herself and know she wasn't on some other plane of reality and that she had in fact heard Rachel correctly. "Why do we have to watch together?"

"Look, Khan, I don't like it any more than you do. But I can't trust you to do your end of the work. Especially with all those labs and hard-core math classes you've got going on. Plus your *cheerleading*. You must be some kind of idealist to say that and think I'd believe you."

Sana sucked in a breath. "Are you calling me a liar?"

"I want to make sure this gets done. I'm volunteering my time to help *you*, you know."

Considering Douga had punished them both with this assignment and Rachel needed Sana to be in her movie not to fail, Rachel was awful sure of herself as holding a position of power in this moment.

But the fight had gone out of Sana. "Fine."

Rachel eyed Sana warily. "Sunday nights?"

"Can't Sunday nights; I've got a standing dinner date with my grandparents." *Good luck finding time for us to watch a movie together.*

"You have a standing dinner date with your grandparents?" Rachel shook her head. "Who are you?"

"Someone who has to explain family time to a lot of people who don't still understand it."

"Oh. Don't you have a social life? Aren't cool girls supposed to go out on weekends? Isn't that like a law or something?" Rachel asked.

"I'm not a cool girl. I'm a cheerleader. This isn't an eighties movie. And I do go out on Fridays, since I can't go do masjid because of the games anyway."

"Okay. Saturdays. I don't work in the evening. Are you free on Saturdays?"

Sana hadn't expected Rachel to give up her Saturday evenings. But maybe Rachel was like Sana and enjoyed having the excuse to stay in and get some work done on Saturdays. "I am."

"Good." Rachel paused for a moment. "Saturday it is."

"Where do you work?" Sana let her curiosity get the better of her.

"Factor's Famous Deli." Rachel raised both her eyebrows. "You can go now. Get some notes on those pages, though. Class dismissed."

"But I don't know where I'm meeting you. I don't even have your info. Am I meeting you at work?"

Rachel got out her phone. "I live off of Palms Boulevard."

"*Palms?*" asked Sana.

Rachel looked momentarily smug. Like she was scaring Sana off from her place.

But that wasn't what Sana was thinking at all. "You drive all the way from Palms up to Royce? You must be exhausted. That's, like, an hour and a half each way at least. Every day."

Rachel's jaw set. "I have a car."

Sana realized Rachel did *not* want to talk about it. *Fine.* "I should be able to catch the bus down to Palms."

"*The bus?*" It was Rachel's turn for incredulity. "Can't you drive?"

"I *can*, technically, yes. But I typically *don't*."

"Crippling fear of operating motorized vehicles?"

Sana cracked a smile at that. "Something like that. Also my mom's on night shoots right now, so I don't think I can borrow the car for nights for a while. I'm only supposed to use ride shares in emergencies."

"I'll meet you at your place, then. Drop a pin and send it to me." Rachel found an errant piece of paper on her desk and scratched her phone number on it.

"Sure." Sana took the paper. "See you there."

"Whatever." Rachel hunched over her work, scribbling across her pages of dialogue.

Rachel usually kept her phone locked away in the break room during work. She didn't want to be tempted by it. But she'd asked Sana for notes. And even though Rachel had told Sana to bring them the next time they met, maybe Sana would send the notes sooner.

Rachel felt her phone buzz in her apron pocket.

She ducked around a wall and checked her messages. An email. Rachel felt her heart kick up a beat.

It was from Sana.

Be cool, be cool. It's just notes.

Rachel clicked through into the message. She felt a surprising twinge of disappointment to see how short it was.

    Project Notes
    Attached.
    s

Rachel opened the attachment.

Helen is an object here.

That was it. The first note. And all throughout—every time Helen was on the page.

Why does she do this?

How is she furthering the story?

Helen. Mythological damsel. She's like a prop. You could replace her with a sexy lamp and the plot wouldn't change.

Sana saw Helen of Troy in a way Rachel never had. To be honest, in a way Rachel maybe wasn't able to. The worst part was the line right at the end—*Helen isn't an object. Everyone just thinks she is.*

Rachel stashed her phone back into her apron. She needed to sit down, think about something else. Keep that last line from reverberating over and over again in her head. She grabbed a seat at the counter, even though she was still on the clock, and thunked her head down on the linoleum slab in front of her. The contact between her head and the counter made a satisfying thump.

Thump. Thump. Thump.

She was never going to figure it out. She was going to live here, at this stool, filled with artistic frustrations until there was nothing left of her but bones and withered dreams and—

Thwack. The counter surface rattled as a heavy plate was set—silverware and all—right next to Rachel's head. "I see you're still feeling sorry for yourself."

Rachel popped her head up. It was Jeanie. Jeanie didn't take shit from anyone, and most particularly not from any of Rachel's sulks.

Rachel put her head back down. Her voice came out muffled, vibrating against the linoleum counter. "I'm not feeling sorry for myself."

"You are. I can tell. Your eyebrows pucker and your whole face looks like a question mark. I know you're feeling sorry for yourself."

Jeanie couldn't even see her face right now. Rachel was going to argue the point, belabor it even, but she caught a whiff of the matzo ball soup. Nobody made matzo ball soup like Factor's. Rachel had grown up with her father's lamb al pastor, her mother's ful medames, but it was this matzo ball soup that got her every time.

Jeanie tsked. "Come on. You've got a customer. Order up."

Rachel turned around to see a tall blond head poking out from one side of a booth. "You have got to be kidding me."

Jeanie hummed, like she'd heard that before. And, to be honest, she had. "I never kid about work."

Rachel picked up the plate, taking it over to the booth where Diesel sat. She clattered it down on his table. "What are you doing here?"

Diesel took up his whole side of the booth bench, his limbs were so long and his body so oversized. He cracked a smile like he'd seen the sun come out after a couple of days of rain. "I heard you worked here!"

Rachel watched his face, checking for any signs of flickering sarcasm. But he held his goofy grin. She understood how he was the kind of boy to break up chorus lines and ruin friendships. When he was genuinely interested, Diesel gave out his full attention.

"I've worked here for three years, Diesel. That is literally not news." Rachel put her hand on her hip, like that would dissuade his cheerfulness.

"Yes, but *I* just found out." Diesel gestured to the other bench. "Wanna sit?"

"Dude, I'm working."

"Hello, ma'am. Is Rachel free for a break?" Diesel was looking at Jeanie, giving her big, pathetic puppy dog eyes. It should have looked cartoonish. Instead he looked handsome and lost, the way a fairy-tale prince might as he went searching for his one true love.

God, did beautiful people annoy Rachel.

Jeanie looked over Diesel once, then looked at Rachel. "He a creep?"

Rachel wished she could have lied in that moment. "No. He's not."

"Do you know him?"

Rachel shrugged. "We go to school together."

"Take your break." Jeanie didn't say it like it was a suggestion.

"Thank you, ma'am," Diesel called out as Jeanie walked away.

Jeanie rolled her eyes and kept moving.

"Ass-kissing doesn't work with her." Rachel slid into the opposite booth bench from Diesel.

Diesel laughed, like that was the funniest thing he'd ever heard. "I like that."

"Seriously? You live your life coasting on charm and a smile and you like when people are immune to it?"

"Of course." Diesel took an enormous bite of his pastrami sandwich. "When people bend to your will when you're nice to them, you end up respecting anyone who sees through the smile."

"You're talking about Maddie, aren't you?" Rachel was eyeing the pickle on Diesel's plate. It smelled sharp and vinegary and perfect.

Diesel caught her looking. He offered it to her wordlessly. And despite herself, Rachel took it. It had the perfect level of crunch.

"Man, you know about that?"

"Yes, even film weirdos hear the same rumors as everyone else."

"Oh, that was shitty to assume. Sorry." Diesel nodded into his sandwich, humming a little like he'd suddenly figured out how good the pastrami was here. "Yeah, she's totally immune. Also, she's really small. I feel like small people are really powerful."

"Says the guy who looks like he could smash a watermelon between his two bare hands."

"But I've got to duck to go into buildings. And I could never sneak around anywhere. I'm too tall."

"What a difficult life you must have had." Rachel rolled her eyes.

"I like you." Diesel said it so simply, so plainly.

"Are you kidding me?"

"Nope."

Rachel put her head into her hands.

"Wanna hang out sometime?" Diesel said this as he slurped his soup.

Rachel must have heard him wrong. Must have been the soup noise garbling the words that were actually coming out of his mouth. "What?"

"We could play *Mario Kart*."

"You do know I'm not straight, right?"

"Yup." Diesel kept slurping his soup, noodles and all. He must have been saving the matzo for last. "I don't ask girls I like to play *Mario Kart*."

"That might be your first mistake. What do you ask them to do?" Rachel watched as Diesel opened his mouth to respond. "Never mind, please don't answer that. I don't want to know."

Diesel nodded. "Fair enough."

"Look, I gotta get back to work."

Diesel grinned like he'd just found out about all the cat videos on the internet. "Rad."

Rachel didn't want to feel so much better after hanging out with a meathead for ten minutes who probably spent more time working out—or working on his tan or his bleached hair—than on his actual future. But she did. He was calming, grounding, annoying.

He was solid, and not just because he was a foot taller than Rachel.

Rachel wasn't even a quarter of the way there, most of the time. She was always thinking, always planning. Her next film, her current film. Projects she'd need a big budget for, the kind that required studio money. Projects she could practically film now with a phone camera, a couple of lights, and a lot of duct tape and dreams. Dreams that she now had less than a month to complete.

Rachel heard the bell ring by the kitchen for an order coming up. She walked over, grabbed the plates, and loaded up the train in her arms.

It was going to be a long April.

9

On Location

Rachel

When Rachel pulled up to the modest one-story bungalow in her beat-ass car, it was yet another thing that she hadn't been expecting when it came to Sana Khan. The house had a seventies vibe, small and beige with a low, sloping brown roof. The watered-down version of what had once passed for high design. Cookie-cutter Americana in bungalow form. Like *The Virgin Suicides* come to life. But way less creepy, obviously.

It was the kind of place you bought because you could afford it, not because you particularly loved it. And something about that shifted more of the footing underneath Rachel's feet when it came to Sana. Because the house was such an unexpected data point, such a radical departure from what Rachel expected of Sana.

Who was this girl?

Rachel rang the bell. She tapped her foot as she waited.

The door swung open and Rachel hardly had time to process Sana before she started talking.

"So sorry, my mom's out on night shoots, which are basically the worst because she gets no sleep and then she needs lots of coffee and then I don't get any coffee and then we're both terrible in the morning.

On the bright side, we've got the house to ourselves, as long as you don't mind being here alone?" Sana was breathless by the time she'd stopped speaking. She looked ready to go on, when she must have remembered that Rachel wasn't one of her real friends, so she snapped her mouth shut, quickly and efficiently. She blinked up at Rachel, as though waiting for a response.

Rachel hunched her shoulders. "Um. I thought we'd see a movie in the park?"

Sana's eyes went wide. "Oh! Sorry! Okay. Wait, come in! I've got to grab my keys and stuff."

Sana practically bounced as she led Rachel through her home. Rachel looked around. This was an original house with all the original suburban fixtures. Wood paneling, ceiling beams, even a brick fireplace. Everything was old and cozy—a mixture of purchases made for practicality and ones that had been worn into something that the owners clearly loved. A TV hooked up to an old PS3 and a VHS player. A lumpy, mottled afghan that somebody had attempted to make into a large square but seemed possibly triangular or trapezoidal. A stack of old *National Geographics* teetering dangerously close to another stack of library checkouts—mostly old DVDs that Rachel didn't recognize with a couple of VHS cassettes interspersed between.

And photos, photos everywhere. Of Sana and another woman. The other woman looked too young to be Sana's mother—her deep brown face smooth and only lined where she smiled at the outer corners of her eyes. But she had to have been related to Sana—she had the same sloping, elegant nose. Same heavy, straight brows. And the same wry twinkle in her eye. Rachel felt uncomfortable, also though she was seeing more than she ever wanted to, as though she was bearing witness to more than she ought to be allowed to.

That was the filmmaker's curse.

Rachel couldn't help but see the signs and signifiers everywhere she went. Once she'd learned how to set a stage, she had learned how to read a person's life like one. It was a blessing when it came to films. It was a curse when it came to interacting with others. Or not feeling ashamed of her own home situation. Not that it was really her fault, her home situation. But it was hers regardless, and she'd have to live with it for now.

"Do you want something to drink?" Sana, ponytail swishing along with her bright tone, interrupted Rachel's thoughts. "Water? Tea? I make dark tea, it's good."

Rachel took a deep breath, trying to steady herself. Unfortunately she ended up taking a deep inhale of Sana's house. Except that wasn't the scent of house. It was Sana. She smelled like jasmine and sunshine. Like too-warm concrete and the salty air from the ocean. And orange blossoms.

She smelled like summer.

"No," said Rachel, at a loss for any other words. "The movie starts at eight, but we need to get tickets before then."

Sana frowned. "Okay."

"And I'm not thirsty." *Oh God, that was an accidentally sexual comment, why was she saying accidentally sexual comments.* She had to fill the void that her accidentally sexual comment had created. But Rachel had nothing to say. Rachel just stared at Sana, hoping she would get this information via brain waves or something.

"I'll just grab my wallet." Sana, clad in vintage jeans and a soft, navy T-shirt, moved into the back of the house at a surprisingly agile pace for someone whose foot was encased in a black boot.

Sana returned, shoving her phone into one back pocket of her jeans and a wallet in the other. She tilted her head toward the door. "What's on the docket for tonight?"

Rachel cleared her throat. "I thought we'd start at the very beginning."

"The very best place to start." Sana's mouth twitched, like she'd told herself a good joke. She grabbed her keys from a hook by the door.

Rachel stopped what she had been doing—which was following behind Sana to the door—and stared. "Did you just quote *The Sound of Music* at me?"

"You teed it up so nicely, I couldn't help myself." Sana shrugged.

Rachel must have entered an alternate universe. There was no other explanation for it. For this joking, movie-referencing Sana. In old jeans and with what could be construed as dirty hair. Still shiny and straight, but definitely not freshly pressed. "*Pretty in Pink.* I thought we'd start with *Pretty in Pink.* They're doing a showing over at a park in Chinatown."

And then maybe, afterward, Rachel would find out where she'd left the universe she had previously occupied and entered this one where Sana had a cozy middle-class home in Studio City instead of a stately mansion up in the hills. A place that looked like it was occasionally cleaned by either Sana or her mother, rather than by professionals on a weekly or biweekly basis.

"That *is* a classic," said Sana thoughtfully.

From the way Sana's mouth twisted to one side, Rachel couldn't help but wonder if there was something else on Sana's mind that she wasn't saying out loud. "Have you already seen it?"

"Not in years." Sana locked the door behind them both. She half hobbled, half skipped toward Rachel's car. "Are all of these movies you want me to watch gonna be, like, conventional Hollywood movies?"

"No, not all of them. Some of them are indie, too." Rachel swung open the door on the driver's side and got in.

Sana's mouth slanted into a disapproving expression. She slid into her own seat and yanked the passenger's door closed. "That's not what I meant."

"Then for the love of God, please say what you mean." Rachel hunched over the wheel and turned the ignition. She could hear the irritation and confusion in her voice.

"Are these all gonna be white people movies?"

Rachel swung around so fast she hit her head on her window visor. *Holy shit* did that hurt.

"Oh no." Sana leaned over, as close as she could get to inspecting Rachel's head without touching. "Are you okay?"

"It's fine." *Just injured my pride.* "I'm fine."

"You sure you don't need any ice?" Sana bit her lip. "I can run back inside real quick."

"NO." Rachel cleared her throat. She hadn't meant to be that forceful, but she didn't want Sana, like, ministering to her wounds, or something totally embarrassing. "Can we head to the movie now, please?"

Sana, mercifully, released her lip. She buckled herself into the passenger's seat. "Okay. As long as I can choose the movie for the next time."

"Fine. You pick next time." *Fucking Sana.*

Sana looked over at Rachel. She had this serious, intent expression on her face and it made Sana want to lean in and ask what Rachel was thinking. Her eyebrows were furrowed and she was watching the line with so much focus, so much determination.

They were slowly creeping toward the front and Sana wasn't sure whether to get out her wallet now, or when it was closer to the time they'd have to actually pay. She discreetly felt for her wallet in her back pocket. Sana thought she ought to pay for at least her ticket and probably Rachel's too, but she didn't want to cross some unspoken line with Rachel.

Too many rules that were too easy to break now.

The line snaked around the park, winding from the entrance down Spring Street and almost to the station for the Gold Line train that ran from East LA through downtown, back out to Pasadena. They had already had a good ten minutes of waiting. Another ten more and Sana was sure she'd go nuts. But couldn't think of anything else to say. All she knew was that she was standing in line to go to a movie next to Rachel Recht and Rachel wasn't yelling at her or glaring at her or telling her to get out already.

It was such a miracle that Sana didn't want to say anything and screw it up.

Sana continued to glance at Rachel, trying to figure out if Rachel was staring off into space as a way to ignore Sana or because she felt as uncomfortable as Sana did. Sana's body vibrated with unspoken words, unspent energy. Her booted up foot rocked against the pavement, back and forth.

Rachel looked up and Sana was unfortunately caught, staring like a total creep. Sana blinked a couple of times. Rachel was making an expression like she'd taken a bite of what she thought was vanilla ice cream but had turned out to be sour cream.

"What is it?" All of that attention, all of that focus that had been directed at the front of the line was now squarely on Sana.

"Nothing." Sana swallowed. She had to keep eye contact. She had to keep breathing like everything was normal, like this was fine. Like she had conversations every day with Rachel about how she wasn't staring at her at all.

Rachel's expression deepened into a frown. "You were staring."

Oh help. "I was just looking off into space."

"Sure." But Rachel's eyes went sharp, keen. Like she hadn't bought that excuse at all. "You said your mom was working a night shoot."

"Yeah." Sana shrugged. *Act like staring isn't a big deal and she'll lose interest. Act like you're totally cool, like everything is okay, okay, okay.*

If only Rachel would stop looking directly back at Sana. "What does she do?"

"She's a production designer. *The* production designer, on this big shoot." Sana was too proud of her mom to censor herself on this, to confine herself to one-word answers. She wanted to see the impressed surprise coat Rachel's face. "She started as a carpenter. Worked her way up."

"No shit," said Rachel, no small amount of awe in her own voice.

Sana liked that Rachel knew how impressive it was. How much steel and determination it took to get from where Mom had started to where she was now. Sana couldn't keep the pride out of her voice, didn't want to, when she said, "She's pretty incredible."

"Did she always know she wanted to make movies?"

Sana laughed. An easy laugh. The first she'd had all night. Possibly the first she'd had in weeks; she couldn't remember the last time she'd honestly laughed. "No. She knew she didn't want to starve."

"Starve?" Rachel shook her head. "Am I missing something? Your mom's in charge of production design on a big shoot. Isn't your dad on TV all the time? Don't you go to Royce?"

"By the grace of my grandparents' forgiveness." Sana shrugged. That was an understatement.

"Forgiveness for what?" Rachel took a step forward as the line surged ahead.

For living life on her own terms. For not following the chosen path. For not living a life they could be proud of, that they could brag about at family gatherings and at social functions. In short, for being the opposite of everything that Sana had strived to do her whole life. Farrah never needed to prove herself to anyone. Sana needed to prove herself to everyone. "For getting a divorce at twenty. Or maybe for getting pregnant at nineteen. Or maybe for running away with me in tow after she got the divorce. Who knows, really."

"Forgive *her*?"

Sana felt a smile pulling at her lips. Felt some sense of solidarity with Rachel, though Sana couldn't quite say how. She just stared into those warm brown eyes again. She didn't know when she'd get another chance to memorize their color. They really were like the color of tea—nearly black one moment, with a flash of red the next. "My mamani was online and she saw a photo of me that my mom had posted. And that was it for her. She needed to know me. Needed to forgive my mom."

"That's it?" Rachel looked like she usually did before she exploded. Her eyebrows were raised, her cheeks pinched in. Like she drew in as much potential energy as she could before releasing it all into the world in some spectacular fashion. "They f—sorry. They cut her off. Told her to leave, and then suddenly they see a photo and all is forgiven?"

Sana tugged at the end of her ponytail, then released it. "They didn't really forgive my mom. But she didn't really forgive them either. It's a mess. But at least they're talking."

"Still doesn't explain your mom's career path, or even the fancy prep school." Rachel watched Sana. Studied her. Looked at her.

People looked at Sana's face all the time. Her body, too. Sana knew that gaze well. But few people ever looked at *her*. In that moment, Sana forgot she was standing in line in a crowded space. Forgot anyone could overhear. She could have divulged every secret she'd ever had. "In those couple of years, my mom had to stand on her own. She took me and everything she felt was really hers, packed it in her old Mitsubishi, and drove up to LA. Decided that there were jobs in the film industry besides just making the movie or writing the movie or acting in the movie.

"She said she wasn't qualified for much at that point—prep-school educated, college dropout, single mom, no work experience except some time filing in her father's office. But she decided it didn't matter. Said she wouldn't leave the lot until she got work. I think it was the Warner lot, though honestly it could have been Sony. She dropped me off at the childcare there and wouldn't let up. So finally some grizzly old carpenter felt bad for her, took her under his wing, taught her everything he knew. And he never regretted it. My mother hardly slept, she worked so hard in those days. Even then, she knew it wasn't a guarantee. But she decided she was going to make it. Through sheer willpower, I think. It's kind of amazing what you can do when you decide you can't fail."

Rachel was too dumbstruck to respond to this. Sana could see it. She lowered her voice a little bit, made Rachel lean in to hear her. Sana needed to know she *could* make Rachel lean in toward her. "And even after they started talking again—my grandparents and my mom—Mom wouldn't take anything from them."

And then, against all odds, Rachel *did* lean closer.

Sana took a deep breath. "Only took the money when it was for my education. Because she said she'd be crazy to turn down that kind of opportunity, not when it was my future on the line."

Rachel bit the inside of her cheek, like she was suppressing a smile. "Your mom sounds kind of ruthless."

Sana smiled. Not the sly one she usually tried out on people. No, this was her real, honest-to-God grin, and she watched as it hit Rachel like a well-executed sucker punch to the gut. "There is something particularly ruthless about my mom. I've always admired that about her. She's so single-minded. Nothing stops her."

Rachel stared for a long moment. "My mom left. A few years ago."

"She left?"

"Yeah. Up and gone. Out of our lives. Guess she couldn't take us anymore."

"But your dad's still around? Or do you have other family?"

"Don't really have other family. My dad was an only child and his parents died before I was born. But yeah, Papa's still around," said Rachel. "He was kind of touch and go for a minute there, but he pulled through. And my mom was an orphan. *Is* an orphan, I guess. But my dad and I, we've got each other."

Sana reached out and touched Rachel's wrist. "I'm really sorry."

Rachel stared at her wrist for a long moment. Sana lifted her hand.

It was tingling and strange and somehow seemed like it didn't belong to her anymore at all. But she knew it did. Knew she'd reached out for Rachel.

Oh no. Sana felt her face flush.

"That'll be seventeen each," said a voice right in front of them.

Sana startled. Even Rachel looked a little bit stunned to have finally reached the front of the line. Sana reached into her back pocket and paid for them both before she'd realized what they had done. Rachel looked ready to protest.

But Sana shook her head. "Just pay for my dinner?"

Rachel snorted but didn't put up any further protest. She just made her way through the crowd of people, trying to find an open spot. When she finally found one, she got a blanket out of her backpack and, still maintaining her grip on one end, threw it out in the air. The blanket landed flat and relatively smooth on the grass.

"Do you mind sharing?" Rachel looked at Sana, but wasn't making eye contact.

Sana shrugged, as casual as she could manage. "Sure."

Rachel sat on one side of the blanket and Sana did her best to sit as far on the other side of the blanket as possible. She needed to make space, to make distance between them. Sana stretched out her legs. She could feel the warmth of the setting sun through her jeans. She leaned back on her hands, tilting her face up toward the sun. She closed her eyes even though she was wearing sunglasses. Spring in Los Angeles was such a fickle thing. One minute it was fifty degrees and too cold for shorts, the next it was eighty-five and required a sundress and a slushie to survive.

Today, this evening, right now—however—was perfect. It was warm, with a night breeze just starting to kick up the dust in the park and the haze in the last of the light. Sana had actually worn the right amount of clothing for the rapidly cooling weather.

Rachel cleared her throat. "I need to ask you something."

Sana leaned over toward Rachel's voice but kept her eyes closed. "Yes?"

"What did you mean—*Helen of Troy isn't an object, everyone just thinks she is?*"

Sana let her back fall against the blanket. Felt her T-shirt grow slightly cold and damp from the dew that was bleeding through the cloth. "She's the most beautiful woman in the world. She's the face that launched a thousand ships."

"I *know* that."

Sana turned, looked at Rachel. She needed Rachel to understand. To get this. To really, honest-to-goodness *understand.* "She isn't just a face. Isn't just the most beautiful woman in the world. She's got thoughts and feelings and ambitions and drive. She's got her own hopes, her own fears. The storytellers take away a lot of her agency, saying she ran off because a goddess cursed her with love. But she could have stayed. You always have a choice, no matter what you feel. She made the choice to leave it all behind. To do what was unsafe and unexpected. She decided to be selfish."

"Aren't all beautiful women selfish?"

The words were so quiet, but they still felt like a slap across the face. Sana rolled back, looking at the sky and the trees that seemed to float on the edges of her vision. "I can't answer that for you. That's a belief you've got. But it's equally selfish to choose home and safety and the familiar as it is to choose love over duty. My mom chose duty and it almost destroyed her."

"She left her children. Helen had a little girl."

The air tensed, charged with something Sana was only beginning to understand. "You can think that's bad or wicked. Immoral, if you want. But there's drama in that choice. You're a filmmaker. You're supposed to see your characters, even the ones you don't like. You don't just take away Helen's agency because you don't like her or don't agree with her. I've seen your other films. I don't think you want to make a movie where you take away Helen's free will. Her ability to change the plot herself."

Rachel stared at Sana with a strange combination of hurt and anger and wonder.

Sana tried to find the right words. "Helen of Troy is more than a plot device. She's more than a beautiful stolen object that needs to be retrieved."

"That doesn't make her good." Rachel hadn't flinched, hadn't looked away.

"I never said she was good. I said she was human. Flawed and real and flesh and blood. Barely older than us and scared out of her mind. Don't make Helen perfect. Make her real. I know you can make her real." And that's when Sana saw it—the moment when Rachel Recht heard exactly what Sana had said.

The moment when Rachel honestly listened. Sana's breath caught.

"Fine," said Rachel. "You can look over the whole project. But that doesn't mean I'll change anything."

"Is it so bad letting someone help?"

Rachel's mouth pulled to one side, like she couldn't decide whether to frown or to smile. "Maybe not."

Sana returned the expression with an unwilling half grin of her own.

"Come on," said Rachel, with a shake of her head. "Let's get in a food truck line before the movie starts. I still owe you dinner."

10

Chew Like You Have a Secret

Rachel

Rachel preferred the city at night, at the edge of winter—the rainy season was over, mostly, but the weather would snap back and forth so nobody knew what to expect. The night air was cool, slightly more cleared of pollution. A metallic tang on the wind, plus the scent of ripening oranges and lemons and whatever other citrus fruit people were growing on their balconies. The jasmine wouldn't bloom until summer—*thank God*—because at this point, Rachel wouldn't be able to smell jasmine without thinking of Sana. But even the jasmine bushes had the best scent at night. They didn't call it *night-blooming jasmine* for nothing, after all.

Los Angeles at night was the thump of the car along potholes, the whoosh of the cold air as the passenger's window rolled up, the distinctive *woompa woompa pop* of a chopper as it shone its spotlight on the latest criminal search mid-city. It was the Santa Ana winds blowing dust and debris and smog into your eyes.

What took hours and hours of traffic during the day to get across West Hollywood a car could fly through at night in five minutes flat.

Rachel took a left down Beverly Drive. She should have taken Beverwil, but she preferred to watch the way Beverly meandered through the upper-middle-class, posturing homes of South Beverly before she had to duck back under the 10 and head into Palms. She liked to turn the old heater on in her car, warming it up until it was stifling hot and she was sweating, then cracking her windows open, taking a relieving breath of cool night air.

She took a deep inhale. Perfect. The air was perfect tonight.

Of course, she'd gone and blown that perfect night all to hell by spending the evening lying next to Sana and trying to watch an eighties rom-com classic.

Rachel should have definitely categorized taking Sana to see a movie as a mistake, but she couldn't bring herself to do it. She couldn't bring herself to cancel the next movie night, either. But it hadn't gone according to plan at all, and Rachel was instinctively uncomfortable with things that didn't go according to plan.

Rachel had to duck off of Beverly and meet back up with Beverwil, the inevitable dead end having forced her hand on the matter of routes. She could drive down Beverly the way some people could drive down Crescent. Forever on a loop, watching the same houses speed by over and over again. Slowing down for the same speed humps. Timing them perfectly so she never had to brake. Finding the rhythm of her foot lifting off the accelerator was definitely better than thinking about Sana as she explained her mom getting pregnant at nineteen and divorced by twenty. Who Rachel couldn't help but for a moment compare to Rachel's own mother, who had gotten pregnant—as though it were the thing to do—at thirty.

But Rachel stopped herself before her thoughts could follow all the way down that path, like a tracking shot cut short. Cut short for good reason, too. Rachel did everything she could to avoid her mother. Thoughts, words, deeds, memories, mementos. Anything. Everything.

The scenery grew less scenic. Still palm trees lining the roads. But more laundromats. Fewer homes, more apartment complexes. More fences, though some of the odd, new gentrification variety. Rachel was glad she would finish high school before she saw the rise of Palms as a neighborhood for young professionals to live in. Her dad wouldn't have to worry about rent with her out of the home. He could get something smaller if it became unaffordable. He could move.

Rachel pulled up to the apartment building she lived in. It had a covered, exposed parking garage, like it had been a motel once, back in better days. But Rachel wasn't sure Palms had ever had better days. To her, it had always been one of those places where dreams and dreamers had gone to die.

Just look at Papa.

Rachel pulled her bag out of the car, sticking her key in the lock to lock it. It was a very manual kind of car, minus the extra-shitty automatic transmission.

When she reached her room, she collapsed onto her bed, shoes and all. She wanted to live here forever in this bed and never get up, not after the day that she had had. But she had to finalize her shooting schedule. She had to get out a pen, get out the journal she kept all of her shooting notes in. She had to check off everything she'd accomplished that day.

She had to make sure she could get through everything for her film by the end of the month. She had to stop thinking about Sana, her unexpected honesty, her unexpected life. She had to conquer this feeling that was welling up in her chest that felt suspiciously like empathy for the girl who had made Rachel tense up throughout the hallways for all of freshman year.

Because this feeling, this one she'd been avoiding for her whole drive home, was almost like caring for a girl who Rachel was supposed to hate.

Sana

When Sana walked into her grandparents' house the following evening, she felt a shiver zip down her spine. Mamani must have set the air-conditioning to full blast.

Athena Mashi had answered the door and was already giving her older sister a once-over. "Can you ever dress like an actual human, didi?"

Sana's mom snorted. "If Mom's not letting me sleep in on my day off, then I'm wearing my house clothes out."

Athena Mashi shrugged. "Your funeral."

Mom hadn't changed out of her sweatpants and T-shirt. She'd called it *athleisure* on her way out the door, much to Sana's frustration. Mom shrugged, leaned in to give her sister the glancing affection of a couple of kisses across her cheeks. "Did she fire her maid again?"

"No, but she's all worked up, so I sent Leni off on an errand away from her. Your ex is here, by the way. I thought I should warn you."

"You didn't warn me soon enough."

"You think they told me ahead of time? I found out after you. *Maman.*" Athena rolled her eyes in a way she never would at her actual mother. She looked over at Sana. "You look perfect, as always."

But Athena Mashi didn't say it like perfection was an ideal or a compliment. She was assessing, because Athena Mashi missed nothing. Sana went in for a couple of kisses on the cheek so her aunt couldn't scrutinize her expression any further.

Athena Mashi let them into the house.

Mom scanned the crowd, catching sight of Massoud. "Hail the returning prodigal ex-son-in-law."

"I wish I could lie to you and tell you he's a horrible slob, but he honestly looks *better* than he did at twenty." Athena Mashi shook her head, like nobody was safe from the cruel humor of the universe.

"I know." Mom made a beeline for Dadu's office. "I need refreshment."

"Kitchen's the other way," said Athena Mashi.

"The good stuff's in here," said Mom, not missing a beat.

"Get me something," Athena Mashi shouted.

"Get yourself something." Mom disappeared into the office.

Athena Mashi shook her head. "Your mother."

People gave that headshake and used those words a lot around Sana. *Your mother* the family reprobate. *Your mother* the wayward daughter. *Your mother* the hellion. *Your mother your mother your mother.*

It was a subtle warning, an everyday kind of hint—Sana was supposed to do everything in her power to become nothing like her mother. Athena Mashi probably didn't even realize she was doing it. Sana didn't know which she resented more, the implication itself or the fact that it had worked so well on her.

Because here Sana was, the potential to be Princeton class of 2023. Here she was in her perfect, knee-length skirt and blouse, her perfectly smoothed hair, her perfectly applied makeup. And there her mom was, getting drunk in her sweatpants in Dadu's office.

The contrast between her and her mother gave Sana the sensation that generations were pressing down on her, like the ghosts of her ancestors could sit on her chest and make her breathing difficult, make her inhales shaky and her exhales sharp.

Mom had been the only one with the courage, or maybe the sheer need, to leave home. Everyone else had stayed, milling about the Orange County scene. Mom's only sister, Athena, had gone into art dealership and done well for herself. She had a husband but she didn't want children, much to Mamani's consternation. Farhad Mama did retirement planning. Zain Mama—well, honestly, Sana wasn't sure what Uncle Zain did other than fly around the world and make buckets of money and refuse to settle down like a proper adult the way Mamani wanted.

Not that Mom had had much choice in the matter. It was either walk the line with her marriage and be the genteel kind of Orange County good girl that made Mom want to scream into the void (and probably played no small part in the decision-making process that led to her unplanned pregnancy) or run away.

Mom had chosen the latter option. And in spite of it, or maybe because of it, she had thrived. She'd worked her way up. She made a good, solid living. She was working on big-budget productions. And if she did this one right, if she got this one in the bucket, she could be up for the kinds of movies that did the rounds on awards ceremonies. She could go on location as soon as Sana wasn't living at home anymore. Not that awards mattered to Mom. But Sana wanted her to get that recognition that she'd worked and fought tooth and nail to have. Mom deserved it.

Not that deserving a thing meant you ever got to have it.

Exhibit: Massoud.

Sana ignored him as he waved at her from the back of the living room. She turned and went to find her cousins.

Jasmine—nearly sixteen—had honey-blond hair and Mamani's eyes. She was Farhad Mama's oldest and half white. She spoke in quick, rapid succession, regardless of whether she was dealing in large concepts or small. Right now, she was talking about her freshly minted boyfriend. "And he loves to surf. I can't imagine dating a boy who doesn't surf. I mean, what's the point of living if you don't date a boy who surfs?"

This last question she had directed at Sana, who raised her eyebrows knowingly back at Jasmine. Her family did this often—halfway forgetting that she was attracted to girls, that she wanted to date girls. They didn't mean any real harm by it, but it managed to sting every time anyway. Like juicing a lemon when she already had a nick in her cuticle. It was a stinging kind of pain—but one she felt like she could have avoided had she done something different. True, they were the ones who couldn't remember a fundamental piece of her unless she drew obvious attention to it. But Sana was the one who had to live with the discomfort.

"Whoops," said Jas, who usually remembered to be sensitive to the people she loved just after she'd stuck her foot in her mouth. "You know what I mean, though."

Sana did. That's why the pit in her stomach didn't go away, didn't clear. Just sat there, in a small but deep pool of hurt and longing and misunderstanding. "I practically go to school in the Valley, Jas. So I've got no surfer vibes to speak of."

"C'est tragique," said Jas, who, like the rest of their clan, had been living in Orange County for her whole life. Then she sighed. "Surfers are where it is at. They've all got like abs of steel or something. It's heaven. Even the girl surfers."

Sana shrugged. If she wanted to look at abs all day, she could stare in the freaking mirror. She didn't need to date someone like a collection of body parts. But maybe it was different with boys. "I'll have to take your word for it."

"She doesn't want to know about your stupid boyfriend any more than we do," said Lilah. Lilah was fourteen and had somehow managed to get her mother's flaxen hair and blue eyes and her father's broad features. She couldn't tan the way her other sisters could. She had the kind of eyebrows that faded into her pale face. This left her perpetually seeking shade and frowning, as though she were missing out on some great rite of life that would never be hers. She tried to give off the impression that she didn't even want that mystery to belong to her anyway. Lilah was a difficult case, so naturally, she was Sana's favorite of the three sisters.

"I don't mind," said Sana. "I like hearing what all of you are up to. How's the water polo going?"

Lilah's chest puffed up with pride and recognition. "Really excellent. I think we've got a shot at the state title this year."

Jas rolled her eyes, but Sana kept focused on her middle cousin. Lilah was the fair-haired child who managed to steal none of the attention away from either of her siblings. She ought to have, the way she so clearly popped out in terms of looks from the entire rest of the family. But instead she faded into the background, like she had been somehow washed out by the Southern California sun.

Reema, their youngest sister, was off somewhere in the backyard. She was still twelve, still full of energy, still full of childhood. She wasn't quite as dark as Sana, but she was nice and brown from all her time in the sun. She would hang on the edges of their conversation, but often found it too boring, too grown-up. She was still made for imagination and adventure. Sana remembered being that age, when anything was possible and nobody made you pay too much attention to what was going on.

Sana had quit flitting around the backyard when she was ten, though. What a luxury those two extra years might have been. She wished she'd taken them when she'd had the chance.

Jas snorted. "*Bo*-ring. Who wants to talk about water polo?"

"Some people have *goals*," said Lilah to her sister. "Like a sports scholarship to college."

"And some people have fun," said Jas, who, for added emphasis and maturity, had stuck out her tongue to her younger sister.

"Girls!" Mamani walked in, catching them at their worst moment. "None of this silly expression! You cannot be serious with your faces like that. Jasmine, apologize to your sister. And to me. I shouldn't have to see my granddaughters' faces like that. It isn't ladylike."

Jas flashed a look in Sana's direction, then gave a pretty apology to Mamani and then to her younger sister. Mamani nodded and went to refresh her iced tea.

The maid, Leni, came in just then, uttering the phrase, "Dinner is ready," and then popped back out of the room.

Sana would never get used to that. She'd forget sometimes that her grandparents had staff in their homes. Mamani still cooked—nobody could make tahdig like Mamani and she wouldn't let anyone know her secrets, not even her daughters or granddaughters. Not yet. The crowd of cousins and aunties and uncles shuffled out of the room and into the dining area.

Sana's father, who she had managed to avoid so far, sat beside her grandfather near the head of the large oval table. Mamani sat on the other end, next to Zain Mama. And because Mamani could be cruel to be kind, she'd sat Mom opposite her father, thinking to rekindle what had been lost sixteen years ago.

It was ironic that the thing that caused such strife between Mom and Mamani was the trait that Mom had inherited directly from Mamani. Neither one would ever give up. Or give in. They had a goal in mind and they would work toward it, come the end of time.

If only they could stop picking goals that were inevitably in conflict with each other.

The family all took their seats around the table. In the middle sat a large platter of saffron rice, surrounded by chicken and lamb and grilled vegetables, salad, and stew. The stew was Sana's favorite by far—chicken so tender it practically fell off the bone, tangy from the pomegranate syrup, a bit of crunch from walnuts, and a perfect cinnamon depth to round it all off. Most of the food served at her grandparents' house was Persian, because Mamani was in charge of the kitchen and Dadu didn't honestly care as long as the food tasted good. It was like some strange separation of church and state—Persian food in the house and Indian restaurants when they went out to dinner.

As soon as Leni had set down the last dish, she scuttled out of the room.

"Eat," said Dadu, spreading his arms wide. "Eat."

Massoud looked across the table at Sana, who pointedly looked away from his gaze. She didn't want to communicate in silence with her father. She didn't want to communicate in any way with him, really.

She wanted him to go away, wanted to ignore the pang building in her chest thinking about how he knew she hadn't put down her deposit, wanted to get up from the table and scream.

Instead, Sana turned to Lilah. "Could you pass the fesenjan, please?"

Lilah passed the stew, a curious look in her eye. "Have you picked your dorm for college yet?"

Fear clenched at Sana's stomach. She hadn't been forced to lie directly yet and she didn't want to have to.

Luckily, Jas snorted and interrupted the conversation. "Can we please talk about something other than school? I get enough of that during the week."

"You'll have no future if you talk like that," said Mamani from their own end of the table.

Sana watched as Jas suppressed an eye roll and a groan. They were all of them constantly doing that—suppressing a feeling and performing another one. The smooth, even keel of a family that behaved well at dinner. That did their duty properly and without fuss.

That was, until Reema spoke up.

"Not everyone excels in school to excel in life." Reema sat up primly.

The entire table's worth of eyes swiveled to her.

The tension in Sana's stomach hadn't subsided. But Reema had struck a nerve, and Sana needed to understand what she meant. Even if Sana's stomach did another flip as she spoke. "What do you mean?"

"You don't have to do well in school to find your way in life." Reema shrugged. "Your mother did all right, didn't she? And she had to quit school."

You could have heard a pin drop around that table, the room went so silent. Even Leni, who had been coming through the entryway to collect plates had paused, and slowly backed away with a light tread.

"I don't think that's the lesson they meant you or anyone to take from my experience." Mom laughed. She was playing it all off as a joke, trying to keep from being the center of this horrible attention. Trying to save Reema from a lecture at home later.

"But you figured it out. You never did well in school. They always say you didn't. And I know they want me to get a lesson about working hard in school. But you don't get to pick the lessons you learn, do you? Even when you're trying to teach something directly. You made something of your life even though everyone said you wouldn't. And it wasn't about school. You worked with your hands, you figured out carpentry. From this house to carpentry." Reema was staring at Sana's mother. Her eyes were unflinching.

Sana stared back openly at Reema, not knowing what to do. Reema was a girl who had seen at once too much and not quite everything. She had violated the one sacrosanct rule of the dinner table—*never stop pretending that everything is all right.*

"I did what I had to do." Mom directed all her attention toward Reema. "I shouldn't be an example of either virtue or vice. We all do what we have to do, Reema-joon. And sometimes that's enough. And other times it isn't. Sometimes we get lucky. And other times we're face-first in the mud trying to find a way to breathe while somebody is trying to kick us in the ribs. Don't make me a heroine. Don't make me a villain. You'll be lucky enough to walk your own path."

Sana's mother took a long gulp of her water, with an expression that longed for whiskey. She looked over toward her mother and, eyebrows raised, said, "I'll bet you never saw that coming."

For a long moment, Sana held her breath. Then Mamani began to laugh, an honest laugh that Sana rarely heard out of her. After that, the conversations around the rest of the table recovered. The rest of the dinner passed peaceably enough, given the circumstances.

After dinner, Sana's mother made an excuse about needing to head back home before the traffic got bad. Everyone knew this was the worst kind of excuse—traffic got better as it got later, not earlier. But nobody questioned it, not after the way dinner had gone. Sana and her mother loaded themselves back into the car and drove up the 405, getting caught in some monster traffic along the way. The heat soaked through the windows and saturated the old car, causing sweat to trickle down Sana's back, sticking to the old velveteen seats.

But it was better than being stuck in that house with the sound of Reema's words reverberating through Sana's ears. Better than being reminded that there were some things that she didn't have to stay silent about.

If only Sana had the same courage that her mother did. The same thread of resolve that had skipped over her and landed in her twelve-year-old cousin.

Instead, Sana let the warm car heat her body back up. Let the cloth seats scratch against her calves. Let the knowledge that she was lying to them all—about Princeton, about her fellowship application, about potentially what she wanted from her life—wash over her in waves that coincided with the thumps of the seams in the freeway concrete.

April 15

16 Days Until Deadline

11

I Know Every Cop in Town, Bucko

Sana

Sana leaned up against her locker. She'd asked Rachel for a copy of the current shooting script as the film stood right now. Rachel had sent Sana the shooting script—the one for tomorrow—and the entire tome of shooting scripts—what Rachel had already used and had footage of. Sana wanted to give the entire movie some serious feedback. Sana had looked up online how you were supposed to print out a script—three-holed paper, but with tiny brads put into only the top and bottom holes. Industry standard, apparently.

That's how Sana was now reading the script, flipping pages and scribbling notes throughout. It was more fun than sitting on the sidelines of her next cheerleading practice. And much easier to face than the packet of dorm selections and deposit materials that Sana was still avoiding. She hadn't heard back from her fellowship yet. Maybe she could spot where Rachel's hang-up was to begin with.

There were three problems that popped out pretty immediately to Sana as she read.

The first was this—*The Odyssey* was really lots of short stories that had been cobbled together to make a much bigger story. It was kind of naturally already a mess. What worked for epic poetry, well, didn't necessarily make a great direct translation onto film. Rachel had been clever—she'd connected all those stories through a character. But Cassandra—the tragic princess of Troy who predicted the city's destruction—was the expected feminist choice. The girl who was never listened to, finally seen through the eyes of a female filmmaker. It was honestly so obvious, so overdone, so *clichéd*. If Rachel was going to use Cassandra, she had to at least find a new way of using her as storytelling glue.

The second problem was scope. Rachel had bitten off one of the longest, largest, most epic stories taught in the English language. Only George Eliot and Charles Dickens could rival the sheer number of plotlines running through this script. But this problem was much like the first—the film needed a strong, continuous thread that kept the whole story together. A through line.

An *unexpected* through line.

But finally, Sana was increasingly convinced that Rachel simply hated beautiful people. There was no other explanation for the sheer disdain that came through whenever Helen of Troy was on the page. Helen had been flattened out into the worst sort of spoiled little rich girl trope. The disdain, the mocking, it came from everywhere—the lines that established the action and the setting, the dialogue of Cassandra as she narrated, Paris when he spoke to her, and even Helen, who couldn't take herself seriously.

All those years ago, Sana had assumed that Rachel's hatred had stopped with Sana.

This was a whole new depth.

Sana was scribbling when she heard a noise down the hall. Rachel had gotten to her locker. Rachel twisted the dial to her lock—once, twice, then the final spin and it ought to have opened. But Rachel's door was jammed. She pulled the metal lever up and down over and over again, to no avail.

Sana pushed on her hand, ready to get up and help, but the locker clicked open, finally, and Rachel swung the door open so hard it slammed and rattled into the neighboring door. Nobody else in the hallway noticed, because few people ever took notice of Rachel.

But Sana saw her. Always had. Maybe she always would.

Sana landed back on her seat on the floor. But she needed to be noticed, needed to be seen, too. "Hey."

Rachel turned around several times before looking down. "Hey yourself."

"I was just reading the latest script for tomorrow. I've got notes." Sana smiled, hoping Rachel would head her way. It was only three or four feet, but it felt like an unbridgeable gap. Like an amount of distance that Sana couldn't cross, no matter how hard she might try.

"We have to *shoot* off the script I gave you. Like, tomorrow." Rachel took the script, began flipping through it, seeing all of Sana's comments. "It's still my film, Khan."

That was the first time Rachel had said her last name without making it sound like she'd meant something unpleasant or disgusting. Like it was a friendly kind of nickname rather than an insult. Rachel walked over. She stood close enough to tower over a still-seated Sana.

Sana wasn't going to flinch away from Rachel, even if her eyes were crystalline and brown and devastating to look into. "But film is collaborative. It's all of our film, too. And I've got notes. Unless you're going back on our deal."

Rachel collapsed into a cross-legged heap beside Sana. Her knees whispered against Sana's. "Fine," she said as she began reading in earnest.

Sana did what she could to keep her voice and her hands steady. "Helen's your through line. The glue to the story. Not Cassandra."

"You're joking." But Rachel was thumbing through the pages. Flipping through the notes rapidly now that she had a sense of them. "Goddammit. How did you see that?"

"If Helen gets to tell the story, she's not an object. I mean, also, she's still your idea of who she is. But Helen has always been that way. Does she run off with Paris? Is she abducted? Seduced? Does she ascend to Mount Olympus in the end? Regret her choices? Hate Paris? Love him? Happily resume the role of wife and queen and mother of Sparta? The only thing anyone can really agree on is this—Helen was found missing from her husband's home and then her husband started a war. That's it."

Rachel snorted, but she leaned closer. She set the paper on the floor and began scribbling her notes across it. "I think you might be the only person in the history of the planet to feel so sorry for a beautiful, perfect princess."

Rachel's hair was accidentally tickling against Sana's knee now.

Sana didn't dare move, didn't dare startle Rachel. If she sat still, maybe Rachel wouldn't pull away. "I don't feel sorry for her."

Rachel looked up and saw how close they were. She scooted away slightly. Their knees no longer touching. Her hair no longer grazing against Sana's leg. "Then what is it?"

Sana didn't know what to do, to make Rachel see. That her attraction wasn't a joke. Wasn't a trick of the light. It was real and solid and had been for years. "I don't think you should underestimate any character in your story."

Rachel put her head in her hand. "Fixing this is going to be so much work. I'm going to have to track all these changes through and change the narrator's dialogue."

Sana scooted closer. "I can help."

"Still. We'll be here forever." Rachel didn't look up—maybe she wouldn't look up, or couldn't.

Sana nudged Rachel with her elbow. "Then let's get out of here."

"What?" Rachel looked up, startled and alert.

Looked like Sana had to surprise Rachel into paying her any attention. "Let's go to LACMA. Better to work in front of pretty things than in this hallway."

"Are you nuts? I'm not driving in this traffic."

Sana grinned. She had the final sucker punch. The kind of shock that Rachel wouldn't be able to resist. "We can take the bus."

"The *bus*?" There it was, Rachel's wide-eyed, incredulous expression. The face of a girl who didn't believe what she was hearing but still had to hear more.

"I take it all the time. Just take the 2 to the Fairfax hub. Be there in no time." Sana gave a lilting shrug, got up, and knew Rachel would follow her.

Rachel

Of all of the luxuries Rachel had been afforded by attending the Royce School, not having to take the bus to school—or anywhere anymore—sat at the top of the list.

And yet here she was, sitting next to Sana on a big, bendy, orange LA metro bus.

Sana was bouncing, vibrating, practically *shimmering* with energy.

Rachel nudged her. "Dude. People are going to think you've never ridden the bus before."

Sana made a quizzical expression—her head tilting just to the right as her mouth pulled slightly to the left. "I ride this bus all the time."

"Then why are you so excited?"

Sana grinned like Emily Blunt—like a woman who could do a one-armed push-up and save the world and still kiss her sweetheart goodnight. Rachel's stomach dropped out from under her, like she was riding an airplane currently experiencing some very unexpected turbulence.

Sana's eyes flickered toward the front of the bus, out the big, open windows. She leaned across Rachel—wafting over a now familiar scent of jasmine and sunshine as she did—and pulled the rip cord. "Come on. We're here."

Sana got up and Rachel had nothing to do but grab her backpack and follow in her wake. The bus rumbled to a stop and made a gassing *whoosh* sound as the hydraulics were lowered and the doors were opened.

Sana jumped down off the steps, rocking unsteadily as she landed on one foot, then balanced on her boot. She skip-hopped ahead into the massive installation of streetlamps. *Urban Light* was the official name given by the artist. Though Rachel wasn't sure who that was anymore. Normally the rows and rows of vintage streetlights made her want to roll her eyes. They made a dense grid of lamplight—with the front row slightly narrower than the rows behind it.

Urban Light was somewhere everyone and their mother in LA took photos. Particularly engagement photos and coupled-up shots. They were so obvious, so overdone that whenever pictures from in front of the lamps at LACMA popped into her feed, Rachel literally muted the original poster. *Oh, how original. Photos of being in love between the lamplights at the magic hour.*

There were even palm trees directly in the background, lest the setting not be quite staged enough for a photographer's taste.

But watching Sana flit and hop with various degrees of success through and around and in between the lamps just made Rachel reach into her back pocket and get out her phone. Sunset in LA really did make the light golden and perfect, combined with the engineered-to-look-incandescent LED bulbs—the lighting *was* off-the-charts beautiful. And that was without Sana fliting through the space like a half-hobbled, dark-haired fairy.

"Could you hold still for half a second?" Rachel was trying to frame Sana, but she kept moving, kept shifting the composition.

Sana popped her head around a lamp and stuck out her tongue. "Catch me if you can."

Rachel caught the photo in one snap.

But Sana wasn't one to be frozen in a single moment in time. She kept moving, kept swishing in and out of the lamp poles, just like her ponytail. Rachel kept taking photos—some of them a blur, a flash. Others more steady, more precise.

"You're not even trying," Sana called out.

She was close now, and Rachel was laughing. Sana reached out from behind Rachel and snatched up her phone.

"Gotcha!" The camera on the phone clicked as Sana took her own picture. Then she turned, got both of their faces in the frame, and snapped a selfie of both of them together. Sana handed back the phone. "Come on. They've got an amazing Islamic arts section. Oh, but we should look at the classics, shouldn't we?"

But Rachel didn't have time to answer that question. Sana was flashing her student ID and telling the woman at the window they were both seventeen, even though Rachel, at least, wasn't anymore. She'd turned eighteen back in the fall. But the woman believed Sana. Her face was so guileless and open.

They were in, for free.

Sana led them into the building to the right of the ticket office and started climbing the stairs.

"Don't you want to take the elevator?"

Sana shrugged. "I like the exercise. I'm not getting as much with this boot on."

"You're a weirdo." But Rachel meant that as a badge of honor. As a good thing.

"Totally," said Sana on a laugh. "Almost there."

And there it was—three flights up—piles of classical marbles and statues. Donated by some rich guy back in the day. A museum never used to be anything without a collection of Greek and Roman statues to lend it gravitas. Rachel snorted.

"You can't do that," said Sana, waggling her finger. "You're using the classics, too. You're redoing *The Odyssey*. So you're just as bad as whoever you're making fun of in your head."

"Who says I was making fun of anyone?"

It was Sana's turn to snort. She stopped in front of a statue on a pedestal. "How's this?"

This was perfect, of course. It was a bust of a goddess—her face tilted down, her robes ceremonial. And on her head was a helmet—the clever goddess of war.

Rachel stared at the marble for a moment. "Athena."

"Athena Pallas." Sana had quite the self-satisfied grin on her face. She knew she'd done well. There was nothing else that half-ticked smile pulling across her mouth could mean.

But Rachel couldn't care that Sana had been right. She was too busy staring at Athena and thinking about the weight of stories and legends. "You know they say she created the whole *Odyssey*? That Cassandra clung to her temple for sanctuary after the fall of Troy, but Ajax the Lesser pulled her away. And invoked Athena's wrath."

"Yeah," said Sana. "And so Athena called on Poseidon to scatter the entire Greek fleet. And inadvertently set Odysseus on his voyage. Though in some versions, she helps Odysseus, working behind the scenes to bring him home. Either way, she starts the story, you know? Doesn't looking at beautiful things help?"

Rachel sat down on the bench, reached into her backpack, and got out her laptop. "It's annoying that you're so right all the time."

"Not all the time. Just with stuff like this." Sana sat beside Rachel. She left an inch between their bodies.

"How did you know?" Rachel pulled up the file. She began typing away. There really was something about looking at beautiful things, at connecting back to stories in a way that was so visceral, so eternal, that gave her the push to keep going.

"My mom. She comes here to think. She's been taking me ever since I was a kid. Helps her with her designs—art in space, or something like that. Sometimes she goes to the Getty, too. But I think this place is her favorite." Sana scuffed her booted foot against the floor.

The movement brushed her knee up against Rachel's, back and forth. The rhythm of it was soothing, lulling. An expected touch— maybe even a bit of expected turbulence. Rachel's stomach fluttered, but not in an unpleasant way.

"She's a smart woman," said Rachel, looking at Sana as she said so.

A smile flashed across Sana's face, and then disappeared just as quickly. "She's definitely more clever than anyone ever gives her credit for, that's for sure. Do you need me to read through your notes as you type?"

"Yeah," said Rachel. "That would be great."

They worked like that—in the otherwise empty room filled with marbles and statues and ancient stories—with Sana reading a mixture of her own and Rachel's notes in quiet tones while Rachel typed, then paused, then typed some more as she worked through her snags in the script. The story was coming together—Rachel could see it now. Could see how she could edit all the disparate pieces of her existing footage together to make a coherent narrative. She might not even need as many reshoots as she thought she did.

Eventually, the museum was ready to close, and they hopped back on the bus and retraced their steps back to school. They made it back to where Rachel had parked her car and, naturally, she drove Sana home. The ride to Sana's was mostly quiet—just the sound of the thumps in the road and the wind whistling through the cracked windows.

It was only when Rachel reached home that she realized she'd spent hours in Sana's company without feeling the need to lash out at her at all.

12

The Correct Term Is Babes, Sir

Sana

When Sana arrived on set, Rachel was nearly ready. The cameras were in place. The crew had the cords coiled into a neat circle on the floor. The lights were diffused, though not clamped directly into position yet. The locker they were using was already opened, already set up with the right amount of decor—the young, modern version of Helen of Troy that Sana was playing had a photo up, just the one, and a couple of magnets. It was a sad, sparse locker. It filled Sana with longing to look at it.

Spartan. That was the word. From Helen's original homeland, Sparta. Utilitarian. Neat. Militaristic, even. The beautiful girl from the most warmongering of the ancient Greek states. If Helen of Troy had really existed, she would have been raised to fight, raised for war. Now she was known for being so pretty, she'd started a global conflict.

Sana turned away from the locker to watch the crew. She would have assumed they would be quiet, subdued, but they were a laughing, unruly bunch. At the far end of the hall was Ms. Douga, the film supervisor, doing her best to look official with her reading glasses and her clipboard and her—was that a whistle around her neck? *What in the world did she need a whistle for?* And at the center of the organized mael-strom was Rachel—her camera on a tripod—adjusting something on the lens. Nobody was paying much attention to Rachel.

Sana walked up to Rachel like it was the most natural thing in the world. Like she'd been doing it for years. Like they'd been friends for ages. She'd envisioned doing this before—in specific, everyday kind of fantasies. Just two girls who hung out like this and nothing strange had ever existed between them. They were muted seventies family photos from the old country compared to this vivid reality.

Sana stopped about a foot from Rachel.

Rachel's hair was pulled back into a low ponytail and covered by a Dodgers hat. She had on leggings and a soft, snug gray T-shirt that made her hair look darker and her skin look a deeper shade of bronze. Her sneakers were beat to hell and back. It took everything in Sana's massive arsenal of willpower not to lean over the camera and flutter her eyelashes. Not to intrude into Rachel's space and make her pay attention to Sana. Make her notice Sana.

"You're in the shot." Rachel did not break focus from whatever she was setting on the camera. She was fiddling with the dials on the lens.

Sana watched as her hands moved deftly across the equipment. *Rachel was good with her hands.* Sana cleared her throat. She would not be distracted by tight pants or an authoritarian voice. "I'm *supposed* to be in the shot."

Rachel looked up then. Her mouth twitched. It was almost a smile. Nearly a smile. So close to a smile. "All right, smart-ass. I'm already using your notes as new scenes. Now you want to tell me how to make a movie?"

Sana chose not to be upset at Rachel's words. She put her hands on her hips. "Maybe."

Rachel shook her head. "Fine. You can stand over there on the tape. That's your mark. I had to estimate your height with a stand-in, but I didn't know when your boot would get in the shot. Since you're here, you can do the boring work of making a movie—standing around a lot."

"Sure." Sana hopped over toward the little taped-down X on the floor. She faced the camera, then angled herself to the left and the right. "Wait, did you just grab a random kid who was walking down the halls to stand in for me?"

"She was the right height." Rachel shrugged. "Now, start with your hand on the open locker door, facing in, please."

Sana did as she was told. She hadn't had years of cheerleading drilled in her only to fail at following simple instructions now. Especially since Rachel had decided to trust her. "Are you always this stressed?"

Rachel's face was obscured by the camera but her snort was loud and clear. "It's the first day. I hate the first day. Sets the tone of the whole shoot and I'm always worried something's about to go heinously wrong. And then it does go heinously wrong. First day is the worst. And this is my *fifth* first day with this film—stay in place, please. I need to make sure your leg stays out of shot. Plus I'm seeing if I need to move the camera for the close-up after the master shot. Your face goes out of frame with the smallest movements."

"Really?" Sana felt a bit breathless. She wasn't used to so much focus on herself. Scrutiny, she was used to. But focus, not so much.

"Really, really."

Sana stayed as still as possible, even as she spoke. "How many scenes have you got left to film?"

"Thanks to your notes? Just a couple." Rachel popped her face back up from around the camera.

"Cool."

"But I might need your help editing. Is that something I can count on?" Rachel was ducked back behind the lens again.

Sana was so startled by the request that she stepped forward, closer to the camera.

Rachel held up a hand. "Don't. Seriously. Stay right there. I just, I think I see where this needs to go, just hold it for like half a minute longer. And then I can call places for everyone else for the opening scene."

Sana didn't move. Barely breathed. Finally, she responded. "I can help. With editing."

"Got it." Rachel popped her head back up, gave Sana a good, long stare. Like she hadn't been staring at her from behind the camera the whole time.

Sana reached out; touched Rachel's arm lightly. It was easy to move away from a light touch. "It's gonna be great. You're gonna do great today."

Rachel nodded, not quite making eye contact. She looked at the place where Sana's hand touched her arm, almost unconsciously.

Sana dropped her hand. She found the bright smile inside herself and said, "Ready to start?"

Rachel looked at Sana. She nodded. Not like she believed Sana, but like she appreciated the effort to find some level of normality here. When she next spoke, she was only loud enough for Sana to hear. "Find your place. I'm gonna talk to the whole crew."

Rachel

For Rachel, there had always been something otherworldly about stepping onto a set, seeing all of the props and the set pieces and the camera equipment and thinking—*I am the god of this world*. The person who determined where they all went and how they all came together in a unifying kind of vision. There was a glow and a magic to the slow-moving process of the motion picture industry that necessarily helped anyone get through the boredom. Because no matter how good the day, boredom still remained. The waiting, the call times, the makeup, and the touching up of the makeup. The costuming, the marking of the lighting, the double-checking the monitor.

Directors were in charge of all the decisions—of the underlying fabric of the film. It wasn't only what shots to take, or what the vision was. It was keeping the actors happy and the crew appreciated (and, not to mention, empowered enough to make their own decisions about where to store equipment and how to set up the props table). Some directors created a general environment of ease and some—in the Rachel's case—terror. That's what kept the ship afloat, what kept everyone in line and moving forward to the same goal.

Because that's what directing was—uniting a whole bunch of disparate people and individual players into a single unifying goal that you had to work together to make. A vision was necessary in order to hold it all together. Call it gravity, call it glue, call it purpose. Everyone on set needed to be pulled in by it, one way or another, if a director was going to make something truly good.

Rachel always had a vision.

Her problem was getting everyone else to see it. She was so visual, she assumed everyone else was. Assumed they saw the world as she did. Saw what she was going for. But after watching Sana read the script in her screen test, Rachel realized that that was the first time anyone got her vision straight off the bat. But even talking over this project with Sana, Rachel realized that two people could come to set with that same vision, but still expecting a different experience.

Rachel knew this, of course.

But watching it in action was different. It was one thing in a critic. It was another thing in a member of the crew. People brought their own expectations and visions and their own ideas and their own experiences to the set. And each of their opinions could be true. They could all be true.

Rachel couldn't believe she'd never noticed this before. Today was the day to change that. "Okay, everyone, gather round."

The whole set stopped. This was unprecedented. Nobody could figure out what was about to happen. Even Douga stopped, the unblown whistle dropping from her mouth. There was a stillness that went around in the air. If nobody knew what could happen, then anything could happen.

Anything.

"We're gonna try something a little differently," said Rachel, ignoring the tension on set. It was hard enough to get through this without having to worry about what people were thinking and how they were going to judge her for this new and unprecedented step. She had to charge through the way she always charged through and hope for the best. Of course, when it came to other humans, the best rarely happened. But when it came to her art, it often did.

Rachel felt she had *at least* a fifty-fifty shot on this one, which was better than most of the times in her life when she went up in front of a group of people and tried to explain herself.

Rachel cleared her throat, though goodness knows she didn't need it. Everyone was as quiet as could be. Unnervingly quiet. "This movie is an epic beast. I've been having trouble focusing on what the actual through line is."

Deep breaths, Rachel. Deep breaths. "And with that in mind, Sana has helped rework the script. Helen is our through line. I've got some revised scripts now."

Rachel had wanted the script to be a tangible, touchable thing. Thank God for free printing in the library or it would have cost her a small fortune. Rachel scanned the crowd to look over at Douga. She was flipping through her script and doing that thing people do when they evaluate work by slightly raising their eyebrows and slightly jutting out their bottom lip.

A hand went up.

"Yes," said Rachel, pointing to Ryan. She couldn't believe he was brave enough to ask a question after their last interaction. Maybe he was made of sterner stuff than he had let on.

"What purpose do the changes serve?"

Rachel nodded. "Good question. *The Odyssey* is, after all, several stories nested within stories. Most of my reshoots have been trying to find a solid strand to connect them. Most of them have failed. But this one won't. Apparently, I've underestimated Helen. At least, until now."

Ryan's hand shot up again. Rachel had barely pointed when he started to ask, "Does that mean that there will be less contained arcs and more of a meta arc by the time the story ends?"

Rachel laughed. The whole set held their breath again. But his eagerness was infectious, if in a slightly irritating but also winning way. "Yes. Anybody else?"

Anybody else was still too stunned to speak.

Rachel called for places and began setting up the shot with the blocking. They had to rehearse a few times. She usually grabbed people and moved them around on set. But she couldn't imagine grabbing Sana and moving her around and positioning her, and since she couldn't very well position everyone *but* Sana (how weird would *that* look, honestly), Rachel just pointed and let people figure out their blocking on their own. For the most part they made better choices than the ones she usually made by manhandling and trying to control the situation.

When they weren't working, everyone was ducked over their script, making the notes Rachel had suggested, highlighting their parts, annotating what the lighting was supposed to be doing in any given moment.

Sana understood that set was a professional space. That she was there to work, do a job. Rachel realized it must have been the years of cheerleading, of running a practice, until a performance was set and practically perfect in every particular. Rachel hated to think that making a movie was anything like cheerleading. But the repetitive, drill-like nature of it, combined with Sana's patient competence, led Rachel to the startling conclusion that the two were not so unrelated as she had held them to be.

Watching Sana performing on set was like nothing that Rachel had ever seen.

Natural was possibly one way to put it. Effortless was another. Fucking fantastic was how Rachel would have put it.

Fucking fantastic.

She really *was* like a South Asian Elizabeth Taylor. At once feminine and aggressive. Threatening and docile. She made a perfect Helen, and Rachel was flooded with regret that she'd underestimated the Helen that she had written—her own character—so much. Without Sana's input, Helen would have remained flat and boring. A basic mean girl villain from a nineties teen B movie. Watching Sana play her was like reading about Helen of Troy for the first time—startling, mesmerizing, and honestly overwhelming at times.

Filming today was somehow the longest and shortest two hours of Rachel's life.

As Rachel was wrapping up cords at the end, most of the crew stayed to help. She couldn't quite believe it. She didn't have to yell or make passive-aggressive, or even aggressive-aggressive, faces. She just called it for the day and started packing up and for the first time she wasn't alone doing so. Everyone pitched in. They were talking mostly to one another. Or Sana. Everyone wanted to talk to Sana. Half of the people were trying to touch her in some way.

A surge of some unnamed emotion went through Rachel. *They shouldn't get to touch her. It's inappropriate.* Rachel watched Sana's ponytail swinging back and forth as she responded to everyone in a friendly, calm way. Like she was used to that kind of attention.

And maybe she was.

"You did well today." Douga was at Rachel's side.

Rachel garbled nonsense for a moment—more guttural than an *um* but just as space filling. That was probably the nicest thing Douga had ever said to Rachel, excepting the time she'd told Rachel that Rachel had talent, way back when she'd been offered admission to Royce. "Thank you."

Douga nodded. "I'm impressed with your work here today."

Rachel coughed. Squeaked her toe against the floor. "Thank you."

Douga reached out and touched Rachel on her shoulder. "You've come a long way in a quick time. Good work." Douga nodded, dropped her hand, and began to walk off.

"You know me, always very non-terrifying," Rachel said to her teacher's back.

A snort sounded. It was Sana. "Sure you are. You're basically the monster in *Young Frankenstein*."

Rachel's jaw dropped. *Was Sana teasing her?*

Sana smirked.

Holy shit, Sana was teasing her. Like they were friends.

"I'm off," said Sana. "You need any more help?"

"Nope. I've got the rest myself."

Sana nodded once. "All right. See you."

Rachel watched the *swish swish swish* of Sana's retreating ponytail with a sinking suspicion that it would haunt her dreams that night.

13

Trying Really Hard, Actually

— Sana —

Mom wasn't available to give Sana a ride home. She'd told Sana she'd be shooting overnight and through most of the day. Even if Mom had gotten home, Sana didn't want to wake her. It just seemed like cruel and unusual punishment. Diesel had already left. Sana thought about taking the bus. She didn't mind riding it out into the Valley. It was usually a solid time she could sit to herself and either get some homework done or listen to a podcast or scroll mindlessly through her feed. But she checked the schedule on her phone and everything was delayed by at least half an hour—traffic combined with one of the lines breaking down.

It wasn't an emergency, so Sana couldn't really justify calling a ride from an app. She remembered one more way she could get home. It was free of monetary charge, wouldn't take an extra ninety minutes, but was probably going to cost in emotional overhead.

Sana rolled the dice. She went into her contacts list. The phone rang once, then twice. Massoud picked up in the middle of the third ring. "Speak of the devil, and she appears. I was just talking about you. I never thought I'd see your name flash up on my screen."

"You've stored my number?"

"Is that a joke?" When Sana didn't laugh, Massoud added, "You're my kid."

Sana was starting to seriously regret this, but she couldn't turn back now. "I need a ride home. From school."

Massoud paused for a moment, but less than a second later he was saying, "Your wish is my command, Sana-jaan. Gimme a minute to wrap up here and I'll be there in a flash."

By the time Sana got to the parking lot, she had only had to wait about fifteen minutes for Massoud to show up. He pulled up with all of the flash and noise and fanfare that Sana had come to expect of him and his love of imported vehicles.

"What happened to your regular ride?"

"I missed it," said Sana.

"Bummer," said Massoud. "Wanna talk about it?"

Sana shook her head. "I appreciate the ride, but let's not play happy families right now."

Massoud gave her a once-over as she buckled herself in the car. "You're the one who made the call."

"You're the one who answered it."

"I'm not the enemy, beti."

"*Don't* call me that."

Massoud swerved—it was a controlled motion, crisp and direct. He pulled over to the side of the road with a screeching halt. "That's it. You don't have to like me. You don't have to forgive me. But you do owe me some respect, kid."

Sana crossed her arms and pointed her knees toward the car door. She didn't have anything to say to that. At least, nothing that would be productive.

"Oh, I see," said Massoud. "I'm the bad guy. I'm the one who left."

Sana whipped her whole body toward him. "You leave over and over again. It's not that you left. It's that you're in a perpetual state of being gone. For some very important reason, I'm sure."

Massoud stared at her for a long moment. "That's rich coming from the kid who applied to a fellowship all the way in India without telling *a single family member.*"

Sana drew in a breath. *Holy Hades.* "You knew?"

"Of course I knew, kid. I got a call from the board for the foundation when you applied. You did, after all, put me on the application. They needed to know you could afford to travel there. That you had family support. Thank God they called me and not your grandmother."

"That's why you called your friend at Princeton." Sana's stomach dropped. It was her one secret, the one thing that had belonged to her from the beginning. And it turned out, it had belonged to her father, too. Somehow, it was worse that he'd kept her secret. Worse that he'd held on to it just as tightly as she had.

Worse, because they were so alike, her father and her. Two tightly wound peas in the same kind of escape pod. Sana resented ever having to confront that truth.

"I needed to know," he said. "How serious you were. I needed to know what you were up to."

Sana's ears were vibrating, somehow. Sound was muted. And an underlying sensation of dizziness, of not quite knowing where her body was in space, overtook Sana. "Why didn't you say anything?"

"I thought you'd tell me." Massoud shook his head. "I thought I could help. I thought you'd need someone to talk to."

He'd held on to the secret just like she had. He'd held on so she would talk to him, which he knew she hated doing. He'd held on to her secret because he knew information was power and in this situation, he held all the power cards and she held none of them.

Not anymore.

The one thing that had been solely hers. The one thing that had belonged to her hopes and her dreams and her honestly admitted doubts. It had been his, too, all along. It had never honestly belonged to her. It was something she'd been allowed. Something she'd been loaned by him. It was an inheritance, and nothing to do with her at all.

Sana had trouble breathing. She took in a ragged inhale, then out again. Her chest was tight, tight, tight with the sensation that she couldn't breathe. That the light was dimming in the car and there wasn't enough air. There would never be enough air again.

"Beti. Breathe." Massoud had a soothing, lulling voice. The calmest voice on the planet. It made him good at his job, those lulling, intense tones.

Sana hated the sound of it. She turned to directly face him and did her worst. "So you're blackmailing me into being your child now, is that it? I have to hang out with you or else you're going to tell Dadu or Mamani?"

Massoud stared—his eyes went wide for a moment. It was only an instant, but Sana registered the shock, the hurt. Then his gaze narrowed, hardened. Turned into the flinty journalist he was on camera. He shook his head and faced the windshield. He turned the car back up onto the road. He turned up the radio, and between that and the thrum of the overturned engine, Sana didn't have to speak or hear another word spoken to her the whole way home.

Rachel

Two weeks. Rachel had two weeks to finish her project.

Rachel was wiping down a table where the customers had taken forever to get up after they had closed out. The rag in her hand was wet and cold. It made this horrifically wonderful sound when she dropped it onto the table.

Splat.

But it was no good. Rachel was distracting herself and she knew it.

The dailies from her first set of reshoots with Sana were good. She'd watched them, edited them down a bit. But still—she had two weeks. That was one week to get all the necessary shots and another week to edit like a damned madwoman. She wasn't sure if it was enough time.

It had to be enough time.

"Rach, I think that table's clean. It only needed a standard wipe, not a full wax and tune." Jeanie was shouting from the counter.

"Right. Sorry." Rachel stopped cleaning table seventeen. She put the rag back away. "Can I take my five now, Jeanie?"

Jeanie looked around the hall. "You didn't take it an hour ago?"

"I forgot." More like, she'd been happy to work through her break. Glad to have the distraction.

Jeanie shook her head. "You gotta take your legal breaks. Go. Be back on time, though."

That was all Rachel needed. She pulled off her vest and apron and went into the break room. She didn't want to check her phone right away. She had plenty of other things to do. Like eat a snack. Or look over her shooting list. Or count the tiles in the ceiling. Anything but check her phone.

Rachel got her phone out of her locker. *Hi*

Rachel wasn't sure what else to say. She knew she wanted to say something. She couldn't get it out of her head. Sana had been so spot on. About Helen. About her story.

You were right. about the script. I'm watching the dailies. They're good

Three bubbles popped up on Sana's end. Then disappeared. Then reappeared.

Rachel couldn't take it. *Sorry I didn't listen.*

It's okay, I get it ⁺✦

No it isn't. I needed to let it out. needed to write it. Rachel had prided herself on being so forward thinking, so feminist. She had thought of herself as the filmmaker who saw every angle. And how had she missed this—that she thought of Helen of Troy like everyone who had written her before, and most of those everyone were men.

Given what you thought, I get it 👍

I hated you. Rachel didn't know why she'd said it. Didn't know what had made her feel so particularly confessional in this conversation. She just had to say it.

I know, wrote back Sana. *and now?*

Rachel thought about that for a moment. What were they now? Not enemies. Not nemeses. Just two people who worked together. Colleagues? But that wasn't right either. That didn't describe what they were. They had some level of mutual respect. Of camaraderie. She wasn't sure how to describe that, but she could approximate as best as she could. *now we're friends*

I'd like that 💚

Then three more thinking dots appeared, but Sana didn't send a message.

Rachel stared at that emoji. Wondering if Sana tacked it on to all her conversations. She seemed like she'd be a prolific emoji user, to be honest. But sometimes Sana went and surprised Rachel, so she couldn't be sure. *So. As friends. I have to bail. I can't meet at your place this weekend. I've got to work late. I have to edit this. I don't have time for more movie watching.*

The trail of thinking dots disappeared entirely. *Okay*

Rachel breathed out a sigh of relief. *it is?*

Yeah. I'll ask my mom for the car. Meet at your place. I can help you edit.

No. God no was more like it.

Oh

That was all Sana sent. *Oh.* And all Rachel could think of was the hurt and the bewilderment on her face before she pasted on a bright smile and made everyone else feel comfortable when she was clearly feeling like hell. Rachel couldn't believe she knew Sana well enough now that she knew how the girl would react. But she did.

Rachel typed out a new response. *Meet me at work?*

Rachel regretted the message the moment she sent it. But it was out there and there was no getting it back now. Maybe she could go to film school in New York or London and never come back to this place. That was a good way to avoid Sana for the rest of forever.

Rad. Back to orgo. See you soon

Rachel sent back a *bye* even though nobody sent "bye" messages and she could see herself staying unread because Sana probably actually did go off to do her homework.

The break door rattled open, startling Rachel.

"Rach. Your five minutes were up five minutes ago. Get to getting."

Rachel stuffed her phone back in her locker and threw her apron back on. Nothing like a conversation with Sana Khan to throw off the rhythm of her entire life.

14

Not on Rex Manning Day

 *Sana*

Sana was up before dawn. Farrah, who hadn't gone to sleep yet from work the night before, was just out of the shower. A hopeful thought threaded through Sana's chest.

Anything could happen today, it was Nowruz. New beginnings, fresh starts. The start of a new year that only spring could bring.

"You cleaned," said Farrah in awe. She was wearing a freshly laundered sweatpants set and she was rubbing her hair with a towel, which you weren't supposed to do because it caused frizz or flyaways and the kind of volume in curly hair that was designated as *unwanted* by lady mags and appearance-conscious mothers. But Farrah seemed to like her hair big and fluffy and full of all the things magazines and her mother were constantly telling women to avoid.

"Of course." Sana had scrubbed the bungalow from top to bottom. She had even dusted the blinds and washed the floors. Vacuumed the baseboards. Everything.

Farrah tossed the towel away. She reached out and gave Sana a bracing hug and kiss on the forehead. "What would I do without you?"

"Have bad luck all year round?"

Farrah laughed, airily and a bit manically. She was, after all, in desperate need of sleep. She pointed to the box of food she'd put on the kitchen table. "Check the clocks. I know I should have fresh food but this is what I could get off of set."

"The caterers made it fresh, didn't they?" Sana went over and checked the box.

Mom had gotten petit fours from crafty—each wrapped in their own clear boxes and tied with a ribbon. Sana had gotten the wheat-grass and the candles, the apples and dyed eggs. She'd set up the haft-seen with bulb of garlic on top of a mirror, sprouts in a dish, coins across the table, and—because she'd forgotten until nearly the last minute—kitchen vinegar in a soy sauce dish. Sana took out the two boxes of petit fours and set each onto the table. Something sweet to start the new year.

"Bless you. I have no idea how you are even mine sometimes." Mom leaned in and gave Sana a kiss on the cheek. She began inspecting the setup. "Did—is that a tulip candle?"

"Someone cleared out the grocery store. Three of them nearby. I improvised." The haftseen was supposed to have tulips. At least they'd had hyacinths at the store. Sana went into the kitchen to grab the vase of water she'd put them into and set it on the table. She couldn't get the aesthetics of the haftseen right, the way Mamani always did. But she did her best.

"Is the jasmine not from the grocery store?" Mom stuck her face in the flowers. She loved the smell of jasmine.

Sana did, too. That's why she used jasmine-scented conditioner in her hair. To Sana, it smelled like the start of spring. It was a smell that would only intensify in the heat of summer. To Farrah, it smelled like Los Angeles and freedom from Orange County. And to Mamani, jasmine was the smell of the old country. Of the life that had been left behind, before she had picked up somewhere new.

"Do you really want the answer to that question?" Sana had ordered a bunch of jasmine online weeks ago. She never remembered about the tulips. They were one of her favorite flowers, but every year she forgot to order them ahead of time.

"Nope." Mom picked up one of the coins on the edge of the table and let it drop with a satisfying metallic *clink* onto the wood.

The wheatgrass had been the easiest for Sana to find. "Just be thankful that you can order those little crates of greens online."

"You can order tulips online, too." Mom ran her hands along the hyacinths, delicately and softly rustling the petals of the flowers without dislodging them.

"Seriously? How was I supposed to know there would be a run on tulips?" Sana huffed.

Farrah laughed. "At Nowruz? In Los Angeles? You definitely should have known."

"Maman." Sana never called Farrah that. Farrah preferred "Mom." Maman sounded too much like what Farrah had called her own mother growing up. And Farrah wanted to be nothing like her own mother.

"Yes, Sana-joon. I understand." And she really did. Farrah rebelled so much against her parents, against their rigidity, their manners. But Mom loved Nowruz. Loved the magic of flowers growing and blooming. The magic of new beginnings and rebirth and the world coming to life again.

They both did.

Not that there was really such a demonstrable shift in weather in LA, or even Orange County. But the flowers knew. They opened and bloomed and understood that they had waited patiently for the right moment—when there was enough light, enough sunshine to keep them flourishing. The flowers had the right instincts about these kinds of things.

Farrah reached out and grabbed the edge of Sana's sleeve. "Are those pajamas new?"

"Yes," said Sana, smiling. It was hard to stay mad at Mom when the new year was starting and spring was happening and the whole house smelled like tulips and vinegar and fresh grass.

Their phone alarms went off—precisely at the same time—and they each untied the bow on the wrapped petit fours in front of them. It was their own tradition, started when Farrah couldn't afford sweets except for stuff at crafty on set. And that first year in LA, on the set Farrah was working on, there had magically been petit fours that nobody had touched. Perfectly new and unwrapped. Mom always said that it had felt like a sign that they were going to make it, that they were going to be okay. Farrah added them to the crafty request sheet now, only request she ever put in. Once a year like clockwork. They still felt like a special gift from the universe to Sana.

"Here," said Sana, handing over a small package.

"Ohh! What is it?' Farrah shook the small box.

"You have to open it!"

"Is it a kazoo?" Farrah shook it again.

"No."

"Is it that Tamagotchi my mom never got me?"

"Mom."

"Mamani refused to get me one and I always hope one Nowruz you'll get me one."

"I'm not getting you a Tamagotchi. Especially not for Nowruz."

Farrah shook her head. "Like grandmother, like granddaughter."

Sana sighed.

"All right, all right. I'll open it." Farrah pulled back the green-and-pink paper to reveal a small box. She opened it, and inside was a miniature enamel tulip pin.

"Oh, honey. I love it."

"I got it off Etsy."

"It's the best, Sana-joon. I'll wear it to work tomorrow and everything." Farrah smiled, big and wide. "Now open yours."

In front of Sana was a small box. She folded back the wrapping paper—Mom had used the obnoxious glitter kind that got all over the house—and she too had a small box. When Sana lifted the lid to reveal a dainty silver ring in the shape of a snake eating its own tail. Its eyes were tiny turquoises. Sana put it on. "Oh, Mom, it's beautiful."

Farrah smiled, smug and satisfied. She got up from her chair at the table and went and gave Sana another kiss on the forehead. "Excellent. I'm glad you liked it. I figured even Mamani couldn't object to a shedding snake at Nowruz." Farrah yawned.

"Go get some sleep, Mom," said Sana, admiring her ring and letting it glint this way and that to catch the new light pouring in through the windows.

"You're coming back to bed, no?"

"Yes," said Sana to her mother's retreating form. But first she wanted to pray. She thought of her focus for the year as she washed her hands and feet and face. As she took off the ring and covered her hair. As she double-checked the direction of Mecca with her phone. As she moved through the motions—up and down, kneeling to standing, to prone across the floor. Her forehead touched the soapstone—cool and smooth and seemingly ancient. She prayed for a new beginning, a fresh start. A way to rewrite the past to take control of the future.

Rachel

The door slammed shut and Rachel nearly dropped the vacuum nozzle in her hand.

"What the hell is going on?" It was Papa.

There were many solid, viable answers to this question, but Rachel went with the most obvious. "I'm vacuuming."

"Mija. I know that. But since it is neither Yom Kippur nor Rosh Hashanah, I am at a loss."

"I'm cleaning." Rachel shut off the vacuum.

Daniel Recht's face remained skeptical, but Rachel's dad began to reverently remove his shoes. This was never his custom. "Look. You don't clean. I don't clean. Unless we are having people over, which is all of never to two days a year."

"I'm having people over."

Papa stopped untying his shoes. "People? You're having people over?"

"Person.. I'm having a person over."

"Were you gonna clear this with me?"

No. "Yes."

Papa made a noise somewhere between a "huh" and a snort. "Right. Does this person have a name?"

"Sana."

Daniel raised an eyebrow.

Rachel gripped the vacuum nozzle tighter. "Sana Khan. She's in my movie. She's going to help me with my film project."

"Right. A cast member. Coming over to work." Daniel's tone was totally flat, like he was asking Rachel to pass the salsa across the table. But he stared at Rachel with his eyebrow raised. He was waiting for her to crack.

Rachel wouldn't crack. She nodded, clutching the vacuum closer. "Exactly."

"Totally normal for you to be vacuuming at two o'clock in the morning."

Rachel opened her mouth, then thought better of it. She looked down and saw she was practically hugging the vacuum cleaner.

Dammit.

"Start over, mami," said Daniel, pointing upward as he spoke. "From the top."

Rachel took a deep breath. "I don't want her to see that this place is a mess." And it was. The apartment wasn't dirty. It was never dirty, per se. But both Rachel and her father were messy people.

Daniel made a sound like an incorrect buzzer on a game show. "Try again."

"You don't believe me?"

Papa thought about that for a moment. He finished removing his shoes. He walked over and sat down on the sun-faded, greige couch. He tapped the fabric of the cushion beside him. Rachel dropped the vacuum hose and sat beside her father.

"I believe you." Papa looked right at her when he spoke. A bit unnerving when so much of their relationship and conversations were conducted in snatched bits of phone conversations. He had dark shadows under his eyes from his hours. Some salt-and-pepper stubble growing across his tan, olive skin. "I don't think you're telling *yourself* everything."

"I'm ashamed." Rachel looked away.

"Look at me, mija. You're a kid. You have no more control over the circumstances of your birth than who you love. And you've never been ashamed of that."

"I know," whispered Rachel.

Daniel put his hands onto his knees, bracing himself. "Are you going to let yourself feel ashamed of where you're from?"

"No."

He inspected her face. "But you do want to keep cleaning."

Rachel cringed. She had to. She couldn't stop herself. "Yes."

Papa pushed himself off the couch, standing with the kind of effort only a long day at work could produce. Rachel knew that kind of bone-deep tiredness like she knew the lenses in her kit. He went into the kitchen, turning on the sink with a squeak.

"What are you doing?"

"Washing the dishes. What does it look like?" Papa put soap on the sponge. "Come and help me dry."

They washed and dried and put away the dishes in companionable silence. When they were done, Rachel felt the tension that had welled up in her chest subside. He gave her a kiss on the forehead, then crashed out on the couch. Rachel took the hint. Enough cleaning for the night. She went to her room and slept—deep, blank, and dreamless.

15

The Trouble with Angels

Sana

The drive down to Orange County was uneventful. The usual amount of traffic, if not slightly less. If everyone was going to their own Nowruz parties, then they were either already there, or they were staying in their own neighborhoods for the day.

Not an option for Sana.

Mamani still cooked to prove that nobody could take the old country out of her. And to reinforce that she'd married a man who had made enough money that she could cook with pure leisure in mind.

Sana had to dress her best. A flowy, knee-length skirt and a floral print top. Her hair smoothed and pulled back, as usual. Sana added a little extra flick to her eyeliner. If she had an extra special game to cheer at, Sana usually would add a touch more highlighter. But Mamani was from a different generation. She didn't understand all these young girls "making themselves shiny on purpose." When it came to special events at Mamani's house, Sana added extra eyeliner, like her grandmother would appreciate.

If Sana thought she could get away with old clothes on Nowruz—even ones Mamani hadn't seen before—she would have armchair diagnosed herself with delusion. Mamani could *smell* new clothes.

Sometimes Sana "accidentally" left the store tags on just so Mamani could fuss over the new item and cut the tags out herself.

It was the little things with Mamani.

Mom rang the bell, and a frazzled Mamani swung open the door. "You didn't park in the drive, did you?"

"No, Maman." Farrah leaned in to brush a kiss on her mother's cheek.

"Because your brother will be late and he'll need the spot." Mamani double-checked the circular driveway from the door.

Farrah leaned into Mamani's other cheek. Farrah's serenity always increased as her mother's plummeted. They were inverse corollaries of each other in so many ways.

"And the other guests." A crash sounded. Mamani started, then left the doorway empty as she went to the noise's source.

"What's the meaning of this? It's clear the house, not wreck it." Mamani's voice faded as she moved, still shouting, deeper into the house.

Dadu appeared, holding two old-fashioned glasses. "You should take this."

"Starting early, Baba." Mom took one of the glasses and gave her father a kiss. She sniffed the glass.

Dadu shrugged. "Suit yourself."

Another crashing sound, followed by the muffled sounds of shouting. Mom nodded and took a swig of her drink. "I think I will."

Dadu chuckled, then turned to Sana. "You're too young for our habits."

"I don't drink, Dadu."

"Good girl." Dadu gave Sana's hand an affectionate pat.

Sana said nothing. True, she practiced her faith a bit more strictly than her mother and her grandfather. She and Mamani had that in common. But Sana wanted to be a surgeon. Drinking could lead to hand tremors. Not now. But ten, twenty years down the road. After education had been paid for and training completed. It wasn't worth the risk, even if it wasn't a guarantee.

"Come," said Dadu. "Your cousin is over here."

"Maman's screaming with company over?" Mom took another swig of her drink.

Athena Mashi came up from behind Mom and stole the drink out of her hand. "No. Just you and Sana-joon and her impressionable cousins. Wants all us girls to know how to manage a household one day."

"Yes, that is so among my goals." Sana laughed.

Dadu's face grew serious for a moment. Sana and Athena Mashi stopped laughing.

"You know," he started, "it was different when your grandmother was growing up. She didn't have the same options, the same choices. She didn't have Princeton or surgery available to her the way you do. But she made brave decisions where she could."

A sinking pit welled in Sana's heart, threatening to swallow her whole. In ten days, she might not have any choices at all. Might not have gotten the fellowship. And she still hadn't put down her deposit. But she didn't let it show. Didn't have her expression slip enough to need a moment to recover. Her face held fast, even as her heart went into turmoil. "You mean when she married you?"

"When she married me? Yes. When she finished her education before she agreed to marry me, too. There weren't many paths open to me then, but there were even less for your mamani. She overcame them all."

Sana wasn't so sure about that. Yes, Mamani had bet on the right horse, so to speak, and triumphed in her marriage. But she had a degree in art history that she used to decorate homes rather than study the classics, the way Sana knew Mamani longed to. Mamani's triumph, her true victory, wasn't in finances or work. Wasn't even in pursuing her academic dreams or publishing a thesis way back in the day. No, Mamani's true path to triumph was her ability to make whatever she ended up with look like what she wanted all along. Mamani made the short end of the stick look desirable.

Sana looked at him, sure he could see the guilt shining through on her face. Sana had nearly every option. She had next to every future still ahead of her. And still, Sana faltered. And still, she couldn't commit to what she had been working toward her entire life.

But Dadu didn't sense any of this. Or if he did, he didn't show it. He patted her hand again and said, "I'm going to make sure your mamani hasn't killed anyone with that big French pot."

And then Sana was left alone. Not alone-alone. She was less than a foot and a half away from Jasmine. She could hear most of the conversation from where she stood. It was an argument, honestly, because it was her and Lilah. But Sana tuned it out.

Athena Mashi walked by and caught Sana's expression; she frowned. "You okay?"

Sana pasted on a bright smile. "Fine."

Sana rolled her eyes at Jasmine and joined the discussion of whether camo pants were now back in style again. It was easier than letting go of her secrets, easier than confessing that she had no idea what her future would look like. It was easier to remain silent.

But for the first time Sana wondered if there was a cost to her silence. An invisible price to keeping the peace.

Rachel

Student filmmakers regularly complained about the editing bay. If you were at the film labs, the room was dark and empty and the software would crash and the clips would misalign and the work was already shitty enough without having to go and do it all over again. If you were at home, the same was true, but usually you were cratering everything running on your laptop and, occasionally, frying out a personal hard drive. There was no win, when editing. Just the slow, methodical clipping and placing, the aligning of the audio, and the smell of an overheating computer running double time to stay cooled off.

Rachel loved the editing bay.

She was cutting up the takes of her last shoot. She liked to make rough cuts as she went. It was easier to keep track of everything. Easier to import chunks rather than do an enormous and terrible editing import at the end. That was how you fried hard drives, not to mention crashed software.

To Rachel, editing was a state of mind. Close the door, turn down the lights, grab a soda or a can of sparkling flavored crap and the kind of food you'd only consume on a road trip and zone out everything that wasn't the focus of the film. Didn't have to be linear, didn't have to be thematic. The work was whatever she needed it to be. The film, the reality of a whole world bending to her will alone.

Except Rachel's will would have had Helen be the victim. The villain, even. The instigator of all of this unnecessary war, unnecessary evil. Rachel's idea for the whole narrative was to have Cassandra be the tragic, truth-telling protagonist.

Sana had gone and thrown a wrench in those plans.

Worse, as Rachel watched and edited, she knew Sana had been right to pull Helen forward. Rachel hadn't been interested in making the most beautiful woman in the world into the most fascinating woman in the world. But this was different. Sana had pulled on the thread of Helen's humanity. Sana had found what makes any character relatable to so many people—her imperfections. Helen here was vain, but also trying to be brave. She was selfish, but also living in a world that had made her be selfless since childhood. She was a woman trying to walk her own path in this world, despite there being no such thing for her.

Sana was perfect. A perfect Helen. Rachel was beginning to wonder if there was anything the girl was bad at. Sana knew where the

light was. Conscious of it after Rachel had pointed it out, without looking like she was aware of any of the individual lamps.

The Helen in the movie was revealing all sorts of things about
Sana. Rachel did a hard save—just to be sure—and then downloaded
the file. She sent a copy of the rough cut—it was only the first thirty
minutes—to Douga, and then closed her laptop. She could save the
rest of the edits for another day. Right now, the clips were making her
dizzy. Right now, she wasn't sure what was real anymore.

16

What's Your Damage?

Sana hadn't meant to lie to her mom about where she was headed tonight. She had called it a school project and had thought about it as a school project, and was currently refusing to give light to any of her other thoughts buried under the idea of *school project*.

So it was startling to realize as Sana took the keys to her mother's car—which were right on top of a note that said *Love you and good luck with your work. Back at dawn* that she had left before grabbing a ride with a coworker—that she felt guilty. She hadn't meant to lie, not really. She had just wanted to keep the truth from herself. But now, with this unsettling pit at the base of her stomach, Sana was starting to think maybe it was a lie, or a kind of a lie.

Was it the kind of lie she was allowed to tell her mother? Was it better or worse than not telling her that she still hadn't sent in her deposit? That she didn't know why she hadn't sent in her deposit? That she had applied for a fellowship halfway across the globe?

But Sana didn't have any sort of satisfactory answer for that.

Sana put the key into the ignition and turned the engine on. She was always surprised when the old boy started up. Mom had kept the thing running on a good amount of basic car know-how and a heavy amount of charm with the local mechanics.

It was a 1993 Mitsubishi Eagle Summit in red—complete with the side faux-wood paneling. The cloth seats always managed to grab ahold of Sana's skirts like Velcro and refuse to ever let go. The car even had a weird holdover safety feature from the early nineties. The top part of the seat belt was attached to the frame—it slid into place as you closed the door. Slid into place at an excruciatingly slow pace. Sana sat, waiting for her seat belt to finish securing itself, when all she wanted to do was set the car into motion.

Mom's attachment to a vehicle had seemed silly, overly sentimental to Sana. But now, driving out to an unfamiliar diner to meet Rachel, Sana felt the comfort of gripping the old, smoothed-down and worn steering wheel. Maybe that's why Farrah liked it. There were so few constants in the life she lived, in the job she did. TV shows would reuse sets, but so many of Farrah's shoots were temporary situations that got pulled down at the end of shooting. This car was as much home as their house was. It even smelled faintly of takeout food and warmed plastic, though not in an unpleasant way.

The worst part about driving anywhere in Los Angeles was that even once she'd gotten there, she still hadn't really arrived, no matter what a map might declare. No, a girl still had to find parking. This was why Sana hated to drive. She could be somewhere and not actually be there at all. She could be on time and also arrive late. She was Schrödinger's dinner date.

Sana did two laps of the block before miraculously finding parking outside the diner. The meter was already paid out for another hour and everything.

When Sana walked in, a small, plump blond woman stared at her for a solid minute.

"Excuse me?" asked Sana.

"You need something?" asked the woman.

Sana smiled her most winning smile. "I'm here to see Rachel. Do you know by any chance if she's off yet?"

The woman's eyebrows disappeared under her curly bangs at that. "Here to see Rachel?"

Sana looked around, to see if there was anybody else who had heard that, yes, that was exactly what she had just said. But the entryway was empty. "Yes."

That's when the woman whistled. "I'm Jeanie."

"Hello," said Sana, a bit at a loss. "I'm Sana. Sana Khan. Are you her manager? Should I wait here, then?"

The woman named Jeanie laughed like Sana had told the funniest joke she'd heard in a long time. "And you're polite, too."

Sana was uncertain of what to say in response. Usually when she was uncertain, silence would do the trick.

"Come on, little lady," and then Jeanie gave Sana a once-over, trying to see if there was another word she ought to use. But after her perusal she gave a light nod to herself. "I'll grab you a seat and a soda. You do drink soda, don't you?"

Sana didn't, not really. "Sure."

Jeanie snorted in a way that made Sana feel sure that the woman hadn't believed her. But she came back in a minute with a menu and a fountain soda with pellet ice. "On the house, little duchess." Jeanie seemed more satisfied with that nickname than the other.

Rachel walked up to the table without looking up. She was digging through her apron looking for a pen to write with, a pan in the other hand. "What'll it be?"

"An order of French fries, please."

Rachel's head snapped up so quickly Sana was worried the girl would get whiplash. "What are you *doing* here?"

"Picking you up?" Sana hadn't meant to make it sound like a question. Rachel had been so startled by her presence. Like they hadn't

166

made plans. Like she hadn't expected Sana to follow through with them.

"You couldn't wait outside?" Rachel hissed.

Sana drew herself up to her full seated height. "I'm sorry. Is my presence here an embarrassment to you?" This time, Sana had meant her tone—loud enough to carry to the next booth over and cause a couple of olds sitting there to turn and take notice.

"I'm not embarrassed." This was more of a whisper and less of a hiss.

"You sure seem not-embarrassed." Sana raised an eyebrow.

"You caught me off guard."

"Do you often find yourself surprised by the people you make plans with being in the spot you planned to meet them?"

"No." Rachel put both palms flat on the table.

Sana's throat went dry. Their faces were so close.

"You're supposed to wait outside. Not in my section."

"Jeanie said I could sit here."

"You talked to Jeanie?"

"Should I add that to the list of definitely-not-embarrassing offenses that I have already committed today?"

The old couple turned again. Rachel stared back at them until they turned around.

Rachel leaned in close, clearly ready to give Sana a piece of her mind. But she was so close to Sana now. Sana fluttered her eyelashes, just to see what kind of reaction she could get. Whatever Rachel was about to say stopped with a halted little squeak. Sana batted her eyelashes again, mesmerized by her own effect on Rachel.

Rachel, however, recovered by pointing a finger at Sana and creating a barrier between their faces. "Don't for a second think you can bat your pretty little eyelashes and make ingénue faces at me and you'll get your way."

"You think my eyelashes are pretty?"

"That's not the point."

"What's an ingénue?"

"It's also not important."

"I'll just look it up later."

"Wholesome. An ingénue is wholesome." Rachel wiped her hand over her forehead.

Sana felt her face scrunch up. "Wholesome?"

Rachel dropped her hand. "For fuck's sake, Audrey Hepburn is an ingénue."

Sana ignored the curse word. "You think I look like Audrey Hepburn?"

Rachel put her head back into her hand. "I don't know what I did to deserve this."

"You're the one who called me wholesome," said Sana.

"I didn't mean it like that."

"What did you mean? Personally, I feel like a perfectly balanced meal. Or like whole milk. Fresh from a cow. Full of calcium. Very wholesome."

Rachel looked up. Her lips parted, her eyes wide. She was at a loss for words. Sana had done that. She had to suppress a smile.

Jeanie came back to the table, refill in hand. "Get out of here, Recht. Your shift's over."

Rachel squeaked again. "But. I've got fifteen minutes left."

Jeanie put her hand on her hip. "You haven't. Besides, I like the girl."

Rachel snorted, like Sana couldn't understand the meaning.

But Sana had, loud and clear.

And Jeanie gave Sana a wink. "You've got to be patient with this one."

Sana nodded. "Oh, I know."

Rachel stared between the woman and the girl like they had both lost their minds.

"Come on," said Sana. "I got a spot right out front. I'll meet you back outside. Thanks for the soda, Jeanie."

"Anytime, little duchess."

Sana waited outside for a minute, the triumph she felt warding off any feeling of cold she ought to have from the brisk night air.

When Rachel came out, she still wore her work uniform, though she had swapped out her apron for a backpack. "I didn't bring a change of clothes."

"We're just going to your house."

"Still."

"What? Did you not think I was going to show or something?" Sana walked over to her car.

Rachel followed her but got out her car keys. They both stood there, each holding their car keys in hand, each refusing to hop in the car with the other.

"More like hoped you wouldn't."

Great. "Seriously? I met you at work and you clearly refused to get in my car. You're ashamed to have me meet your coworkers. I thought we were over this by now. Past it somehow. What gives? You afraid I'm going to contaminate your precious home?" Sana was breathing heavy by the end.

Rachel went silent. Didn't say a word in response. Sana knew something was amiss. She'd misstepped again. She didn't know when or how, but the stricken look on Rachel's face spoke volumes.

But Sana couldn't seem to stop herself, couldn't contain her irritation. "That's it? You won't tell me? I've screwed up yet again and I have to berate myself for an unknown crime. Speaking to you? Asking questions?"

"Jesus Christ," shouted Rachel, like she'd remembered it really upset Sana to blaspheme. "I'm embarrassed of where I live."

Sana opened her mouth, but all that came out was a puff of air and a sound resembling "Oh."

Rachel heaved a sigh. "Whatever. Follow me there. I'm in the black Lincoln Continental right around the corner." And then she walked off without waiting for any kind of confirmation from Sana.

Silent, Sana got in her car, letting the door slowly block her back in. *Ashamed of her home. Where she lived.*

Sana felt about as big as the tip of a razor-sharp scalpel as she drove around the corner to find Rachel. Rachel was pulling out of her neighborhood parking spot. Sana followed her into Palms, wondering the whole while how she could possibly make it right again.

Rachel and Sana sat a foot apart on the couch like everything was perfectly fine. This was all okay and nothing weird had ever happened.

Just admitting to shame over my current home. Nothing to see here. Move along, everyone. Just Sana sitting on the couch like that greyhound in a sweater labeled "Nervous."

They were fine and this was fine, and if the earth could just open up right now and swallow her whole—that would be ideal for Rachel, honestly.

Sana looked straight ahead and politely at the screen. She'd been doing that since she arrived—looking at nothing and touching nothing without seeming like she was consciously touching nothing. She didn't even touch the computer when suggesting edits. She just pointed vaguely in the direction of the right minute mark on the timeline of the film. It was like treading lightly and looking nowhere were natural to her state of being. It was so awful Rachel didn't even have a sarcastic thing to say about it. She willed Sana to say something that wasn't directly about the film. *Say anything.*

Because Rachel certainly couldn't. All she could see were the chips in the paint on the walls—*had those been there before?* And the dust she missed while vacuuming. She only now remembered she was supposed to use a special attachment to vacuum the baseboards. Not that their vacuum even had that attachment anymore. It had been lost in one of the moves and they had simply soldiered on in their infrequent vacuumings without it.

Sana took a deep inhale. "I brought a movie."

"Oh." It was still all that Rachel could manage.

"I mean, we don't have to watch it." Sana sounded so sad and dejected. "We can keep editing."

"No," said Rachel. "We can. Sounds fine."

That's when Sana reached out and finally touched something— Rachel's hand. Rachel's eyes snapped to Sana's.

"I'm sorry, you know. I shouldn't have pushed. I get an idea in my head and I can't let go. I'm like my mother. And my grandmother."

Rachel imperceptibly winced at the mention of mothers. Sana must have thought she was flinching away.

Sana released her hand. "I can go."

"No," said Rachel, hardly sure of herself. "I don't want you to go." *Where the hell had that come from?*

Sana must not have known either because she stared at Rachel all agog.

But it was true. Rachel didn't want Sana to leave. "I didn't want you here—" Rachel helped up her hand to stay Sana's movements. "I didn't want *anybody* here. Not ever. But now you are and the worst is over. Let's watch whatever you brought. I don't think I can edit anymore right now anyway."

"I brought *Pakeezah*." Sana ducked her head into her bag, her normally swishing ponytail now arrested upside down. The only sound in the room was the cars going by outside and the clattering of the impossible amount of crap Sana carried around in that tiny bag.

How did she even fit that much stuff into such a small receptacle?

Sana finally pulled the movie out. Relief coated her face.

Rachel wished she could go back in time and unsay what she had said. How had she let her embarrassment get the better of her? How had she managed to *say it out loud*? That was the worst. Even worse than

Jeanie winking at Sana. Like Sana could possibly be into a girl like Rachel.

Rachel didn't want to melt into the couch. She wanted to turn into the couch and never regain sentience ever again. That was the only way these moments would stop looping over and over again in her head like a blooper reel from hell.

Why did all of Rachel's worst moments always have to involve this impossible girl?

It was one thing to relive your own worst moments. It was something else altogether to have to relive them standing next to a girl who looked like she had stepped out of a reel from the golden age of Old Hollywood. Rachel didn't even look like the leading lady of her own memories.

Rachel was jolted back to reality by singing that started ringing through the still apartment. Sana began scrambling for the remote, trying to get the menu to stop playing and getting the movie to start. It was refreshing, honestly, to watch Sana scramble at anything. Even if situationally, it made sense that she had no idea where the remote was in another person's home.

The movie opened up with a tragedy. A woman was meant to go from courtesan to wife, but her lover's family shamed him into giving her up. The woman fled, dying in a cemetery, but not until after giving birth to a daughter. It was the stuff of classic melodrama, no matter what tradition of cinema you followed—would the tragedy of the mother revisit itself on the daughter?

Would it indeed.

But Rachel could see why this movie was a classic, why Sana had picked it. It was the lead. She was clearly too old to play the ingénue, but it didn't matter. She was shining, magnetic. Gorgeous, too, but that was beside the point. Her beauty was almost like a costume—an adornment to be put on, a piece of a character, another bit of backstory. No, the actor, she had a tragic face. A tragic pull. The way Billie Holiday had a tragic song inside of her. The way that Emily Dickinson poetry that they had been forced to read sophomore year had a tragic literary tone.

Tragedy was in their bones.

This actor pulled it out of her character, she pulled it out of the story, and she pulled it out of the audience, even though she was probably long dead now. And Rachel was reading subtitles. She couldn't imagine what it would have been like to a native speaker.

"Who is she?" Rachel whispered.

The woman onscreen was doing a dance of lament, cutting her feet on glass, bleeding her love out, quite literally. This level of melodrama made Joan Crawford look tame, made Bette Davis look subtle. Rachel lived for this kind of shit. It was incredible.

"Meena Kumari," said Sana. The reverence in her tone was plain. "Queen of the Bollywood Tragedies."

"Ah," said Rachel, like she understood. Because she did. She really did.

"Yeah," said Sana, her voice still hushed, her attention still singularly focused on the screen. "She died from alcoholism, basically. Nobody could rival her, not for tragedies, for years. Not really."

"That I believe."

"Plus, dying young, she was immortalized a bit. The way Marilyn Monroe was. Forever young. Forever beautiful."

Rachel had nothing to say to that. She had too much to say to that.

But Sana, still mesmerized, didn't seem to notice. She kept on talking. "I wanted to be her when I was little. 'I wanna look like Meena Kumari when I grow up,' I used to say. My dadu is from what's now Pakistan, but his mother was Bengali. The same as Meena Kumari. I felt like I understood her, somehow. Then Mamani would give me a lecture on the tragic lives of Bollywood actors. Especially the actresses.

173

Loose morals, Mamani would say. But that only added to the prestige for me. I think I was so obsessed with the idea of being tragically beautiful, from all these old Bollywood films."

"My mom was beautiful like that." Rachel felt Sana's gaze snap from the TV to her. Rachel didn't know where that confession had come from. Didn't know how Sana managed to pull them out of her. Maybe that was Rachel's tragedy. She just wanted to tell Sana things, wanted to let her in.

But Rachel kept on talking anyway, careless of the consequences. "She looked like Hedy Lamarr. A little darker. But tragically beautiful. Femme fatale. She had it, looks-wise. But she couldn't get a toehold, acting-wise. Happens a lot in this town, when everyone thinks pretty girls, even stunningly beautiful ones, are a dime a dozen. Especially when they've got a bit of a Mexican Spanish lilt to their English. And then she hit thirty and her acting career was over. Imagine your career ending not by even looking thirty, but by casting directors knowing you were. I think she thought having me would fill the void. Give her life meaning. Purpose. That's what everyone told her. Settle down. Have kids. She'd find that peace again." Rachel laughed, a harsh, bitter sound she hadn't meant to release. She looked away from the TV and saw the intensity of the sorrow in Sana's eyes. Not pity, thank God. Just a bone-deep sense of sadness.

And that's when the floodgates really opened—when Rachel realized there was no going back and she didn't want to go back in any case. "When she left. We—my dad and I—we thought she had run as far and as fast from the town that had eaten her alive. I guess it kept us from taking it personally. Or more personally. But she hadn't run far at all. We ran into her at a Pavilions in Brentwood. She was with some guy—looked like a manager or a producer or something. She nodded our way, once, and changed aisles. That was it. She was done."

"That's awful."

"Yeah. I spent so much time being angry. At her for leaving and not even having the decency to run far. At a world that told her motherhood would give her meaning. A world that took her career and twisted it and warped it until her looks were all she thought she had to sell. Dad fell apart after that."

Rachel couldn't look away from Sana's unflinching gaze. Maybe this was what people meant when they said cleansed by fire. Her ears were ringing, her whole body was flush with fresh anger and resentment, yet she could not look away. And Sana wouldn't.

The credits were rolling and Rachel had no idea how the film ended. "That was the day we met, you and I. The next day. The morning after. I wish I could forget that, but I can't."

Sana's mouth pressed into a firm line. Disappointment? Determination? Rachel didn't know her well enough to know for sure. Sana looked away then. She grabbed the remote, clicking the TV off. She got up, smoothing out her skirt as she did. "Come on, let's go."

"Where?" Rachel felt as bewildered as she knew she sounded.

Sana turned, flashing a brief but full smile. "We're getting fro-yo."

17

Retro Classic

Sana watched as Rachel waited for the seat belt to slide slowly, click-ingly, into place. Sana was ready with her usual apologetic explanation. "It was like a thing in the nineties. Before everyone wore seat belts. They made them automatic. Safety first."

Rachel raised an eyebrow. "Safety first? That's it? These are the most annoying seat belts known to man and all you've got to say about it is 'safety-fucking-first.'"

Sana frowned.

Rachel sighed. "Sorry. For the cursing. But really."

"My mom paid seven hundred bucks for her freedom. She didn't care if it came with literal strings attached. As long as the strings weren't attached to anyone else. That's just how she is. She'll take the horrible car, as long as it's hers and its quirks are hers and its problems are hers."

"Ah," said Rachel, like she understood. And maybe she did.

"She could afford a new one now. I mean, it's never fun to buy a new car. But she's got the cash to do it."

"Why doesn't she?"

"I guess she likes to remember where she came from. After the pregnancy, after the divorce. Like she can handle anything life throws at her."

Rachel didn't say anything to that.

"But I think she also likes being the production designer, head of all that she's head of, now on a big-deal production and driving one of the crappiest cars on the lot."

Rachel laughed. "That I understand. I think if I could, I'd keep my beat-ass Continental. There's something about it. It's mine. Somehow it's mine."

Sana turned off of Palms and onto Centinela. "Exactly. That's how Mom feels about it exactly. You can't tell her anything."

Rachel shook her head. "I see where you get it."

Sana's jaw dropped. She looked over briefly, still affronted. "Excuse me, people can tell me things."

Rachel scoffed. "Like what?"

"Like," said Sana, suddenly at a loss. "How mitosis works."

"Oh, how mitosis works. Excellent. You don't think you're innately an expert in cellular biology. How gratifying to know."

Sana made a noise between a squeal and a grunt. "Says the literal director of a project who couldn't give up control if she ever wanted to, which she also doesn't."

Sana flicked her gaze over to Rachel. Rachel was grinning. A real, honest-to-goodness grin. It nearly caused Sana to swerve, it was so potent. It was like the rain after a drought. Two days of torrential downpour that threatened to destroy as much as it provided life-giving water.

"Says the perfect athlete with her hair always slicked back in the sleekest ponytail I have ever seen." Then Rachel pointed, nearly smacking the dashboard. "Hey! Watch the road!"

"Right." Sana shook out her head, focusing ahead. She shouldn't have taken her concentration off of the road. She had the ability to focus, to hyperfocus, to zone in on one thing so intensely she saw nothing else. Right now, nothing else needed to be anything that wasn't the road. But Rachel seemed to be forever pulling Sana's focus.

"I'm not perfect and neither is my hair." Sana didn't know why she needed to say it, but she did. She needed Rachel to understand. "And neither is Helen of Troy. We're people. You aren't the only one to miss that. But we're just people who are trying to get what we've always wanted. It's just, sometimes you don't realize what it is that you've wanted until you've had it. And then it's too late."

"And what did you want?" When Rachel focused on a thing, she gave it all of her attention. It was dizzying to be on the other side of it.

Sana kept her eyes on the road. "To go to Princeton."

Rachel was still looking over Sana, like she'd been given an opportunity and she wasn't going to waste it. "And how does it feel now that you have it?"

"I don't know." And then Sana said something she'd never told another living soul. Never let out. Never confessed one hundred percent, even when her dad had said that he knew. He didn't get why. He didn't understand her anxieties. "I haven't put down my deposit. For Princeton. If I don't do it by May first, I'm toast. I pulled all my other applications because I applied early."

Rachel drew in a breath, drew away from Sana. "You're just going to throw your future into the wind?"

Sana shook her head. She felt a pressure in her eyes but she kept watching the rhythm of the road. The movement of the lights of the cars. The city was passing her by. But she was in the driver's seat. She could stop the car anytime she wanted; she kept driving. "I applied for a medical fellowship in India."

"Why?" asked Rachel.

"I don't know," Sana confessed. "I just had to do it. Had to have something that was mine."

Rachel reached out, her hand hovering over Sana's on the gearbox. But Rachel pulled her hand away. "Look. Don't let other people force you into a decision just because it sounds good. I've seen what that looks like firsthand. It's better to screw up on your own terms than to screw up on somebody else's. It's better to have something you know is yours rather than what everyone tells you that you should want."

Rachel turned away, breaking the moment. Like she needed not to focus on Sana for a moment. Like she too needed to watch the palm trees and the jacarandas and the jasmine bushes swooshing by as they drove.

Sana made it the rest of the way into Beverly Hills without incident. Rachel seemed to understand that Sana needed to not be distracted as she drove. And the silence—which should have been, if not tense, then at least awkward—was a calming, reassuring thing.

She drove to the frozen yogurt shop. Not like those photo-worthy shops that were popping up all over downtown LA and beyond. This was old school and authentic LA. The kind where you could get four types of frozen yogurt and sixteen types of toppings and nobody could or would say a thing. A palace of infinite possibility, a temple to every hedonistic impulse Sana possessed.

Well, maybe not *every* impulse.

"This looks legit," said Rachel, looking out the window.

Sana finished her parallel parking before responding. "It's the best. I mean, it's my favorite."

"The best, then." There it was, that grin.

Sana felt her heartbeat in her throat. She couldn't look away from Rachel. Her eyes flitted from the other girl's eyes to her mouth back to her eyes again.

Don't stare at her mouth, oh my goodness, do not stare at her mouth.

Except, when Sana's eyes flickered back up to Rachel's, Sana realized Rachel was staring at *her* mouth.

The air in the car went very still. Maybe it left the car entirely, because Sana couldn't breathe. She felt like some horrible frozen robot.

Sorry, no longer computing. Rachel Recht just looked at my mouth. Impossible to say if this model will ever reboot again.

Then Rachel licked her bottom lip and Sana was pretty sure air was overrated and she really didn't need it anymore to survive. But she did need to know desperately how soft Rachel's lips were. She might die if she didn't learn that in the next ten seconds. Some doctor would have to write that down under "Cause of Death" on the form, right next to "Time of Death," which was, for sure, seconds away.

And then Sana saw it, Rachel pushing the button to unclip herself from the seat, watched Rachel leaning in toward her. It was magic and perfect and probably about to be one of the most romantic moments of her life.

That's when Rachel's body went slamming backward into the chair. "What the fuck?" That was Rachel.

Sana couldn't even be mad about the swearing. Because, *what the fuck indeed.*

It had been the seat belt. Still around Rachel's shoulder, still attached to the car. The safety-first seat belt. Sana wanted to be like liquid nitrogen—go from a solid directly to a gas. To disappear, with no trace left of her but a slight fog where her once corporeal form had been.

Sana closed her eyes. "I've never hated a car so much in my entire life."

And then a miracle happened. A real, live miracle. Rachel Recht laughed. At Sana's joke. Sana opened her eyes, staring at Rachel in what must have been awe. That's what she felt. Awestruck.

Rachel opened the door, sighing her relief when the seat belt began sliding away from her. "Come on, let's try the best yogurt in LA." Rachel was out of the car before Sana could open her own door and release her own seat belt.

Mom really needed to get a new car like ASAP.

Rachel got cookies-and-cream frozen yogurt with strawberries and a few strawberry boba. It was a tame choice, by Sana's standards.

Sana, for her own part, got cheesecake and passionfruit and milk chocolate yogurt with Oreos and strawberry boba and gummy bears and actual chunks of cheesecake. Not everyone was into the cold, hard gummy bear thing, but it was one of Sana's favorites. She loved chewing through the tough sugar until she released its inner sweetness.

Sana had a red gummy bear in her mouth, clacking against her teeth as she ate the rest of her bite of yogurt.

"You know." Rachel was eating her yogurt in these large, fantastic spoonfuls. She made the fro-yo look better than anything that could be eaten on planet Earth. "I think you're brave."

Sana nearly choked on the gummy bear. "What? Why?"

Rachel shrugged, like she hadn't been upending Sana's world all evening. "I always wanted to get my helix pierced, but I've never been able to work up the nerve. You've got your nose pierced. That's gotta be even worse."

Unconsciously, Sana raised her hand to the gold ring on her nose. She forgot she was holding her spoon and dotted fro-yo in her hair. She wiped the yogurt away on her arm. "You can always work up the nerve for a piercing."

"Maybe. Usually I chicken out."

Sana turned to Rachel then. "Hey, would you mind driving?"

Rachel stared at the offered keys for a moment. "You want me to drive?"

Sana nodded, very sure of the decision. She'd used up all of her focus driving them to the fro-yo place. And that was *before* the almost but not quite kiss moment. "I'm too easily distracted. And you're done with your fro-yo already anyway. Please?"

Rachel stared for a long moment and Sana couldn't read her expression.

"Alright," said Rachel.

Sana dropped the worn, smoothed-out keys into Rachel's hands.

Rachel

Rachel was paying attention as she drove. She knew she'd been entrusted with a great privilege. But she hadn't been one to let great privilege make her cocky.

No, if anything, being afforded more privilege made Rachel more careful, more cautious. There was now more in her hands to screw up. Not just a movie. Not just a friendship. Or whatever this was. But somebody's car.

Somebody's car that meant something to them.

That, Rachel had understood from the beginning. It was strange really, how much about Sana that Rachel did understand, implicitly. It was stranger still to realize that the understanding went both ways.

Mutual understanding. Rachel shivered.

"Are you cold?" Sana asked, concern in her voice. She was reaching for the old vents in the car. There must have been a trick to getting them to blow air the exact right temperature.

"Yeah," said Rachel, even though she wasn't.

Sana fussed with the direction of the vents, turning one off to one side and another off to the opposite direction. The air streams blew into one another and skidded away from Rachel. Then Sana turned up the fan but turned the temperature one tiny, almost imperceptible tick up.

Sana smiled. She had such a pleasant smile. A ray-of-sunshine kind of smile. A Debbie Reynolds kind of thing, it was. "There, that should do it. You should be comfortable now."

Rachel was sure that she'd never be comfortable in Sana's presence again.

I almost kissed her.

Thank God for safety belts. Rachel wasn't sure what had possessed her to do it. Sana was just sitting there, flitting her gaze between Rachel's

182

mouth and Rachel's eyes like that wouldn't have some kind of effect on any normal person from even the most average-looking of people. And Sana was not average-looking. And for some stupid reason, the worst idea in the world had popped into Rachel's head. *Just lean in and kiss her.*

Right, like that would ever happen. Sana just looked like that. Rachel had seen it, on camera. That was just the girl's face. Thank God for weird nineties seat belts or Rachel would have made a real ass of herself.

Safety first, indeed.

Except Sana had looked as jarred by the seat belt snapping Rachel back as Rachel had felt. If Rachel hadn't known better, she would have called the look on Sana's face disappointment. But it couldn't have been that. Rachel couldn't even entertain the idea of it having been that.

Sana was still eating her fro-yo. She'd gotten a hell of a lot more frozen yogurt than Rachel could have ever stomached, but Sana was one of those people who savored dessert. She seemed to really enjoy it, slowly taking bite after bite. Chipping away until eventually there would be nothing left but small puddles of melted yogurt—remnants of what once had been but now no longer was.

Rachel really needed to watch the road and not Sana's mouth. That was definitely what needed to happen. Rachel was so busy, so determinedly focused, that she missed whatever Sana had been saying. She knew this because Sana pinched at her arm.

"Ouch. What was that for?"

"You were ignoring me."

"Right, that's totally an acceptable reason to go around pinching someone."

"I'm an only child, I'm used to getting all the attention."

"I'm an only child as well and I can assure you that is not always the case." Rachel snorted.

"Aren't you at least going to tell me what you think?"

Rachel looked over and Sana was batting her eyes theatrically. At least, it looked like she intended the move theatrically, but the batting of Sana's eyes, even as a bit of a joke, just did things for Rachel that she wasn't quite sure how to process.

Rachel fixed her eyes on the road. "Think about what?"

Not your mouth. Not almost kissing you. Not your stupidly long eyelashes. Definitely not your near-black eyes.

Sana sighed so performatively that Rachel could hear the eye roll that went along with it. "The fro-yo. What did you think of the fro-yo?"

"It was good." Rachel was determined. She was staying safe, staying aware of traffic. She would not be distracted. She would not let her thoughts be distracted. She was driving Sana's mom's car. She had to give the driving one hundred and ten percent of her attention.

"Good? Just good?" Sana was clearly incredulous.

But Rachel didn't have any extra willpower to spend on Sana right now, not even fighting with her, no matter how much fun it was to fight with her. Looking over at Sana was like pointing a camera directly at the sun. The light cleared away the entire picture, left no room for anything but itself in the frame. Rachel couldn't stare straight into the sun and drive at the same time. That way was how accidents happened. Bad ones.

"It *was* good," said Rachel.

"No," said Sana. "It was the best. I can't believe you didn't think it was the best. You ate yours in like four seconds; how could you not think it was the best?"

"A truly dizzying argument, I'm not sure how I could possibly respond." Rachel gripped the wheel tighter. She was holding at nine and three and she was using a signal before changing lanes.

"Man," said Sana. "You're a safe driver. I don't think I've ever met anyone who was so thorough about checking their blind spots before."

Rachel snorted. They had nearly made it back to Rachel's house. They were in the neighborhood now. Fewer cars, less traffic. Rachel could almost relax. But she still didn't. She knew better than to relax right at the end of any journey.

And that's when a cat with a long bushy tail ran into the middle of the road. Rachel tried to brake but she was going to hit it, going to kill a cat.

She couldn't kill a cat.

She might be the most terrible director in the world to work with, she might have originally written a movie about how Helen of Troy was the worst and then cast the girl who reminded her most of Helen of Troy as the lead of the show, but she wasn't someone who killed animals if she could help it.

So Rachel swerved.

She swerved, and as she did, she watched everything go in slow motion. Somewhere in the back of her mind she heard Papa's voice telling her that if the choice was between swerving and hitting an animal, to hit the animal. But it was too late now. There was a telephone pole right there, right in their path. It took less than half a second to realize they were going to hit it. Maybe it took five minutes to realize they were going to hit it, realize that she could do nothing to stop it. Time was doing funny things right now. Speeding up and slowing down. Like she watched them hit the pole before they did. Like it happened twice. Same with the airbags. Same with hearing Sana thud against them.

God, was Sana okay?

But the words didn't come out. Rachel was groggy, disoriented. But also, somehow, hyperaware of everything that had happened. She was trapped between the airbag and the seat. She moved her jaw. She took a deep breath. "Are you okay?"

"Yeah," said Sana, equally disoriented, equally visiting from some land other than this one. "There's a thing. Behind your seat."

Somehow, Rachel knew what she meant. She could get her left

arm around, it hadn't been pinned the way her right one was. In the back of her seat pocket was one of those windshield-shattering things. But it had a razor attached to it. Rachel punctured her airbag. Then reached for Sana's.

She looked Sana in the eye then, once the airbag was down. "You sure you're okay?"

"Yeah," said Sana. "I just can't move my left arm."

18

Suffer Love

Rachel

Rachel couldn't believe it. She jangled her leg against the brightly lit, overly clean linoleum floor. Emergency-care clinics always had floors that were at once stained and overly clean. Must come with the territory of constantly shuffling in people with an assortment of severe but not-quite-life-threatening ailments. The scent of the place alone was enough to burn through and preserve her nostrils forever.

But still she jangled her leg, like she was the boyfriend, girlfriend, loved one in some terrible episode of *CSI*. Close up onto the leg. Pan up. Stay with her face. Her worried, nervous face. The face of someone who is trying to prepare themselves for what they cannot possibly know, cannot possibly prepare for, yet are trying to anyway.

It was only a broken arm.

That's what she'd been telling herself, over and over and over again. Only a broken arm.

But Rachel had been the one driving. She'd been driving and she'd never gotten in an accident, despite being able to drive a year before most of her peers because her dad worked and she needed to get to school so she'd declared a hardship with the state.

Sana was only getting a cast and she had only broken her arm and she was fine, fine, fine.

It was all Rachel's fault.

The nurse came out into the hallway. He had on fun, printed scrubs and was clearly about to tell Rachel something when what could only be described as gale-force Santa Ana wind blew through the emergency-care-clinic doors.

The woman had dark, wild hair pulled back into a tight ponytail. She wore jeans with a thick, black, practical sort of belt that a walkie-talkie was still attached to. She wore a dark T-shirt that could have been black but also could have been navy. Her skin was deep brown. She was also, despite what was a clear attempt to appear somewhere between casual and professionally neutral, so stunningly good-looking that nearly everyone in the waiting room decided to stare at her. It was Sana's mother. Rachel recognized her from the photos in Sana's home.

Also, she had Sana's eyes.

"Where the hell is my kid?" Her voice was direct and frantic all at once. It was not the kind of tone anybody messed with, especially not in an emergency-care clinic.

The nurse directed his attention to Sana's mom at once. "And you are?"

"Farrah. Farrah Akhtar."

"I'm sorry, ma'am, we don't have anyone with that last name in right now."

"Don't ma'am me, kid, I'm not in the mood. Just because I kept my name doesn't mean she's not my kid. Khan. Sana Khan."

The nurse took in the sight of her then—steely-eyed, sharp cheek-bones, an outfit built for no nonsense, built for function on a set. She had on flare jeans, not because they'd come back in style again, but because she'd clearly never let go of them in the first place. Even Rachel could tell that by the fraying on the bottom of the hem.

The nurse gave a nod. "Right this way."

Sana's mom blazed through the double doors, and the nurse followed. Rachel had been asked to wait outside since she wasn't family, even though it wasn't serious. But she took the nurse's distraction and Farrah's intensity as an opening. Rachel slid through the doors as they swung shut.

Sana sat upright on a doctor's table. Her feet were thudding against the wood and making a gentle *swish, swish* of paper sound. Her left arm was now encased in plaster and whatever that netting, wrapping material they used was, in neon pink. She smiled as she looked up at the opening door, clearly expecting someone.

Whoever she'd been expecting, her mother wasn't on the list. Sana's smile dropped. "Hi, Mom."

"Don't you dare *hi, Mom* me."

But Sana, who seemed like the kind of girl who had good sense and who Rachel *knew* was the kind of girl who generally did what she was told, didn't stop there.

"Mom, I'm okay."

"Your arm is broken. You broke your arm."

"It was an accident. There was a cat in the road. I had to swerve." Sana stopped swinging her legs.

What.

Sana hadn't been driving. Rachel had been driving. In fact, even though Sana's eyes hadn't once flickered toward Rachel, Rachel knew that Sana had noticed her enter, knew that Sana knew she was here. Sana could easily get out of at least half the trouble by saying Rachel had been driving while Sana finished her yogurt.

As it was, Sana was making sure all eyes in the room stayed firmly on her.

"You know better than to swerve because a cat runs into the road." Sana's mom put her hand on her hip.

"She didn't," said Rachel.

Unfortunately, this caused all the eyes in the room to turn to

Rachel. She couldn't know for certain why she'd said it. She didn't want to watch Sana get grilled all over again by her mom. Not when it was Rachel's fault. Rachel's responsibility.

"I was driving. I was the one who swerved." Rachel said it louder this time.

Farrah looked between Sana and Rachel for a long moment, her head swiveling on a pivot. "And you are?"

"Rachel Recht?"

"And how long has this been going on?" Farrah put her hand on her hip.

Rachel was dizzy. *How long had* what *been going on?*

"Nothing is going on, Mom. We were getting fro-yo."

Farrah seemed to be rendered speechless. She lifted her eyebrows and stared disbelievingly at Sana.

"We were working on a film project," said Rachel lamely.

But Farrah was done with Rachel. She didn't seem to care that Rachel had been the one driving. She had that single-minded, focused intensity that Rachel had noticed in Sana during filming. Once Farrah got ahold of her target, she wasn't one to let go, that much Rachel was sure of.

"You're sneaking around behind my back, letting strange girls drive my car, doing God knows what, going God knows where, and saying it's a school project? Is that about the sum of it?"

"It *is* a school project," Rachel tried interjecting. But nobody was listening or paying much attention to her.

"Do you want family to intervene? Do you want me to have to tell Dadu and Mamani that I have no idea where the hell you are when I'm filming on set? Because they'll make you stay with them. Don't think because you've finally hit eighteen they wouldn't make you stay with them."

"They can't intervene. I'm not supposed to be dating according to them." Sana raised her eyebrows.

"Neither was I. They still intervened."

"That was different. You know that's different."

"It was almost exactly the same."

"Not even close!"

The two women stared each other down.

"I was filming a project and grabbing frozen yogurt. It was the kind of accident that could happen to anyone. How much trouble can I get into eating frozen yogurt?" asked Sana.

"You'd be surprised, kid."

"But you wouldn't." Sana crossed her arms. "You'd know *exactly* how much trouble I could get into getting frozen yogurt. Worried I'm going to go out and come home knocked up?"

Farrah's eyes went wide. Sana's expression didn't back down. Rachel could tell that Sana had crossed some invisible line. Some point of no return in the fight. Even the nurse had stopped fussing with his equipment to watch. The force of these two women was like watching a clash of titans. Amazons. Warrior women. Goddesses. Ancient and powerful—typically unknowable and unseen by mere mortals.

That's when a man came crashing into the room. Slim, below average height, but again, powerfully good-looking. A salt-and-pepper streak running through his hair. He wore an expensive, well-tailored suit and he had all of Sana's bone structure.

Dear God, was anyone in their family even mediocre-looking?

"I came as soon as I heard," said Sana's dad. "How are you? Are you okay?"

"Your daughter went on a date without telling me, then let the other girl drive, and now she's got a broken arm."

"It wasn't a date," Rachel tried, but nobody was listening, and Rachel had never felt more like an interloper or an intruder. She slowly backed out of the room, unable to hear anymore. Felt like her ears were ringing, but that couldn't be. She hadn't been going fast enough to cause any concussive damage. The emergency clinic tech double-checked her while they were putting Sana through X-rays.

If she was fine, why couldn't she hear the rest of their conversation? Why was it difficult to breathe? Why did she have to get out, get out of this room, get out of this clinic, before she passed out, or vomited, or *something*.

Rachel took big gulps of air when she reached outside the sliding glass doors. She put her head between her knees and kept breathing deeply until she could hear again, until the nausea passed, until that closing-in, dizzying sensation floated away.

Then she got out her phone. "Papa? Yeah, it's me. I need a ride home."

Sana watched as Rachel left the room. Sana didn't blame her. She glared at her mother. Farrah glared back.

"Look." Massoud held out his arms. He was clearly trying to find a way to keep the peace. "Everybody's upset right now. Tensions are understandably running high. Sana, your mom is worried because she didn't know you were out and then next thing she knows she's getting a call about your arm being broken. Farrah, Sana is going through a lot since she still hasn't put down her deposit and I think you should cut her a little bit of slack on this, okay?"

"What deposit?" asked Farrah.

Oh no.

Massoud looked at Sana, his face wild with uncertainty. He'd assumed, as anyone might assume, that she had told her mother that she was having second thoughts about Princeton. His voice was quiet. "You didn't tell her?"

Sana shook her head. Shame was flooding through her and she didn't have words. She'd told her mother nothing.

"Tell me what? Didn't tell me what?" Farrah was too confused to hold on to her anger, at least in her voice.

Massoud looked at Sana for some kind of cue. But she didn't have one. She was without words, without an answer for Mom's question. Without answers for herself. If she had them, she wouldn't have this problem in the first place. She'd have put down her deposit like a normal person who was excited to be accepted into an Ivy League school. Sana didn't answer.

Farrah thought she *wouldn't*. She turned back to Massoud again. "Somebody tell me what the hell is going on."

"Sana didn't put down her deposit for Princeton."

"I heard you the first time. I just don't understand." The look on Farrah's face was like the wind had been knocked out of her.

"I didn't put down the deposit."

"No," said Farrah. "I heard you giving your commitment. I heard you."

Sana swallowed. It was so difficult to breathe right now. Her chest had gone tight, her throat was smaller somehow—closing up and shutting down. She swallowed again, hoping that would push down the feeling rising up through her ribs, clenching everything from her waist to her throat. "That's not the deposit."

The nurse took the tray of instruments and put them over on another counter, away from everyone. Their voices were approaching a shout, approaching the edge of unforgivable things that could never be unsaid. Or maybe they had already passed that point.

Farrah flung her arm out. "And when is the deposit due?"

"May first." Breathe in, breathe out. It was fine. Everything was okay. This was what happened when Sana thought about the future. Her vision pinholed, her throat closed up, and her chest compressed until the weight of a small car rested on it. The tips of her fingers went numb, like blood forgot to flow there when she was in this state. Like her body forgot how it worked once breathing became difficult.

"Thank God." Farrah slumped into the one extra chair in the room. "We can still get it in."

"No." It took a moment before Sana recognized that voice as her own.

"No?" It was the second time Farrah had looked punched in the gut. Lost. Without an anchor. Her voice was at a whisper. "Why the hell not?"

Sana shook her head. She didn't want to say about the fellowship. She wasn't ready, wasn't ready at all. "No. I can't."

"You told them you would. You pulled your other applications." No question there. Just a raw, horrified statement. Farrah stared at Sana.

"I can't," said Sana.

"No." Farrah shook her head. "You *won't*."

"Get out!" Sana wanted to throw something, honestly at anybody at this point. Maybe that's why they kept the tray of instruments out of the patient's reach. The safety of others.

"Whoa, I *just* got here," said Massoud.

"Not you!"

Massoud looked around himself, bewildered that Sana could be talking to anyone else.

Farrah, meanwhile, had known what Sana meant almost instantly. Hurt flashed across her features, but not for long. Quickly a quiet rage coated her expression, pushing her eyebrows together, pursing her lips, giving her cheekbones a feral quality.

"You're gonna put this on me, then? It's your dream. It was always your dream."

Sana turned away. "No. It's your dream. It's Mamani's and Dadu's. It's not mine." That wasn't quite true, but it was close enough that Sana let the words out of her mouth. Let the hurt that would be done by them flow freely.

"Great, now you're blaming me for my parents' sins."

"No, you're blaming me for yours."

Farrah sucked in a breath. "I don't know what's going on but you can't send me away. I'm your mother. I belong to you and you to me.

194

You'll always be mine even if you leave home for school and don't want me anymore. That's how it works, kid."

"Go to hell." Sana crossed her one good arm over her chest and turned away.

The air had long gone out of the room. But now the only sound left was the faint buzzing of the overhead fluorescent light as it twitched in and out of two different shades of brightness. The nurse had even stopped shuffling papers. He froze, probably unsure of how to get out of this room, out of this situation. Sana was right there with him.

"It's been a long night," said Massoud. "Why don't I take Sana home. You can collect your thoughts and put through the insurance stuff."

"And you'd want that?" Farrah directed her question at Sana. She didn't have any fight left in her.

Sana couldn't face her mother anymore. Couldn't believe she hadn't told her. She took her out. "I would."

"Okay then." Farrah looked away, started talking about payment information with the nurse, who seemed happy to have any other topic of conversation to discuss.

Sana hopped off the table, onto her left foot, using her right hand as an aid. She knew her mom thought she was blaming her for her side of the family. For her Dadu's conservativeness. For Mamani's controlling nature. For her yelling. But Sana needed to get away. To think. To keep from wallowing in this horrible sinking feeling that flooded her whenever she looked at her mom. To keep these complications from spinning everything out of control.

Massoud unlocked the car and got in quietly. Sana followed suit. He drove, not at his usual breakneck pace, but smoothly, fluidly. In a way that Sana had no idea he knew how to do.

After a long stretch of silence, filled only by the thump of the road underneath them and the whoosh of the wind over the aerodynamic lines of the car, Massoud cleared his throat. "Do you like her? And don't pretend not to know who I mean. The girl you were with. Do you like her?"

"She's just a friend. We're making a movie together." Sana looked out the window. She'd had enough embarrassing public confessions for the day. She didn't need to pile on.

"I'm going to take that as a yes." Massoud glanced over from the road for a moment.

Sana's eyes snapped to Massoud's.

"Damn," he said. "You really do have your mother's eyes."

Sana looked away again, embarrassed and enraged all at once. "And my grandfather's."

"I know you don't like me. And I know I'm the last person you'd want advice from. But as someone who's been down this path before, who's seen how this goes, I'm going to offer up some anyway. I don't know if you like her or you're serious about her. But if you are serious, even if you don't want to admit it yet, don't let family intervene like I did."

Sana looked over, ready to snap.

Massoud held up his hand. "I'm gonna cut off whatever biting yet witty repartee you probably have lined up. Trust me. Don't let them intervene. Make up your own mind first. It'll be hard enough to sort through without everyone else making up your mind for you."

And then he turned on the radio, blasting some horrible rock from his own high school years so Sana couldn't reply.

19

How to Eat Pizza Without Burning
the Roof of Your Mouth

————————— *Rachel* ————

Rachel collapsed into the passenger's seat of her dad's car. It was an older sedan, but clean and not so ancient that it would scare off any potential clients when they called for a ride.

"Rough night?" asked Rachel's dad, not taking his eyes off the road.

And Rachel, too tired to come up with a version that sounded better than the truth, told him everything. About the car and the cat and the movie night and the frozen yogurt and showing Sana where she lived. She didn't add that she was embarrassed of their apartment; her dad didn't need to hear that yet again.

"Mija," he said.

Rachel prepared herself for the lecture.

"Are you okay?" he asked.

Rachel looked over at her dad and blinked. "I wrecked some kid's parent's car and you're asking if I'm okay?"

Her father looked stunned. "Of course I'm asking if you're okay. I picked you up at a clinic. Did they check you out too or just her?"

"They checked me out, too." Rachel felt her voice go soft. It wasn't like Rachel forgot that Papa cared. But the reminder was good, necessary even. Rachel didn't want to, but she needed that kind of reassurance every once in a while. "No concussion. No head or neck damage. I got really lucky, they said. The car took most of the impact."

"Thank you," he said. "For telling me."

Papa got that stoic look on his face. The one where he bottled up his feelings and didn't express them. Rachel hated the expression. She wanted to wipe it off his face. She wanted to wipe the idea that men couldn't express their feelings without being weak off the face of planet Earth. It had hurt him so much. It had hurt her so much. It was the kind of idea that had nearly destroyed them both.

"Papa?"

He humphed, still distracted. "Yes?"

"I'm okay," she said.

He looked up then, like he'd understood what she was trying to say. *Don't worry about me, Papa. Don't be stressed. It'll be okay.*

He nodded. "I'll always worry about you. That's how it goes."

Rachel didn't know what to say to that. She worried about him, too.

What a mess.

Sana's arm was broken. Rachel felt worried and bruised and uncertain and banged up. She couldn't imagine how Sana was feeling. Being yelled at by her mom after breaking her arm. And trying to cover for Rachel.

Trying to cover for Rachel and being accused of being on a date with her.

A date. Like the one Sana had asked her on all those years ago. Except not as a joke. As a thing Sana's mom believed that Sana could actually be on.

A date with a girl like Rachel.

With Rachel.

Theoretically.

Every revelation was a wave of relief and nausea and fear. It was like she got to rewatch old memories from a different angle. The angle where everything that had been hidden in the first shot became clear. A flashback at the end of the film that changed everything. If she'd been sitting in the audience, watching the movie of her own life, Rachel would have probably yelled *FINALLY* at the screen.

Had she honestly hated Sana all those years?

Why had Rachel thought being asked out was a joke in the first place?

What the hell was she going to do?

All Rachel knew was, she had to try. She had to reach out and do the right thing, had to keep doing the right thing, had to set this all back to some kind of an equilibrium.

Rachel looked over to her father. "Do you mind if I make a call?"

Papa waved in the air. "Call away."

Two rings and the phone clicked over. "I swear to God if this is another marketing scam, I will sic my lawyer family on you so fast you won't know what hit you."

"Hi, Diesel," said Rachel, overly bright.

"Uh. Hi."

"It's Rachel."

"Oh, hey! I thought you were one of those guys that calls and breathes on the other end, recording people's voices."

"You know they make call blockers for that?"

"True," said Diesel, clearly unfazed by this discovery.

Rachel took a deep breath. "I was calling because I was working on some stuff for the project with Sana and we were taking a break and grabbing some dessert and this cat ran into the middle of the road and the car swerved and we got in a wreck and anyways Sana broke her arm."

There was nothing but silence on the other end.

For a moment Rachel thought the call had dropped.

It was eerie, that silence. It took a moment, but Rachel almost longed for Diesel to yell at her. Or at least talk in his overly friendly way for too long and give more details than Rachel ever needed about his life. This stunned, horrible quiet was beyond anything that Rachel had ever dealt with.

"Okay, anyways, thought you should know. I'll go now. She was at an emergency-care clinic in Beverly Hills but I think she's going home with her mom. Which is where you can reach her. On her phone. With her mom. I just thought she might need a friend right now. Okaythanksgoodbye." Rachel hung up.

Rachel shuddered out a sigh. Two thoughts fought for top billing in her mind. Neither was particularly good for the hushed ride home. She wasn't sure which was worse: that awful, ongoing tension that had crackled across the phone or the realization that maybe Sana hadn't asked Rachel out on a date as a joke at all.

Sana

It was noon when Sana woke up again. Her arm was throbbing. Small throbs at first, but pitching to a large swell. The intensity of the throbs got so bad she couldn't sort through her own thoughts. All she could do was breathe deeply and pray for a little bit of mercy on this one. Eventually the throbbing declined in intensity again. The low level was nearly forgettable, except for when she thought about it and she realized she was *at best* going to be in low-level pain for the next however many days. Weeks, even.

Sana pushed herself out of bed.

The house was quiet—not silent, because there was always creaking and cracking and whirring in an old house. Always a small shift, a noise, a little bit of movement here and there. She was used to it, this kind of silence. The house was hers, not the way it was her mom's through regularly installed payments, but because they kept each other company through the long, quiet hours. They were companions, this house and Sana. She did her best work, studying and reading, when she was home alone. It gave her time to think, time to breathe.

Sana didn't want time to think right now.

She went into the kitchen and fiddled with the pantry stuff in there. Oatmeal, toast, cereal. She picked one and ate it. But the oatmeal could have been toast and the toast could have been cereal, for all she was paying attention.

Toast, she was having toast.

It didn't taste like much, even though she'd remembered to put on the almond butter and the jam that she liked. She'd never been in a fight like this with her mom before. She'd never said anything that crossed the line, that she desperately wanted to take back but couldn't. At least she wasn't stuck in a car with Farrah for two hours trying to get down to Orange County.

The toast tasted like those awful, dry, brittle crackers Mamani was telling Sana were so healthy for her. Sana put it down, checked her phone instead. She only had one notification. It was from Diesel.

You on? He was asking about *Overwatch*, because that was how all their messages about gaming started.

She wasn't, but it was a good idea. *Gimme five*

Sana booted up her well-loved laptop with the shitty graphics card.

She logged into her *Overwatch* account and selected, as she always selected, Pharah.

On

Get ready to rumble

Diesel played as Tracer because he liked the speed and to move through time. Also, he liked heckling the opposing team with his own terrible British accent.

Diesel was the worst. Unless he was on your team, then he was the best.

Sana, for her part, liked taking her giant rocket launcher and blowing whatever came into her path to bits. Sana didn't like real guns. She played with a character with a grenade launcher. Maybe that was semantics. Adults liked to say that playing violent video games made a kid violent. But for Sana they helped her let off steam. Helped her express violence on a plane where it hurt no one. Particularly when she couldn't run or jump and now she could only play, essentially, one-handed.

She and Diesel were losing pretty spectacularly.

Diesel didn't seem to mind, though. He kept his comms on and chatted through loss after loss. The other team members they were being assigned to were less than generous about it.

"You wanna talk about it?" Diesel asked.

"Nope." Sana had fired at someone flying through the air who was playing as Mercy.

"You should, though."

"And yet, here I am, aiming at digital strangers instead." Sana finally got her first kill of the day.

"One, never call them digital strangers."

"Whatever." And there it was—someone launched their own rocket at her—and she was done. Dead. Wiped out. And now to sit here, waiting to respawn. Her screen went dim with a countdown timer.

"It's not whatever, dude. You gotta let it out. And not on the unsuspecting people of the internet. Especially since you're really bad at this right now."

Sana snorted. "You can say unsuspecting people of the internet but I can't say digital strangers? Ugh. I wish I could actually reverse time and undo last night."

"Why is that?" Diesel was on the other side of the map, laying waste to the other team.

"I might have yelled at my mom for getting pregnant with me at nineteen."

"You didn't." Diesel ran out of charge in his weapon and started punching someone on the other team. It looked so satisfying.

"I mean. Basically I did. Once you take step one down that path, you don't have to go all the way to step eighteen for it to hurt like hell, do you? It's all there. It's all implied." *Fill in your own horrible, slut-shaming adventure.*

"True." The best thing about Diesel was that he never lied to you. It was the worst thing, too.

Sana finally respawned and was dropped back into the game, but she still wasn't quick enough compared to the other players.

"Geez, I know you broke your arm but come on, I *know* you can click faster than that."

"You're a jerk." Sana found a bit of high ground with cover. If she could possibly not bring her whole team down this game, it would be a Nowruz miracle.

"Does she ever ask about me? On the squad?" asked Diesel after a long pause. He'd been blinking across the map and lobbing strategic time bombs.

"Who, my mom?" *Honestly, how did everyone she played against know she was the weak link on her team today?*

"No. Maddie."

Sana wasn't feeling very generous. She'd taken a huge hit to the chest and she was nearly dead again. She played as a tank and she was still being taken out, left, right, and center. It was so embarrassing. Normally she could rain hellfire on her enemies. "Nope."

"Great."

"You're the only jock in the history of jocks to not get the girl." Sana hopped behind some more cover, trying to run from this fight. At least she was quicker at that in the game than she was in real life now. Her leg was closer to healed, but she was still in a boot.

"What about you? Aren't you the one making a movie with someone you *definitely don't have a crush on*?"

"I hate you, Diesel."

"Just saying, we're both sad and alone and playing video games on a Sunday rather than hanging out with the girls that we like."

"You're honestly the worst."

"Nope, I'm the only reason we're even playing ranked right now. You're the worst."

"We should definitely *not* be playing ranked when I have a broken arm. This is why I am dying every five seconds. You are not helping your case at all." Sana finally died after limping across the map, trying to save herself. Her respawn would take longer than the time that was left in the match. "Okay, that's it. I've had enough humiliation for one day."

"Feel any better?"

"A little. But normally I'm better at this."

"Normally your arm isn't broken."

"True. And Diesel?"

"Yeah?"

"Try not flirting with other girls in front of Maddie. She hates that."

"She does?"

"Yeah. See you Monday."

Sana logged off, closed her laptop, and shoved it into her bag. She could take a shower, but that would involve wrapping her arm in a baggie and keeping it out of the shower and washing her hair with one hand, while standing on one foot. She was well and truly not in the mood right now. Sana climbed back into bed, curled up, and went to sleep.

20

Double or Nothing?

———— *Sana* ————

Monday was a rainy day—oil-slick roads and unsure drivers making a mess of the city—even if it was only a light, sprinkling kind of rain. Sana had slept past the time to grab the bus to school. She begged Diesel to swing by and give her a ride—which she never normally would have done on a rainy day. Mom was still sleeping off her night shoots. And there wasn't a replacement car for the Mitsu. Sana felt too much pride to call a ride and charge her mom. She'd get to school on her own, thank you very much.

Sana had a message from Massoud when she checked her phone. *Sorry*

Yeah, they were all sorry about something right now. Sana didn't answer him. She got her bag for school together, grabbed a piece of toast for breakfast, and was out the door by the time Diesel arrived.

Right now, Sana didn't need an umbrella, so she didn't grab one on the way out. It was probably a mistake, but you could never tell if it was the kind of weather that would get worse or suddenly clear up. Sana wasn't in the mood to carry around any more garbage with her this morning.

"You look like hell," said Diesel.

"Good to see you, too." Sana buckled herself into Diesel's tiny Mazda Miata coupe. He was a contrast in opposites most of the time.

"It *is* good to see you, you just look like hell." Diesel shrugged, like it really was that simple for him.

Sana pulled out her makeup bag and began swiping concealer under her eyes.

"That's not what I meant, either," said Diesel. "I don't even mean your arm. I meant the fact that you've got this, like, punched-in-the-gut look in your eyes. I mean, what is going on with you?"

Sana blinked back tears. She didn't know where they had come from, but she sure wasn't letting them out now. "Everything."

"This isn't just about your mom, is it?" Diesel looked over while he was driving.

Sana looked away. Careful for him not to see the sadness pooling in her eyes. "I can't be perfect anymore, Diesel." It was the only thing Sana really knew anymore. The only true thing. She couldn't be perfect anymore.

"Nobody asked you to be perfect."

"Yes, they did. When I was a little girl they asked me to be good. Impossibly good. I know it helped my mother. My grandmother. 'Look at our respectable granddaughter.' 'Look at the beautiful, good girl I made.' I could see the relief in them. Maybe they didn't ask with words. But they asked. All the time."

Diesel made a turn, winding up into the hills on the way to school. Up the bumpy roads that needed repaving. The concrete mixed with the quick fix of asphalt that hadn't been enough to stop fault lines. "So fuck 'em."

Sana startled. "What?"

"Tell 'em all to go to hell, Sana. Do what you want to do."

Sana shook her head. "It's not so easy."

"It never is." Diesel found a parking spot and they both gathered up their bags and books as quickly as they could in the misty, spitting weather. The day was gray and humid and still not raining enough to justify anything but a quickened pace and a hunched posture.

As Sana walked to her locker, everyone stared. She couldn't really blame them. Her foot still in a boot and her arm now in a pink cast. She hoped there was a way to frame the shot so her injury didn't totally ruin the continuity in Rachel's final shoots. That was the best that Sana could hope for on a day like today.

Rachel

Rachel got called into Douga's office after her last class. She had been dreading this. The moment where Douga told her whether or not she was on track. Douga never emailed back her notes. She gave them in person. Probably because they were more intimidating that way.

Rachel knocked on the glass.

"Enter," said Douga.

"Hi." Rachel's voice was so much quieter than she would have liked.

"Sit," said Douga, not looking up from her laptop.

Rachel sat.

Douga did a few quick keystrokes, then finally pushed her laptop off to the side and looked up at Rachel. "I got your rough cut this weekend."

Rachel waited for the death knell to sound.

"Good work."

Rachel blinked. "Excuse me?"

"Good work. You've saved this project from the brink of extinction. I'm looking forward to seeing it officially on May first."

Rachel felt relief on a cellular level. She closed her eyes briefly. "Thank you."

"I do have a couple notes, since you're still working on your edits.

I don't get the Helen of Troy changes that you've made. Why does she suddenly have so many lines? Why is she *talking so much*? Go back to the original stuff. Keep Sana as Helen. She nails that ice princess thing so well. It's a great visual. But go back to using Cassandra as your narrative through line for the piece. That's so much more the style of film you should be making here."

The air vacated Rachel's lungs so quickly it was nearly like the time she'd fallen with all of that camera equipment strapped to her. Rachel had just begun to understand, to see what Sana had been talking about. She'd finally gotten to the point where she saw where her project was going. She'd finally seen how she could make a film beyond anything she'd ever done before. New, different. A film built on the foundations of what she had learned in the past four years, but actually moving forward. A film that stretched her creatively. Now Douga was telling Rachel to go back to what was safe, what was comfortable, what was known.

Rachel cleared her throat. "You know, you got me to work with Sana, and I think she had a lot of good points. About Helen of Troy. I'd really like to see how it develops as I edit. I was as skeptical as you are, but the more I watch, the more I understand the points Sana was making about the character. I understand the depth she was bringing to the role."

But Douga had switched over to her monitor and was clicking through something on her screen. "Look, I'm sure she's smart. But she's not a filmmaker. Make the edits, Rachel. This is not a suggestion. Do you understand?"

Rachel did. She was being told what would help her pass. She was going to have to throw Sana under the bus. Throw all her suggestions out the window and act like they were still working as partners.

Rachel nodded, a lump of guilt forming in her throat. "Understood."

"Excellent," said Douga, typing again. "That's all."

Rachel got up and exited the office. If she wanted to pass, if she wanted to make sure her scholarship wasn't in jeopardy, she had to make Douga's cuts. It was an easy choice, as far as life goals went.

Then why did she feel so uneasy about it?

When Rachel walked out of the Royce campus, the weather had shifted from a light sprinkling to a real storm. The rain splatted against the concrete. Large, unforgiving plops of rain. The kind that would soak through to the bone, never relenting.

Rachel made it to her car just in time, having only gotten the tops of her thighs and the top of her shirt wet. The car steamed and fogged up immediately, from the humidity and the heat coming off of Rachel's body. She turned on the ignition and set the wipers on. But the rain was so heavy now, the wipers barely cleared the view for more than half a second before the rain came pouring back down, sheeting the windshield and blurring the view so that Rachel was making out the general shapes of things more than the sight of them.

As Rachel turned the corner, through the carpool driveway, the one always lined with luxury SUV after luxury SUV, she saw a blur of bright red. It could have been any of the cheerleaders. But it wasn't. Rachel didn't know what was worse, that she knew Sana by a cardinal blur or that Sana knew her car and waved Rachel down as she drove by.

Rachel pulled up to the curb, the tires sloshing as she slowed. She drove the fine balance between flooding her car and splashing Sana's pristine cheerleading uniform. Rachel leaned over and unlocked the passenger's side door with her hand. Sana waited patiently until Rachel was halfway back to her seat before swinging the door open and sliding in.

Rachel drove a Lincoln Continental that had been in production before a woman had ever been nominated for directing an Oscar. It was an old clunker. She'd never found it to be anything but serviceable before, but having Sana swing open the door and slide in drew attention to the age of the car. That it had seen better days in an entirely different century. Hell, in a different millennium. But Sana slid into the passenger's seat as though there were nothing better in the world. And, given the weather outside, maybe that was true.

And Sana, well. Her uniform was not pristine, but it was as close to it as a uniform could get while still being drenched all the way through. It stuck to her legs, and her ponytail was plastered straight to her neck. Her makeup had been mostly washed away. She ought to have looked like a drowned rat. But she didn't. Rachel watched as a drop of rain slid down and dripped away from her face.

Sana had been hiding.

True, everyone was hiding something. But Rachel hadn't thought that anyone would hide under the veneer of harmless, pretty girl. But there Sana was—perfection gone. She had dark circles under her eyes, cheekbones that were a little too sharp without the gloss of highlighter. No swishing ponytail to counteract the rigidity of her jawline. This was Sana, in essentials. Sana minus the glamour.

"Oof," said Sana. "Thanks for stopping."

"Of course." Rachel didn't know what to say. She could only stare.

Sana had blurred her power with softness—her cheerleading uniform covering up the clear muscles of her body. Her makeup blurring her cheekbones with soft highlights, her mascara coating her lashes to a doelike state. And Rachel had fallen for it. The softness was a game, a play, a trick of the light. Sana had greased the lens. She had softened everything that was a threat about her. She had hidden herself so perfectly, nobody had dared to look beyond it. Sana had completed the illusion so thoroughly that its exposure was so startling, so revelatory that Rachel laughed.

Sana's eyebrows snapped together at the sound of that laugh. "What?"

There she was. Uncovered. Striking, spellbinding. Rachel couldn't look away. "You've fooled everyone, haven't you?"

Sana sat up straighter. "I don't know what you're talking about."

But that had only made Rachel believe herself even more. Sana's reflex was to cover herself in more primness, to cloak herself in lady-like behavior. She was *Cléo from 5 to 7*. But now the wig was off and the baby doll dress was gone and what was left was a girl in a plain black dress and a hell of a lot of interior life.

And then Sana shivered.

Rachel did the only thing she could think of. She reached into the back and grabbed a hoodie. "Here."

Sana took the hoodie. She threw it on over her wet clothes. "Thank you."

Rachel began to drive, but as soon as she turned the corner, the visibility became the least of her problems. Pothole after pothole was covered by the water flooding the streets, and if she wasn't careful she was going to either flood her car in half an instant or be waylaid in the road. Or both.

"Shit," said Rachel. "Double shit."

Sana sighed. "Use the median, up there."

Rachel's eyes followed the direction of Sana's fingers, where they pointed to.

An extra four inches was an extra four inches. That could be the difference between no car the next day and continuing to keep this old thing running. Rachel changed lanes slowly, sloshing her car through, then hit the accelerator, slowly building power so her tires could climb over the curb to the median. She'd beached their car on a patch of curbed grass, between two trees. But at least they wouldn't be flooded. Hopefully.

Sana laughed. She was so small inside Rachel's hoodie, she was practically swimming in it. And just when Rachel thought it shouldn't get any worse, Sana tucked her arms in and the sweatshirt swallowed her whole. She wiggled and fidgeted, and then her head ducked in. Without any warning, Sana's cheerleading top came sailing overhead onto the dashboard, quickly followed by her bra.

Sana sighed her relief. "Oof, that feels better."

Rachel swallowed. Sana was naked in her hoodie. Her brain was short-circuiting with the thought. But she couldn't let that show. She had to be normal. Only nothing about this was remotely normal.

Sana's lips curled upward without fully forming a smile. "Something wrong?"

"Don't block the heaters with those things," said Rachel, more gruffly than she knew she could.

"I wouldn't dare," said Sana, all propriety. But it was a lie, that propriety. She was naked underneath that sweatshirt. *N a k e d.*

Cool cool cool cool cool. Totally fine.

"I don't have any sweatpants," said Rachel.

Sana shrugged. "My legs'll dry much faster than my uniform."

"They can't be that bad; aren't they designed for athleticism?" Rachel was eager to talk about anything that distracted her from the fact that Sana was so dressed and undressed right now.

Sana tilted her head and for once, her ponytail was too stuck to her neck to tilt along with her. The move looked more bold now without that nice swish to counterpoint the seriousness of her face.

How had Rachel never noticed how serious Sana's face was before this? She was all angles and pointed focus.

"Har, har. Very funny. You've really showed me."

"No," said Rachel. "Seriously, aren't those designed to wick sweat?"

Now it was Sana's turn to laugh. "You are joking, right? Those are designed to keep their shape despite whatever position I take, including being thrown into the air. They're supposed to be crisp and perfect and beautiful, even when I'm doing a backflip. They are definitively *not* designed to wick sweat. They're designed for preservation. I bet when I'm thirty I could put it on and relive my glory days and it won't have lost a single pleat." Sana snorted.

"You seem pretty sure that these aren't your glory days," said Rachel. "I mean, aren't they supposed to be? The young and beautiful and talented cheerleader when she's at the top of her game? The best of her looks, the leader of her pack?"

Sana's eyes went sad, then she turned and stared pointedly at the old heater. Sana held her fingers up to it, the tips of them having gained a slightly blue wash, even with her brown skin. "No," she said quietly. "At least, I hope these aren't my glory days. I hope these aren't my best years."

And there it was, another secret. Another side to Sana that Rachel hadn't seen before. No, that was wrong. Rachel had seen it, she'd just ignored it before. Assumed that the reason was something superficial. But here in this warming, humid car, trapped on a median in the middle of the road, Rachel knew that whatever it was that made Sana wistful and sad, whatever it was that made her hide behind soft makeup and feminine clothing was not anything superficial or minor at all.

No, it was something terribly important that Rachel needed to understand right away. Especially before Sana found out that Rachel had cut the best parts of her work out of the film and left in only the hollow shell of an ice princess trope. "I hope they're not your best years either."

Sana turned then, her intense, dark eyes looking straight into Rachel, piercing her with a gaze that Sana must have used all the time. But now, with her mascara dripping under her eyes, it was a ferocious look, a fervent one. This was not a simple glance, a surprised look, even a question. It was a demand, a probe. Rachel squirmed.

"That's the nicest thing, I think, that you've ever said to me."

"It can't be."

"It was."

Sana wouldn't look away and Rachel couldn't. And to be honest, even if she could have looked away, she wouldn't have wanted to. She wouldn't have wanted to lose a moment of being able to look at this bright and shining Sana. This girl who pulled focus from herself so easily that the core of her was lost on them all.

"Sorry," said Rachel.

"Sure," said Sana.

"No." Rachel cleared her throat to be extra sure. "I am. Sorry. I've misjudged you. I can see that now. I'm sorry. It wasn't fair and it wasn't right. And you don't have to believe me. But I am sorry."

Sana didn't take her eyes off of Rachel and she lifted herself off of the seat, unsticking her wet legs and wet clothing from the passenger's seat, slid herself so she perched on the console. She swung one leg into Rachel's side of the car, leaving the other on her own. Sana's leg dripped lightly onto Rachel's leggings. The water was warm from her skin.

"Say it again."

Rachel sat transfixed for a moment. "I'm sorry."

"Me too." Sana licked her lips.

Rachel couldn't breathe. "For what?"

"I'm sorry I wasn't clearer with my intentions."

Rachel just kept staring into Sana's eyes. "Your intentions? What intentions?"

"That day freshman year. When I asked you out. I didn't fight back, I was too stunned."

A pit welled in Rachel's stomach. Anxious. No, that wasn't right. This wasn't anxiety. This was another feeling. A humming, stomach-clenching anticipation. But it wasn't anxiety. "It's okay. It was a joke."

Sana shook her head, slowly and clearly. "It wasn't a joke. It was never a joke."

Rachel opened her mouth, then closed it.

Sana's eyes dropped down to Rachel's mouth. "I can't believe I let you think it was a joke."

Rachel swallowed hard. She blinked. No. That wasn't blinking. Her eyelashes. They were fluttering. *For fuck's sake.* Rachel tried to think of every girl who could manage to keep it together in a moment like this so she could channel them. But her mind had gone completely and devastatingly blank.

Sana was close enough now that Rachel could feel her as much as she could hear her speak. "So what's it gonna be?"

The car, which had already been humid from their rain-soaked clothes, suddenly felt like a sauna. The coziness of the atmosphere had evaporated, leaving behind a steamy mess.

Rachel swallowed. "What are my options?"

Sana held up a finger. "Option A is I go back to the passenger's side, buckle myself in, and we wait out the rain. You drive me home, and when we shoot again come Tuesday, we pretend like none of this ever got aired out."

Rachel's stomach dropped out from under her. She should take that one, she knew. They should go back to being enemies. Or at least, quasi-indifferent acquaintances. Work colleagues with a healthy level of disagreement. Instead she opened her mouth and said, "And Option B?"

Sana batted her own eyelashes. She leaned in so there was a millimeter of space between her mouth and Rachel's. She raised a second finger, right alongside the first. "Option B involves my kissing you and taking it from there."

"You're usually more of a detailed planner," said Rachel.

Sana didn't say anything at first. Her mouth just quirked into half a smile. "Your call."

Rachel's mouth went dry. She should definitely go for the first option. The safe one. The one that didn't end in horrible disaster and her film being unfinished because she had hooked up with her lead actress just like every idiot Hollywood director on the planet. Instead, her mouth let out the words, "Option B. Please."

Sana's mouth hovered that millimeter above Rachel's for an instant, then lightly, gently brushed against her own. For a moment Rachel was too stunned to return the kiss. Sana's mouth was soft, full. She tasted like vanilla. That must have been the flavor of lip gloss she used. Like baked goods. The rain had intensified the salty-sweet scent of her skin, and that light scent of jasmine was wafting off of her hair as per usual.

Then Rachel's mind went into overdrive because this was Sana Khan and she wasn't sure how many opportunities she was going to get like this in her lifetime, but she sure as shit wasn't going to waste them over the mental poetry of what Sana's hair smelled like.

And as soon as Rachel added pressure from her own lips, as soon as she started kissing Sana back, that was when the floodgates really opened. Sana slid further off the console and climbed into Rachel's lap. Rachel wrapped her arms around Sana, pulling her in closer, needing her still closer. She wanted to run her hands through Sana's hair, but her ponytail was still wet and slicked back. She took hold of Sana's face instead, steadying it so their mouths could find a rhythm.

Sana pulled back suddenly and took a deep breath, as though she were desperate for air. As though she had run a mile and needed to catch her breath. "You're so soft everywhere."

And between the pulling away and the words themselves, Rachel would have flinched had she not heard the wonder and desire licking through Sana's tone. Had she not felt Sana's hand—her uninjured hand—dig into the flesh at Rachel's hips. The tips of her fingers in her casted left arm added a light pressure. A thought nestled deeply and immediately into Rachel's subconscious, taking root there: *She likes this about me.*

It was strange, nearly foreign, to be wanted for what she felt so unloved for most of the time. For what the world so typically resented in her. For what she had told herself over and over hadn't mattered but nearly always had.

And then Sana's mouth was moving along her jawline, down her neck. *Oh God, her neck.* Rachel would never be able to think about washing behind her ears the same way ever again. Her whole body had become more potent than she ever could have imagined. Because Sana was kissing her in spots that had never felt particularly sexual before, until that girl had set her lips to them. And now everywhere Sana touched was going up in flames like a storehouse of old celluloid did with the flick of a single match.

Arson had never been so wonderful. So dizzying.

Eventually the rain stopped. And sometime after that the kissing stopped as well. Rachel pulled off the median, driving Sana back to her house. But the spinning—like watching an action movie that had refused to use a Steadicam for the effects—that didn't go away for hours.

April 23

8 Days Until Deadline

21

Take Me by the Heart When You
Take Me by the Hand

Sana

Sana had never hated cheerleading practice before.

Then again, she'd never had to stand on the sidelines of practice while everyone else actually did things. Yes, she was correcting form on stunts. She was making sure they went through the proper sequences. But she wasn't *doing anything*, not physically. She didn't do cheer for the opportunity to teach. She did it for the opportunity to use her body, for the ability to flex her muscles and fly.

Running practice with a foot in a plastic boot and her arm in a plaster cast was the opposite of everything Sana loved about the sport. No, it wasn't a sport, not technically. It was technically an athletic *activity*, because she lived in a world where chess players were Olympic athletes and cheerleaders were brain-dead airheads.

Sometimes sexism really sucked.

Sana was watching practice, vibrating with energy and inaction. She couldn't even go on her regular runs. She'd never realized before how much she relied on them to stay calm, to stay sane. To help her focus and get through the day. She'd never felt their absence before.

She'd been lucky to have been running and cheering for as long as she had without any incident or injury. Because now, now that she was sidelined by her sprained ankle, she felt like a racehorse put out to pasture. Testy, snippy, shuddering with the force of a body at rest. Three weeks without running. Three weeks without flying, without stunts, without choreography. She was bursting at the seams.

Sana tapped her uninjured foot. "No, no. Do it again. You have to keep your arms *locked*, Alexis. *Locked.*"

Alexis looked ready to break into tears. Sana ought to have waited, let Maddie correct Alexis. But Sana's whole body was waiting, waiting, waiting. She had to do something, for goodness' sake. "Alexis? If you don't lock your arms, your flyer could wobble. She wobbles, the base falters. Base falters, and she falls. Do you get it?"

Alexis sniffed. A single tear streaked down her cheek. But she still didn't nod.

"Alexis. I don't need you to cry. In fact, I'd prefer if you didn't. I need you to acknowledge that you understand. And then I need to see you do it right. Or I swear, I will pull you from this stunt. You get it?"

Alexis's eyes went wide like saucers. The entirety of the squad stopped what they were doing to stare. Sana didn't look away. Didn't see what looks she was getting from the rest of her team. She needed Alexis to *listen*. Finally, Alexis nodded, ever so slightly.

"Good. Run it again." Sana turned, finally registered the rest of the squad's notice. "What are the rest of your standing around for? Do you already have the stunt perfect?"

The girls shuffled into position. Even T didn't bother to give an eye roll or throw a look of disdain Sana's way.

Maddie waited until everyone was busy practicing before she tugged on Sana's arm. She spoke quietly, though with her usual authority. "Look, I'm as mad at Alexis for dropping you as anybody. But making her cry won't help."

Sana pulled her arm away, slowly but with intention. She kept watching Alexis run the stunt. "She's gonna drop someone else if she doesn't pay attention to her stunts."

Maddie rolled her lips in, clamping down on them with her teeth briefly before releasing the expression. "Shame isn't gonna fix that."

Sana straightened her stance. "Somebody has to teach her."

Maddie called for a boom pyramid. Sana was usually the peak. But Maddie made Alexis take the top position, to teach her to trust her teammates, to understand what it was to be reliant on them. It was a better strategy than Sana's, to be sure.

Sana watched them build the pyramid, watched as each level of girls used the rhythm of the chant to boost, step, position themselves. Watched as the whole pyramid came together from an assembly of girls in a series of lines to a pile of girls in a rigidly geometric formation.

And then it came crashing perfectly and spectacularly back down. Just as they had all wanted it to.

Sana had wanted to be captain of the squad since she'd started cheering in the eighth grade. Back then, she had been too quiet, too new. But she'd worked hard toward the goal. She knew she could be in charge, knew she'd be good at it.

And she had been.

So why was it all falling apart now?

Sana blew her whistle every minute, calling out everything everyone was doing wrong.

The squad didn't stand a chance.

The boom pyramid, one of the most fail-safe of all the stunts that they could do, didn't stay up more than three counts.

It took at least eight to build a decent one.

All this work and it ends here.

The boom pyramid came crashing down on count two—Sana was clapping the counts out now so that the squad would get the rhythm.

Alexis and T were glaring Sana's way. Sana called for the pyramid to go back up again. The squad groaned in unison.

Alexis, her frustration having finally overcome her shame, looked right at Sana as she faux-whispered. "She doesn't even do anything anymore. I wouldn't mind the injury if she wasn't using it as an excuse to slack off and get famous."

Then T did her signature smirk in response.

"You think this is funny?" Sana stared T down. "I can name at least fifty reasons why this isn't a joke. Starting with your attitude."

"Whatever," answered Alexis. "You're the one who's in charge with a bad attitude in the first place. If you can't keep it tight, why should we? You went soft, Khan."

The squad all stared pointedly away from Sana.

Coach K, who had taken a pretty laissez-faire approach thus far, blew her whistle. "If you girls cannot get it together, I am canceling the next pep rally on the grounds of disarray and ill-discipline."

Alexis raised an eyebrow at Sana. "That's true for one member of the squad."

T snickered.

"Okay, that is it." Sana threw her clipboard down.

Alexis looked startled. T looked away, since she was rarely the one brave enough to say her undercutting thoughts out loud. And Maddie, Maddie could only stare.

"I get it, I'm the injured screw-up. But before I was the injured screw-up, I was the horrible, insufferable kiss-ass. So which do you want? The girl who goes one hundred, or the one who phones it in?"

T sputtered. "You, you said ass."

"Yeah. Ass. The one you dropped me on in the middle of a stunt, which you wouldn't have done had you been paying attention at all during practice. But instead you were snickering with Alexis and making jokes and rolling your eyes. And because you were too busy with your judgmental social schedule, she *dropped me on my ass on the hard gym floor.* So yeah. Kiss my freaking ass, T."

Coach K blew her whistle. Maddie sucked in a breath. Alexis's jaw hung, swaying in the air-conditioned breeze of the gym.

"Khan. Language."

But Sana was just getting started; she ignored the warning. "I'm handing the squad over to one of you two next year—you're the only juniors left—and neither one of you can keep it together for a whole practice. You could step up to the plate. You could give Maddie a break. You could call a stunt. Show some initiative. But no, you'd rather whisper and talk shit."

Coach K blew her whistle again. "Khan. Language. This is your last warning."

Sana looked Coach in the eye. She'd had it. With all of it. She'd had it with watching practice and barely cheering. She'd had it with working so hard to climb up something without any idea of what happened once she got there. She'd been living her life like a boom pyramid, climbing to the top only to come crashing back down. All for no apparent reason other than the entertainment and pleasure of others.

Sana smiled, bright, pretty—her signature Sana Khan smile. Alexis and T relaxed slightly, thinking the fight was over. But Maddie watched her with narrowed eyes. Because Maddie saw the storm beneath the calm. She saw what nobody else saw, what no one, not even Coach K, knew was coming.

Sana held up both middle fingers. Dragged them along Alexis and T's line of sight. "Fuck. You. Both."

Then Sana didn't wait. She walked over to her bag, grabbed it, and left the gym. Even the boys' basketball team watched her exit.

Rachel was standing on set, talking over script changes with Ryan. She had expected Sana to go into hiding after that kiss. It must have been

225

a one-off. An aberration. An intrusion into an otherwise ordered and tidy life. But instead Sana had walked onto set and given Rachel a public wink. She'd even leaned over her, grazing her shoulder as Rachel went through script changes with her.

If Rachel had done half of the things—touch an arm, swish her hair, bat her eyes—that Sana was doing, everybody would have known she was at least attempting to flirt. But when Sana did those exact same things, people assumed she *was* just friendly. It was like eyes glazed over her and everyone filled in a totally different story.

Sana had come out, must have been ages ago. But nobody remembered. Not on a day-to-day basis.

And then there was Sana's frustration. Rachel could see it. See it when people dismissed what she was doing as some kind of normal girly behavior. Some kind of regular girly-girl dance. Sana hid her frustrations behind a mask—the good girl on the surface—but now that Rachel had seen what lay beneath, Rachel couldn't unsee any of it—the frustration, the flashes of anger, the desire, and so, so much hurt.

Maybe it was because Sana was clearly more frustrated in general, so that the low-lying, deep-seated version she always held on to was coming to the surface more quickly.

Sana caught Rachel looking at her and she gave one of her signature megawatt grins.

Rakish. Sana Khan had a rakish grin.

The girl opposite Sana—Lacey—caught the direction of Sana's gaze, looked back at Sana, and rolled her eyes at the girl. Trying to win favor with the cheerleader by undercutting the power figure, aka the director, aka Rachel.

Sana ignored this and headed directly for Rachel. A strange, determined expression lighting her eyes.

Holy shit.

Before Sana could do something truly exposing, Rachel had to do something. *What if Sana eventually changed her mind?*

"Do you remember your mark from last time?"

Disappointment flashed over Sana's face, then was gone. She shrugged. "Sure."

"Okay, I'm gonna need you to run through your blocking with Lacey. Lacey, get over here. Mostly I just need you two to face off in this. It's not complicated blocking. Do you got it?"

That smirk. That Natalie Dormer–level smirk popped up across Sana's face. She winked again, like she got that Rachel wanted this to be between them only for now. "Aye, aye, captain."

Rachel went back, fiddling with the camera. Figuring out the angles. She did it longer than she needed to. Because Sana Khan moved through this world trying to tell everyone in tiny, everyday ways that she was attracted to girls and nobody registered any of them. Flirt, touch, wink, bat her eyelashes. Kiss girls, hold hands. Brush up her insane body against Rachel's. Be obvious in the way everyone could see but that nobody seemed to care about. Not if you looked like Sana.

Sana wasn't trapped in a closet. Other people just kept building one around her. And as she kept walking out of them, they kept building new ones around her. Sana, the girl who could say she loved Joan Jett and simply get an ironic giggle in return. Like the listener thought she didn't get what she was saying.

You have now crossed over into the Twilight Zone.

This truly was a dimension as vast as space and as timeless as infinity.

The day's shoot went by quickly. They had been flying through her shooting scripts and her sheets ever since Sana had taken over as the lead. Douga hardly paid attention, which was a miracle in and of itself. She trusted Rachel now. Trusted her to keep set moving like a well-oiled machine. Trusted her to take Sana's acting work and turn it against everything Sana had thought she had signed up for the project to be. And Rachel did keep it moving. In a way she hadn't, not before Sana.

Rachel was relieved when filming was over. It was a dance, filming

Sana while hiding that the overall goal of the film would have to change. A strange, horrible dance that a better person might have called a lie. Especially when Sana registered that she didn't have any lines in this take—confusion had washed over her face, but Rachel had covered the moment by calling action and moving through the last of the close-ups.

She's going to hate me.

Of that, Rachel was certain. But Rachel kept going. Until she'd shot the last of the footage that she needed. She hadn't gotten this far only to trip at the finish line. She didn't care who she'd been kissing. "Okay, everyone, that's a wrap. We did it."

A few whoops and hollers emerged from the crew. Nobody thought they'd get to the end of filming on this project, least of all Rachel. And yet, here they were.

Everyone packed up the equipment and took it into the film lab. Rachel's days of hauling the cameras and lenses and lights by herself were over. Her days of doing anything totally by herself were over. She thought she would have felt weak or unbalanced, but instead she felt this immense sense of relief. This was what she had been missing while making films for the past four years. Camaraderie. She had that because of a girl the world refused to see beyond the scope of their own limited imagination. A girl she herself had refused to see.

A girl she was lying to.

The thought was haunting. Kissing Sana was one thing. Seeing her, really seeing her, was something else altogether. Rachel was packing the last lens back into the bag for the camera when she heard the squeak of Sana's shoes.

Rachel got up, grabbing the camera bag. "I gotta drop this back off in the lab. Do you need a ride?"

"Sure do," said Sana, linking her arm through Rachel's.

It was a relaxed and easy move. Rachel's shoulders tensed and she pressed her lips together until her mouth formed a straight line.

"You okay?" asked Sana.

"Oh." *Don't say fine. She'll know something's wrong if you say fine.* "I'm alright."

But Sana saw through the *alright*, just like if Rachel had said *fine*. "Don't worry. Here, I can help by distracting you."

"And how would you, like, distract me?" Rachel hadn't meant any innuendo at all. Hadn't planned on the deep raspiness in her voice. It had just happened.

Sana's eyes went wide for a moment. But then Sana recovered, the right side of her mouth twitching.

Oh God, she's going to kiss me in the school hallway.

Rachel couldn't tell if she needed Sana to kiss her in the school hallway or she needed Sana to never kiss her in the school hallway.

If she kisses me here there's no going back. And the way forward had to be heartbreak. Has to be. Because Rachel was going to use Sana to get ahead in her future, just like every horrible person in Hollywood who had ever succeeded.

But Sana, ever attuned, sensed Rachel's hesitancy. She gave a quick peck on Rachel's cheek, then skipped out of reach. "That wasn't quite my idea, though I do like it. I had something else in mind."

Disappointment welled in the pit of Rachel's stomach. She had wanted the kiss after all. Even if she didn't deserve it. "What's that?"

"Come on," Sana said, skipping down the hall. "Let's go get your ear pierced."

22

A Girl After Midnight

Rachel

"You want to go do *what*?" Rachel must have misheard. There was no way Sana had suggested that they go and get a piercing right now.

Sana grabbed at Rachel's hand, tugging her playfully along. "I know a guy on Hollywood Boulevard. He looks intimidating but he's honestly the biggest teddy bear in the world and he does the best job. No swelling or bleeding."

"Mentioning swelling and bleeding does not help your case." Rachel let Sana drag her along. She'd never had this before. Someone dragging her to do something, not out of exasperation or teaching her a lesson, but simply for the sheer joy of making her go along. Rachel felt a bit dizzy with it, whatever this new feeling was unfurling out of her chest and expanding outward, all the way to her tingling fingers and bouncing toes.

Bouncing toes? Keep it together, Recht.

"Don't you want to be brave?"

Sana had her there. "Well. Yes."

Sana smiled. "And you said you always wanted one."

"Yes, but—"

"But what? Is your dad going to be home early?" Sana's face was so eager, so bright, so ready for adventure, come what may.

"No, he works late on Thursdays."

"There! See!"

"But . . ." Rachel was running out of steam in her arguments. "What about your mom? Doesn't she hate me? Are you allowed out with me ever again?"

Sana laughed. God, that laugh. Rachel could listen to it forever and probably still not get tired of the sound. A bright, tinkling bell with a grand sense of sarcasm that bit through its natural sweetness.

"My mom's at work. She won't even know I'm out. Besides, I'm in trouble, not you. My mom—" A sad expression crossed Sana's face, but then faded quickly. "She at least knows where to place her anger. It's squarely at me. Not you. Never you."

Never you was a strong sentiment that Rachel couldn't quite bring herself to believe. But instead of snorting, she stared into Sana's earnest expression and felt herself melt a bit.

Oh no.

This was why it had always been easier to imagine that Sana was joking, imagine that she was a mean girl with a mean prank. Because at least that way, she could hate Sana. This way—this new one where she saw Sana as she was—she'd end up half in love with the girl. And Rachel had a feeling Sana wasn't the kind of girl you just got over.

Did Sana have exes? How many other girls had she kissed?

A look must have crossed over Rachel's face, because Sana squeezed her hand. "Don't worry. I'll hold your hand. It'll only hurts for like a second."

Rachel nodded. Yes, it was the piercing she was worried about. Not all the girls Sana may or may not have kissed over the course of her lifetime.

"Okay, and then it throbs, like, after. I mean, it hurts. But you don't have to go."

"I want to." Rachel got in the driver's side of her car, leaned over, and unlocked the passenger's side.

Sana got in and directed them to a piercing place near Hollywood and Highland. They managed to find parking, despite the fact that the area was a tourist trap and a parking nightmare. The shop had a door that Rachel might have driven by a hundred times already. Maybe a thousand.

"You ready?" Sana looked over, her hand on the door.

"As I'll ever be." Rachel tried to sound braver than she felt.

The bell jangled as they walked in. There was something both comforting and incongruous about the fact that a bell jangled, like they were walking into a neighborhood coffee shop rather than a store that said TATTOOS and PIERCINGS in neon lights across a dusty window on Hollywood Boulevard. The walls were covered in flash, there was a jewelry case up front, and the whole place smelled like acrid cleaning solution—nearly like an antiseptic doctor's office. It turned Rachel's stomach, until she remembered she wanted her piercers to smell like a doctor's office. They were, after all, about to put a hole in her body.

The shop had checkerboard floors and a big glass case full of new jewelry in all sorts of shapes that Rachel didn't want to think too closely about. She stuck with the obvious ones—hoops and studs. She leaned over, trying to see if she even had any options among the cheapest of the earrings, when a big, booming voice rang out.

"Look who it is." Approaching was a bull of a man—covered in tattoos and wearing all black. He even had the septum piercing and everything.

"Maybe this isn't such a good idea," hedged Rachel.

Sana just laughed. "Don't worry. We go way back, Wild Bill and I."

Rachel tried to make sense of this. "You got any piercings I don't know about?"

Sana blushed. "Just my nose."

"Then how does this guy know you like you're a repeat customer?" Rachel put her hand on her hip.

"This guy knows her," said the man in question, "because that girl has the meanest left kick I have ever seen on anybody. Was showing how to do a nose piercing to a trainee, which she was cool with letting me do. And I didn't hold her down as much as I normally would, because the trainee needed a good view and I figured *what damage could a girl like that do?* Turns out the answer is *a hell of a lot*. Nearly thought Bones had a hairline fracture. Turned out to be a deep bruise."

Sana looked sheepish. "Cheering."

"Cheering?" Rachel was incredulous.

"Exactly," said Wild Bill. "I didn't believe her either."

Wild Bill had to be about six foot five. His T-shirt showed off his full-sleeve tattoos. He looked like the kind of guy in a movie that a character would be trash talking until the guy stood up and showed just how big he was. Then the character would stop talking and back away slowly, practically groveling as they exited the bar.

Bill was sizing up Sana, but not in an unfriendly way. Like they were on good terms, this huge, hulking man and Sana. "What happened to you?"

Rachel held her breath, waiting for the answer.

"A string of bad luck, man." Sana sighed. "A string of bad luck."

"That's a bummer." Wild Bill shook his head. "Come on in, don't be shy." This second part was addressed to Rachel; he was waving her into the back area, where a door was open and waiting.

"Do you want me back there?" Sana's hesitance was endearing.

"If you don't come back there after this being your idea, I will never forgive you."

Sana smiled and Rachel suddenly understood every stupid poem comparing the beloved to the sun. "It wasn't *my* idea, strictly speaking."

"Lead me to my fate. I am ready, Oh Enthusiastic One." Rachel held out her hands so that Sana could drag her along again.

Back in the side room, Wild Bill was swabbing things and setting up paper. He told Rachel to lie down. She closed her eyes. A warm, small, soft hand gently grabbed on to hers.

"It's gonna be cool."

"I know." And Rachel believed it.

"The helix, correct?"

"Yup."

"What jewelry do you want?"

"Whatever is cheapest and meets the safety requirements."

Wild Bill laughed at that. "I'll go grab it from the front."

Alone again, with Sana. Rachel had that same heart-hammering she'd had in her car in the rain. Only this time not because they were nearly about to kiss, but because Sana was holding her hand and lightly stroking her knuckles.

"It's gonna be okay, you'll see. One moment of pain and then you get what you've always wanted." Her voice was like a lullaby. Or what Rachel imagined a lullaby was like. She didn't have any memories of them. "You're so brave, you're being so brave."

Rachel hadn't noticed before how deep Sana's voice was. Resonant and commanding, sure. But never deep and low and soothing. A tiny girl with a husky voice, trying to lull Rachel into a calm state.

Of course, it couldn't work. Because as soon as Sana's hands and words and tone soothed Rachel, calmed her nerves down, Rachel realized it was Sana gently brushing a thumb back and forth over her hand and whispering near her ear. Then her heart would start hammering all over again and then she'd remember that she was about to stick a whole new hole in her body and the panic crested anew, a confused wave of fear and excitement.

"Got it," said Wild Bill, coming back into the room.

He sat down, swabbed her ear. That's when she really felt light-headed, like she was about to get a shot or something, but it wasn't a shot, it was a hole in her body that she'd have to take care of forever and ever and might get infected and might bleed and—

"It's okay," said Sana, her voice cutting through Rachel's wild thoughts. "You've got this."

A wash of calm ran through Rachel right as Wild Bill ran her through with a needle.

"SHIT."

Wild Bill snorted with a light laugh. Even Sana managed to find it funny.

"Nearly there," he said.

"AreyoufuckingkiddingmeBill?"

"Gotta get the jewelry in," said Wild Bill matter-of-factly.

"Oh fuck fuck fuckity fucking fuck," Rachel whimpered. "I thought you said it was one thing. You didn't mention the jewelry. You lied."

"I forgot!" said Sana. "I always forget about the jewelry. Worst part."

"Now she tells me," said Rachel.

Wild Bill laughed. "Okay, you can sit up now. And take this."

Rachel got up slowly. Wild Bill handed her a lollipop. Rachel popped it into her mouth and the sugar took the edge off.

"You're driving home," said Rachel once the throbbing had stopped making her too dizzy to think.

"I've got a better idea." There was that smirk on Sana's mouth, and Rachel knew beyond a reasonable doubt that she was in real trouble.

"Come on, Recht. Let's get a little bit reckless."

This was probably the worst idea in the history of ideas.

But for once, Sana didn't care. They had grabbed a burger on the Strip. It had been the sloppy, greasy kind but it had put life back into

Rachel's face. They'd made their way down to Koreatown, the breeze cooling as the sun set. The air tasted better at sunset, smoggy but also refreshing. Full of potential. Full of the night ahead.

They had parked on a side street and now they were walking down Wilshire, passing doughnut shops, bars, and the errant laundromat. But none of those places were Sana's aim. No, she had bigger plans for their night. Rachel was letting Sana drag her along. She wasn't sure if it was the delirium from getting a piercing or a newfound sense of trust. Whatever it was, Sana would take it.

That's when she caught sight of the strip mall she'd been looking for. The one with the half-lit sign and the L-shaped parking lot.

Karaoke.

She caught sight of a group of olds already in line. They had to be in their thirties, from the sheer polish on them. There were at least fifteen of them. Hopefully, they were celebrating someone's birthday. Hopefully, they wouldn't notice when she and Rachel snuck in with them. Somewhere in the middle of the group, but toward the end. "Let's go in with these people here."

Rachel looked around. "They look way older than us. I doubt they would be cool about us sneaking in with them."

Sana shrugged. She felt like she'd taken Felix Felicis tonight. Nothing could go wrong. Everything would go their way. "We gotta at least try."

"We do?" Rachel sounded reluctant. And confused that she had become the voice of reason for the night.

"Yes," said Sana. "Because you and me, we gotta do something for once. You watch the world from behind your camera. And I let girls toss me into the air, flying high, but I've never actually gone anywhere. I've never even been on an airplane."

"What does that have to do with karaoke on a school night?"

"Everything, Rachel. We've gotta have an adventure. And adventures rarely come to you."

"Adventures come to people in the movies all the time." Rachel crossed her arms.

"That's movie magic." Sana crossed her arms back, mirroring Rachel's posture. "They're headed in. It's now or never."

Rachel nodded. She uncrossed her arms. For a second Sana thought she was going to turn around. But then she reached out, offered her hand. "Now."

Sana took it.

They blended into the crowd of adults. One of the women in the group had attempted to smuggle in an entire thirty rack of beer in her tote bag and the bouncer was totally preoccupied with taking each individual can out. The woman had an incredulous, that's-not-mine look on her face.

The bouncer had his own incredulous, how-is-this-my-life face.

Sana and Rachel had made it to a dark, narrow hallway when a hand reached out and grabbed Sana by the upper arm in a tight squeeze. "Okay, kids. What are you doing?"

Sana turned around, sure they were about to be booted out by management. But it wasn't management. It was the woman who had attempted to smuggle all the beers by the bouncer. She had on high-heeled booties, vintage denim, and the most perfectly winged eyeliner that Sana had ever seen. She was eyeing Sana and Rachel skeptically.

"Doing karaoke?" Sana tried.

The woman tilted her head. "Come on. I know I'm old, but I'm not *that old*."

"We don't drink," Sana tried again.

The woman put her hands on her hips.

But before she could say anything, Rachel interjected. "We're having an adventure."

The woman gave Rachel a once-over, seemed to believe her, and gave a nod. "Fair enough. But you're sticking with us. I'll believe the 'no drinking' when I see it for myself." Skepticism slashed across the woman's face.

Sana was so relieved to not have to leave as soon as they had gotten in. "Oh! Thank you!"

"Calm down, ladies. I'm Pooja. In case anyone asks how you ended up at this birthday. Say you're with me."

Then Pooja turned heel and they followed quickly behind her.

The adults were a raucous crowd. They hardly noticed Sana and Rachel's presence.

Rachel looked startled, a bit frozen. Like she wasn't sure how much longer she could sit here and hang out at someone-she-didn't-know's birthday. "Look, we got in, isn't that enough?"

Sana wanted this to be fun, to be a real adventure. To be the kind of thing they would remember forever, even if they had to part ways and never see each other ever again one day. Sana got out her phone and got out the app that allowed her to add a song to the karaoke queue. "Wait," said Sana.

"What are you doing?" Rachel hissed. The remnants of her good mood had evaporated. She was all worry and pragmatism. And nursing a still-throbbing ear.

"Just wait" was all Sana could say in response. None of the adults noticed when she added her song to the queue. Even Rachel was too busy worrying and fretting to see it flash across the screen briefly. "Give it a minute, okay?"

"One minute." Rachel held up a single finger.

Sana tapped her feet, a bundle of nerves. She hoped her song came on soon. She knew she had probably closer to five minutes before Rachel really started to kick up a fuss and tried to get them to leave.

But five minutes wasn't long when you considered most songs were three and a half.

The grown-ups were all singing with off-key enthusiasm, and the lyrics were displayed over a screen playing old K-dramas. Right now, a girl and a boy were floating down a river in a small rowboat, their expressions sad and meaningful. Except the song playing was "Wannabe" by the Spice Girls and the incongruity of the moment caused a giggle to bubble and burst out of Sana's mouth. Rachel cut a glare in Sana's direction. The message was clear: *Do not draw attention to us, Khan.*

That's when Sana saw the prompt pop up—"Whole Wide World," by Wreckless Eric.

"Whose song is this?" asked Pooja, a bit of a slur on her lips.

Too late to back out now. "It's mine."

Sana took the mic and stood up. Rachel looked like she was ready for a hole in the earth to swallow up the entire karaoke place to avoid all of the attention that Sana was drawing to herself. But Sana had meant what she'd said. She was going to make adventure.

And possibly, a little romance.

The opening bars kicked in and Sana started off a little quiet, a little unsure with her opening. The guitar was so quiet. Sana could feel her voice—warbled and tense. The opening guitar was so light, so barely there. She'd forgotten that this whole song opened on the sound of the lead's voice.

Deep breath. And Sana began to sing, let it out as she sang the words. About going to find the world just to find the one girl who was meant to be.

She got a whoop from one of the olds. Sana winked in their direction. Rachel stood and stared. The olds, of course, got it right away. They all stared between them like something sweet and good and true was happening in front of them. Sana had seen it in their eyes. Could feel it in the air.

Young love, they seemed to be saying without words.

It took Rachel a little bit longer. Must have been the shock, the attention, all of it. Her eyes went as wide as those lenses she was constantly carrying around with her. But she didn't duck or hide. She looked back as Sana looked at her. And logically, Sana knew she was in a room full of strangers singing a serenade to another girl. Knew she was declaring herself in a big, public way. But she kept on singing, kept on staring at Rachel. Because right now, they were the only two people who mattered, the only two people in the room, the only two people in the world, the only two lovers left alive.

Keep breathing. You can do this.

And then the refrain ended and the heavy, bass-filled guitar dropped and Sana didn't care anymore. Bass could do that to a girl. Give her more confidence. The guitar thrummed out the beat, was practically percussion in itself. She brought the mic up, tapped her feet, swiveled her hips as she sang the chorus.

Deep, deep breaths. Because the next line was real and true and Sana felt it in her bones that if she sang it out loud, she'd never be able to get them back, never be able to hold on to the feeling inside of her. It would be beyond her control.

"I should be lying on that sun-swept beach with her." Sana could only look in one place—at Rachel. "Caressing her warm, brown skin."

For the first time, Sana wasn't really performing. Not for a goal, not for a cheer, not for a team, not for an eventual position. She was singing—making an idiot of herself, honestly—because she wanted Rachel to know how she felt. She wanted her to express the joy buzzing inside her. Wanted to share what she felt rather than keep it tamped down and locked inside.

Last chorus. Hope she doesn't wanna kill me. Sana kept singing, kept reading the prompter. But she didn't look away from Rachel as she sang. About going the whole wide world, just to find the one girl she was meant to be with. The whole wide world just to see where that one girl had been hidden.

Except Rachel had never been hidden to Sana.

Maybe Sana had been the one who had been hiding all along.

But that didn't matter anymore. Sana was letting out the best kind of secret. The kind she never wanted to keep to herself in a million years.

Wham wham wham wha-wham. Bang bang bang sha-bang.

The song ended and Sana was startled back to reality by the whoops and cheers from her audience. She ducked her head, feeling a blush creeping up her face all the way to her hairline. She didn't blush often, but when she did her skin went a bright, hot red. Practically magenta. Sana handed off the mic, not noticing who she passed it to.

And then Rachel was standing in front of her, giving Sana a look that she couldn't quite read. "Sometimes I really hate you, Khan."

And then Rachel leaned in, wrapped her arms around Sana's neck, and kissed her.

Rachel Recht is kissing me. The thought flashed and was gone. Because for once in her life, Sana was done thinking. She was too busy kissing Rachel like a madwoman. All hands and mouth, everywhere. Anywhere she caught sight of a flash of skin. She was beyond volition, beyond thought, and into pure and unadulterated instinct.

Rachel pulled away first, breathless. She looked over Sana's shoulder, maybe gauging whether or not the adults were paying them any attention. But they must not have been. "Let's get out of here."

And then Rachel was pulling Sana out the door, through the dark hallway. She was trying every door down along the way. She apologized a couple of times when she walked in on another group's private room. She hit a few locked ones. But then one door handle slid down with only the tiniest of clicks—unlocked—and the room inside was dark, empty, and entirely their own, at least for the moment.

Rachel clicked the door shut, pushed in the button for the lock on the door. She found a notice on the wall—about returning mics when done with them—and taped it over the one window on the door. The room got a bit darker, became a space that belonged only to them, only to this moment that was somehow frantic and still all at once. Then

Rachel pulled Sana toward her. Sana did her best to suppress her laugh; she didn't want Rachel to think she was laughing *at her*. But she didn't need to worry.

"You can laugh," said Rachel. "I love your laugh. You sound like a subversive Victorian lady when you laugh."

Now Sana did laugh, her lips nearly brushing against Rachel's. Their breaths mingling together. "I don't feel like a Victorian lady right now."

"Good." And then there was no *nearly*, no *almost*. Just two lips meeting—softly at first. Quietly. Sana smiled, and then she felt Rachel's mouth pull into a smile, and that's when she used the opportunity to test her tongue against Rachel's lips.

The kiss changed after that.

It was as though every untamed thought Sana had ever had about Rachel hadn't been tucked away and buried down deep as she had so desperately tried all those hours working together. No, instead the thoughts had been tagged and filed *NSFW*, so that Sana could boot them up, all at once, with perfect recall for here and now. And now this running catalog of ideas wouldn't stop, couldn't stop. It was too much and not enough. Each idea flashed, then was replaced by the next and then the next and then the next.

She pulled Rachel over her, onto the bank of cushioned benched seating in the room.

Sana wanted it all. Big curling hair, soft rounded shoulders, wide thick hips. That mouth that so rarely pulled into a smile. All Rachel. Each a smaller piece of an irresistible whole. How could she prioritize this staggering list? It was incomprehensible. She couldn't keep her hands still. Sana felt short of breath, like she was being tossed in the air over and over and over again without ever having to land. Her hands were frantic—even the one in the cast—her mouth couldn't keep up with her thoughts, and all she had humming through her was *yes* and *now*.

She leaned back again, desperate for air. Desperate to regain some level of control over her wandering, and now shaking, limbs.

"I want you." Sana's hands hovered above the button of Rachel's jeans.

"You've only got one good hand." Rachel's words came out in puffs of breath.

"You'd be surprised what I can do with one hand." The only thing Sana could hear was Rachel's breath as she steadied herself. The only thing Sana could feel was her own thumping heart. "May I?"

"Yes," said Rachel, like she was answering

"Are you sure?"

"Yes," said Rachel.

Sara's hand went back to the button. She tugged it open, then put her hand under the now opened waistband.

Rachel yelped. "Your hand's cold."

Sana moved to pull her hand away but Rachel grabbed her wrist. They looked at each other, and then they were kissing again. Sana kept her hands light at first. She kept her attention on Rachel. When Rachel deepened the kiss, Sana knew she was on the right track. When Rachel grabbed at her wrist, digging nails into Sana's forearm, Sana knew she was close.

"This is not a great way to get me to give up swear words," said Rachel, catching her breath between each word.

Sana leaned in close to Rachel's ear, kissing her way along Rachel's jaw to get to her. "You can swear as much as you like."

But instead of swearing, Rachel kept quiet by kissing Sana, so that there were no cries to echo out into the room. Just a kiss to take in what belonged to them.

After, Rachel nestled her head into Sana's shoulder, fitting where she should not have. "You're wrong, you know."

"How so?"

"I'm not surprised with what you can do with one hand," Rachel said. "But I am pretty impressed."

Sana giggled and Rachel returned the laugh. They stayed there, wrapped around each other, refusing to let the rest of reality intrude for as long as they could.

There Goes Your Social Life

Sana

The door snicked shut behind Sana. The porch light was on, but that was automatic. The hall light was off. The entryway was dark. The car wasn't in the driveway, but it was likely that the old Summit Eagle would never be in the driveway again. And while Sana knew where to step so as to not make a sound, she didn't bother. She hadn't expected for Farrah to be home and all signs pointed to the assumption being correct.

Except the light clicked on in the kitchen and Farrah was standing there looking like the reaper of death. "Have fun?"

It was such an unexpected question, Sana nearly stumbled. "Yes."

"Good. Because you're not having fun for a very long time after this."

"There it is. I guess I'm grounded."

"Don't be flip about this, Sana. You're in trouble."

"Don't be flip? Don't be flip? When in my life have I ever been flip about anything? Ever? I took my Brownies meetings seriously, Mom. I was seven and I did the minutes because I thought Ms. Piper was writing them too casually."

That didn't slow Farrah down. "You never used to come home at one in the morning either, so I'm having to improvise."

"And what would you know about my coming home at one in the morning? Are you home all the time?"

"That's it. You're not to see that girl again. I don't know what she's doing to you but you're not acting like yourself."

Sana laughed. A harsh, bitter thing. "You know what, for the first time in a while I have honestly been acting like myself. Not Perfect Sana. Not Future Ivy League Sana. Not Cheer Captain Sana. Just me. And it's driving you nuts. You go on and on about how Mamani and Dadu ruined your life and made you be something you weren't and here you are doing the exact same thing to me."

Farrah sucked in a breath. She stared at Sana. And then she left the room. Vacated it like a coward.

Sana followed her. "You're going to leave in the middle of this?"

"I don't have to put up with this, not from you," Farrah shouted.

"But I have to put up with it from you?"

Farrah turned around, stared for a long moment. "That's it, huh? You're going to throw your life away over some girl the way I threw my life away over some boy?"

"I'm not throwing my life away over a girl!"

"Really? Because that's not what it looks like from here. Go ahead. I can't stop you anymore. You're eighteen. You can do what you want. You're a grown-ass woman. Make sure she's worth it."

"And I wasn't?"

Farrah shook her head. "You're smarter than that. This isn't about you. I love you. You've always been worth it. You know that I gave up so much of my own life to have you. And I don't want you to have to give up your life, not like I had to. I want you to be able to make your decisions on your own terms."

"You mean your terms. You're the one who never sent me to see the old country with Dadu and Mamani. You're the one who kept me from them. So I could be like you and not like them."

"You really feel that way?" Farrah stepped back, stood motionless.

"I do."

"All right, then." Farrah nodded. "Ruin your life. Throw it away. You're still grounded. But do whatever it is you're gonna do. I can't stop you."

And then Sana was left standing in the hallway. The floors creaked and the pipes hissed as she went to her room.

Rachel

Rachel sat at her laptop in the Royce film lab. But she was staring at her phone.

The message was from Sana. *Can't make it to the lab today. Grounded. Will come up with a plan for tomorrow.*

A reprieve. That's what Rachel was being given. An extra day where Sana still wanted to hang out with her. Where Rachel wasn't a pariah to Sana. Because once Sana saw this cut of the film that Rachel was making, Rachel would definitely be a pariah to Sana.

She had one more day. Twenty-four more hours before Sana came by the lab and helped finish up the editing of the project. Rachel had been rewatching the cut before Sana had messaged.

It sucked.

Not, like, it was the worst movie ever. Not even like it was actually bad. Douga would be impressed with this cut. She would be happy that she had been listened to—*obeyed* was the better term, really.

It was just that—this cut of this film, it didn't hold a candle to what the movie could be. This edit was fine. It was solid. It was technically well done. And the acting was good. But the totality of it, the sum of the parts was shitty. It was something you could get anywhere. It was exactly what someone who had seen Rachel's earlier work would assume she would go, if she went down a commercial vein with her films. Rachel wasn't against making commercial films. She was against turning a film that didn't need to be commercial into palatable schlock.

It was easy to digest, this film. A consumable kind of feminist vision. The pretty girl was bad and the quiet girl was good and she had warned them all. But it didn't question why those women had been pitted against each other in the first place.

Rachel had never wanted to make a movie that was easy to swallow. She had wanted to make art. This wasn't art. This was expected. This was going to ruin the only good thing Rachel had ever had going on in her personal life.

A knock sounded at the door.

Rachel started. "Who is it?"

"It's me," said the voice. A male voice. Young.

"Ryan?" Rachel looked up from her laptop.

"Yeah," said Ryan, walking into the room. "Douga gave me a key finally and I thought I'd come in and work on my freshman project, but then I saw your car and I figured you were out here and I didn't want to disturb or anything."

Rachel waved him in, turned back to her computer. "Can't disturb me while I'm editing unless you're gonna ask a hundred questions or you click super loudly with your keyboard shortcuts."

"I promise to do neither." Ryan took a seat two away from Rachel. Nearby, so not like insultingly across the room, but also not directly next to her, which she appreciated.

She stared at the screen for a while longer before she heard a cough.

"You need to talk about it?"

"Didn't you promise to stay silent?" Rachel was starting to see double she'd been staring at the screen in a darkish room for so long.

"You looked stuck. I thought it might help to talk it out."

"I don't need help. I know what I'm supposed to do."

Ryan turned back to his screen in his whirly, twirly chair. He didn't even glance over. *Damn.* Rachel had done that. Had taught people to turn away immediately and instantly and not even press for help. In the early days, it was because she knew if she took a single wrong step she'd be labeled as someone who didn't deserve her spot, as someone who had been given a chance and found wanting. She'd had to figure it all out on her own and she would. But now, that just seemed like the norm. Rachel does it all on her own, even though that wasn't how most people got anything done in the film world.

To be a woman, to be on scholarship, to always be looking over her shoulder had taken so much from Rachel. But this, this was the worst thing it had taken. Because nobody asked if she was okay after the first try. Nobody pushed even a little bit harder to get underneath the surface.

Except for Sana.

Rachel had to avoid that thought. Had to push that idea away for now. Had to keep away the anxiety that pressed against her chest, that stuck to her ribs, when she thought about Sana right now. "Okay, I'm stuck."

Ryan turned again, his expression overeager and excited. "What's wrong?"

"Nothing is *wrong,* per se. But nothing is clicking to be all the way right. I know I'm missing something. I'm not sure what." That was a lie. Rachel *was* sure what was missing. The heart of this goddamned story.

"Have you tried cleaning up from the beginning? The knot is almost always earlier than you think it is. In the story. In anything."

Rachel narrowed her eyes. "That's a fair point."

"It should be; I learned it from you."

"You did?"

"Sure. You're always saying, 'Wait, go back to the beginning,' when we're filming and it stuck. Because you're right. Sometimes you gotta go back to the beginning and see where it all went wrong, you gotta find the turn or the knot that needs to be untangled before you go any further, or you'll be pulling the knot tighter and tighter and making it harder and harder to undo."

"Good advice. Even if it's mine. I guess thanks for listening. Both times. All the times."

"Sure thing, boss," said Ryan with a shrug. He went back to his own project.

Rachel stared at hers. He was right. Or she had been right all along. Maybe she could find a spot earlier in the film to squeeze the newer Helen scenes back in, in the right way. The narration had to go somewhere. Maybe she needed to fix that first thirty minutes, the rough cut that Douga had seen. Maybe she could find a way.

She was in for a long night of it.

24

Putting Baby in a Corner

—————— *Rachel* ——————

Rachel was bleary-eyed. She couldn't stare at another screen ever again. She was sitting in front of her laptop again, except instead of being in the nice film lab with the ergonomic chairs, she was hunched over her laptop like a computer gremlin on her bed. But she'd have to get up and do all of it again tomorrow if she was going to finish this project in time to hand in next week.

She was still trying to solve for Helen of Troy. It was a three-dimensional math problem from filmic hell.

Her phone went off. She went to pick it up when she saw it wasn't her dad calling.

A new inbox notification.

Rachel checked it, expecting nothing. Maybe a camera equipment sale that she couldn't afford. Maybe a price drop on some items she was currently watching on eBay. You could find some good camera equipment that rich people had bought and didn't use for next to nothing on eBay if you knew how to look.

It was a notification from NYU.

Rachel clicked it. *Your financial status has been updated.*

Cool, cool, super cool. Rachel was probably going to vomit on the floors she had cleaned not a couple of weeks ago.

She sat down. She cracked her fingers. She could do this. She would do this. She clicked through the link. She typed in her password.

But she couldn't click through just yet.

The mouse hovered over the log-in button. All she had to do was click it. All she had to do was see her status update and she'd know her future. It was second away—clicks away. But every confident mantra she'd told herself faded away. Revealed itself for the trick that it was. She was just a girl, applying to a school, against the odds.

Because the odds were against everyone, particularly when applying to one of the best film schools in the country. It took talent, yes. It took hard work, yes. It also took luck—luck that Douga had found her work in that program. Luck that she'd applied when the world was looking for filmmakers like her. That admissions counselors were looking for students like her.

Rachel didn't want to click. Didn't want to know if she'd been wrong all that time. If she had pinned all her hopes and dreams on a future that she had only imagined and would never be realized.

Rachel took a deep breath. She thought about what Sana would say. "Come on, Rachel. Let's go. Just do it."

Sana was always saying that. *Come on. Let's go.*

Rachel had to face it eventually. One more deep breath. And she clicked.

She'd gotten it.

Rachel was going to get out of LA for at least the next four years. Study film and art in a city that *cared* about film and art and not only how pretty all the people you cast were and how bankable they were in terms of box office results. Rachel had lived in LA long enough to know the business of film.

NYU had given her enough scholarship money—not something

they were particularly known for. Relief flooded through Rachel, practically from the ends of her hair to the soles of her feet. She'd done it. She'd said she could do it and she'd known she could do it and she'd believed she could do it. And here it was. Proof.

Rachel Consuela Recht had done what she set out to do. She'd gotten into film school and was going to NYU, virtually for free.

Rachel screamed into a pillow so she didn't freak out a neighbor. She needed to release the energy vibrating through her. She got up, went back to her computer, and switched to her editing software. A cold, icy dread unexpectedly wrapped around her stomach.

She had something to lose now. Not just the theory of something. Not just the dream of something. The reality of something that she'd worked toward for years. It was the potential to lose that reality that made the roaring sound in her ears and the whooshing sound of her dreams float away. It was the knowledge that if she screwed up this film, if she didn't get it in on time, Douga could write to NYU. Pull strings. Maybe not pull her admission, but pull the scholarship that Rachel needed in order to be able to work as a PA on a crappy salary those first few years out of school.

Rachel sat down on her bed. She didn't know how any of this was going to turn out okay. She had to choose. Between love and money. Between her future dreams and getting this film out the door.

Rachel closed her laptop.

Fucking Sana.

When Sana walked into the living room, she did not expect her mom to be sitting there, coffee in hand, waiting.

"Good, you're up." Farrah took a sip of her coffee. She was using a mug that said *A WOMAN'S PLACE IS IN THE HOUSE AND SENATE*, which normally Sana loved. Today the mug looked ominous and foreboding.

Mom only used that mug when she needed to face something truly heinous. Mom usually used the mug when she had meetings with producers and people directly from the studios. Except today, Sana had a suspicion that the truly heinous thing was her.

Sana went to the coffee maker. She was going to pour her own mug of coffee if she had to approach Mom while she was in this kind of mood.

Farrah didn't interrupt the coffee-making process either. She just sat there, sipping from her threatening feminist mug, and stared. She was waiting.

Farrah could outwait anyone. She was just like Mamani.

Sana took her mug of coffee and sat on the couch, a foot over from Mom. She angled her body toward her mom and sat upright. She took tiny, slurping sips. Her mug said *Don't Fuck With Me, Fellas* and had a drawing of Joan Crawford on it.

They both sat there, sitting on the cold couch that the sunshine hadn't warmed up yet, facing each other but not looking directly at each other, waiting for the other to speak. The classical music that Farrah put on in the background was tinkling away in the kitchen.

It wasn't soothing.

Farrah opened her laptop. It had been sitting on the coffee table in front of them. She clicked through and opened up a call.

It rang twice before Sana realized the laptop was dialing out to Dadu and Mamani.

"Are you kidding me?" Sana set her coffee down so hard on the table that it sloshed.

"I can't handle you anymore." Farrah calmly took a sip of her coffee.

On the fourth ring—before Sana could respond—Dadu picked up and his face popped up across the screen. "What is it, beti?"

"Hi to you too, Baba." Farrah waved at him, still holding her coffee mug in the other hand.

Mamani picked up next. Her face took up the other half of the screen. "What's wrong, maman-jaan? Che daste gol be âb dâdi? Are you in trouble?"

"You know," said Farrah, a touch of annoyance in her voice, "I'm not always the one that's in trouble."

Mamani snorted. "You're usually the one that throws the flowers into the water."

It was Farrah's turn to angrily set down her mug on the table and slosh coffee. "Don't blame me. Your precious granddaughter hasn't put down her deposit for Princeton. And she only has six days left."

Mamani and Dadu began shouting in unison. Sana couldn't make it out for a minute.

"What is this?"

"Why would you do this?"

"Why are you doing this to us?"

"Log kya kahenge?"

"Yes, what would people think?"

It was an unending barrage and it was, languages aside, difficult to tell who was even saying what. Mamani and Dadu spoke multiple languages each. Mamani with her French and her Farsi, her Bengali and her Urdu. Dadu with his Urdu and his own Bengali and his Arabic.

Sana was done with it all. "I DON'T CARE WHAT PEOPLE THINK."

The voices on the other side of the computer went silent. Mamani and Dadu stared silently from their positions on the screen.

"I don't care what people think," said Sana. "I can't care anymore. I've been caring for so long. I haven't screwed up since I was eight years old. I can't breathe anymore. I can't put down a deposit on my dream school. I don't even know if it *is* my dream school."

"Poti, this is American nonsense. There is no dream school. You go to the best school you get into." Dadu nodded as he spoke.

Mamani tsked and waved her hand like she was pushing the screen away. "Tell her, mama. This idea of dreams is nonsense."

Farrah put her head into her hands. "I don't think dreams are nonsense. I need you to talk sense into her. Not yell at her for her beliefs."

"We can yell at her for her beliefs if her beliefs are wrong!" Dadu's voice warbled and warped through the laptop speakers, so it was less like he was shouting and more like there was static interference with what he was saying.

"You can't make me turn in my deposit!" said Sana.

"We're family. We can send it in for you." Mamani nodded.

"I'm eighteen." Sana was shouting back now, a first for her. She'd never even shouted at her mother before this week and now she was yelling at her grandparents. She'd never felt more like she had entered a circle of hell before than in this moment.

"This is a ridiculous argument, poti." This was Dadu.

Sana clenched her jaw. She was going to go around and around in circles with her grandparents at this rate. They would never see eye to eye on this.

The only bright side was that Farrah had a look on her face like she was regretting this call as much as Sana was. *Good.* At least someone else was suffering alongside Sana.

"Poti, tell me why you can't answer me?" Dadu was looking at Sana.

"This is just a phase," said Mamani so definitively. "Send her here. She can miss a little school. She is already into Princeton. We can help."

This was it, then. This was as close as Sana would ever get to being sent back to the old country for misbehaving. And all she'd done was not put down a deposit. She felt herself starting to dissolve, where the edges of her were starting to disappear, beginning to break into pieces that were ready to fade into the wind and become nothing at all.

"No," said Farrah.

Sana looked at her mom, feeling hope for the first time in the whole conversation.

"I'm not sending her to you. And that's final." Farrah shook her head.

"But, beti—" but neither Sana nor Farrah got to hear the end of whatever Dadu was going to say, because Farrah closed the laptop before he could finish.

Farrah folded over herself for a moment, her head in her hands. Then she sat up, composed herself, found her posture again. She stood up. "You've still got school."

Farrah left the room without looking at Sana.

And that's when Sana knew she'd broken her mother's heart.

25

Nobody Expects the Spanish Inquisition

———— *Rachel* ————

The Santa Anas were blowing today.

Rachel hated admitting she was a romantic about anything, really. But there was something about the Santa Anas. The winds swept through Southern California September through May, but they were the most notable when they could really kick up some dust and destruction during wildfire season. They should have been almost over by now. The rain should have wiped them out entirely. But these were the Santa Anas.

Anything was possible.

There was a knock on the door.

"Yes?" Rachel didn't turn around. This entire project was turning into a nightmare. Her future was a nightmare. She'd gone over from the beginning like Ryan had suggested. Like Ryan had suggested that she had suggested. It made it all worse. Rachel ended up doubling down on Douga's notes. Doubling down on her future in film rather than her precarious future with Sana. They were both leaving for college soon, anyway.

And Sana was maybe leaving for India.

There was that knock at the door again.

Please don't be Sana.

Rachel didn't want Sana to see this version of the film. It was cut so that Helen was back to a two-dimensional, Hollywood-standard beautiful woman. It was exactly the kind of role that had been tossed haphazardly at Rachel's mother. It made Helen of Troy *look like* beautiful garbage. It made the entire film beautiful garbage.

Sana walked in, the door shutting it behind her. "Oh good, you're here. I brought *A Little Romance*."

"Why would you do that?" Rachel didn't turn around. She couldn't face Sana. Not after she'd finished editing this film the way she had.

Hesitation entered Sana's voice, but none of her words faltered when she spoke. "I thought I'd swing by the editing bay and we could watch it. Together."

"I'm editing." But Rachel wasn't, not really. She was adding the final touches. The film was basically done at this point.

"Oh. Can I see it?" Sana's voice came out small and distant.

Rachel turned around and saw Sana standing there, her face twisted in confusion. "I don't know. It's not in a great spot."

Sana's face slanted into a little, subtle frown. Rachel might not have noticed it if she weren't looking for it, but she always seemed to be noticing Sana, looking at her, trying to understand what was going on underneath the surface. Because if the last several days had taught Rachel anything, it was that Sana had an entire reel of subtext going on below the surface. She was like some series of rewrites and postproduction shoots where most people only saw the final, polished picture. The one the studio okayed for the world to see. Rachel preferred the part that hadn't been okayed for release. Not even a director's cut. The rough cut. The raw footage. She wanted to see all of it, know all of it.

The impossible. That's what Rachel wanted. The kind of thing that only happened in movies. The kind of thing that could never happen once Sana saw this cut.

Sana looked over Rachel's shoulder. "Oh! That's my favorite scene."

"Wait!" shouted Rachel.

But she hadn't been quick enough.

Sana reached over Rachel's shoulder and hit the space bar easily. She'd been built for stealth and speed, and despite her injuries, she was still quick.

Rachel watched Sana watch the edited scene.

Sana looked over again, from the screen, a strange light in her eyes. "You changed it."

Sana paused, unsure of what to say next. No, not unsure of *what*—Sana was unsure of *how* to say what she was saying next. Rachel was learning to read Sana like learning to dial in a camera. Rachel needed the right settings, the right lighting, with Sana. But clarity wasn't impossible.

"I did," said Rachel.

"Why did you change it?"

There were so many ways that Rachel could have answered that question. *Because I had to. Because I had no choice. Because there was no other way.* But Rachel knew those were lies. She had a choice. She'd just picked the option that made sure her bright and shining future in film stayed intact. Directors had to make these kinds of choices all the time. "Douga gave me notes. It's stronger this way."

"Is it?" Sana set her hand on the desk, like she needed help propping herself up.

Rachel had to look away. She felt naked and raw and exposed. More naked than she had when they had been alone in that karaoke room.

God, she had to not think about that. She needed, desperately, *not* to think about that. Anything else, really.

"I had to do it." Rachel pointed to the screen. It was the worst subject change in the history of subject changes. But she needed space, to think. It was difficult to breathe right now. Difficult to think. "Douga said I had to."

"Did you?"

Rachel shook her head. "Do you have to keep asking questions? Can't I get a straight response out of you?"

"It doesn't matter, then. That you saw Helen in a new light. All that matters is that in the end it's a better film to go back to your original vision. You see her the same, like you always did."

It did matter. But Rachel didn't dare say that out loud.

"Tragedy is tragedy." Rachel swallowed back the nausea climbing up her throat. *There was no way this could last. She had destroyed it.*

Sana took in a deep breath. "You used me."

Rachel shook her head, like shaking her head would make it true. "I would never use you."

Sana turned, slowly, away from the screen. "I'm having a hard time taking you at your word."

It was like the movie had hushed itself for the conversation. It should have. Maybe that was Rachel's brain fogging out any noise, any additional input, that wasn't Sana's voice, her expression.

"No. I didn't use you. Not intentionally." Rachel really was going to throw up now. She was going to throw up in her own editing bay. Her one sacred space.

"It's okay then if it's not intentionally, isn't it? It's okay to accidentally use people, right? Because if you didn't mean it, if you only accidentally benefit from it, you can maintain the moral high ground. Right?"

Rachel could have screamed into a void. Fallen on her knees in epic fashion with a nice slow-motion shot that circled around her and her frustration, her pain. Instead she felt her voice go cold. "And you would know that better than anyone."

"Excuse me?"

"You take your grandparents' money, even when they hurt your mom. You take the education they provide, and all the strings that go along with it. You're not any different from me. You avoid shit when it's uncomfortable, too."

261

Sana sat up straighter. "Go to hell."

"Learning to swear, I see. What about keeping your good girl mouth unsullied by curse words?" Curse Sana's swishing ponytail and Sana's belief in this project and Sana's big, accusing doe eyes. Everything. All of it. It was life-ruining and it was enraging and Rachel wanted to pick up one of the most expensive pieces of equipment in the lab— probably the data storage—and smash it onto the floor, just to watch something break. To watch destruction in its purest form.

Rachel couldn't take it anymore. She wasn't going to sit around and let Sana get the best of her. To let Sana dump her and let her down gently so everyone knew how sweet and kind she was. Let Sana tell the story so that Rachel became the villain. Rachel was done and she was done right now. "Get out."

Sana shook her head. "Are you kidding me?"

"Get out. Don't come back. I don't want to see you again." There, Rachel had said it. Maybe now the nausea would subside and she could stop paying such close attention to Sana and her expression and her feelings.

But the nausea somehow intensified and Rachel was locked onto Sana's gaze as though she were a camera clicked in for a tracking shot. She had one fixed view and one fixed point and one fixed height and it was all toward Sana.

Sana's eyes were shining. Not in a good way. Not in a bold way, either. In a sad, defeated sort of way. "Don't you dare call me after this, Rachel. Don't you dare follow me either."

But Rachel could only wait a beat before fleeing the premises of the lab herself. She raced outside—luckily in the opposite direction that Sana had gone. She found the first large trash can and retched into it. Rachel spat a couple of times, then wiped her mouth on the back of her hand.

Christ.

As she walked back to the door into the building, a palm front blew across her path.

Fucking Santa Anas.

It was then that Rachel remembered that anything being possible meant that lives could be destroyed, burned all the way down to ash, with a change in the wind.

Sana was lying across the couch.

Sprained ankle. Broken arm. Crushed heart.

She'd gotten there the evening before, and she was still there. She must have gotten up at some point to take off her school clothes. Must have eaten something that her mom put in front of her, but she didn't remember it. *Say Anything* was on the TV; it was some kind of straight romance torture loop.

"Don't you have school?" Farrah walked into the room; she was adjusting her belt and doing her check for phone, keys, wallet before she had to jam out the door.

"Probably," said Sana. Lloyd Dobler was driving around the streets of Seattle with Diane Court. It was the beginning. New love, fresh love. The kind that inspired Sonnet 130. Maybe even 116.

It was doomed.

"Are you going to go to school?" asked Farrah.

"Nope." Sana's pajamas were comfy and the couch was cozy and this movie really was just getting good.

"Are you sick?" asked Farrah.

"Sure." Couldn't Mom leave her alone? Let her sit here by herself in silence. No words. Words were awful; words could hurt. She wanted to watch a nice, doomed, straight romance where everything turned out okay in the end because it was so the opposite of her life. She needed the opposite of her life right now. She needed a reminder that everything with Rachel had ended and Rachel had ended it and Sana had made it final.

Why had she made it final?

Why had Rachel changed the movie? Why had she reverted to the old Helen of Troy?

Why had Sana even bothered?

Maybe Sana ought to have softened her anger. Made it sound more palatable. Made it more pleasing. Less jarring of a sentiment. Girly cheerleader expresses actual displeasure that has nothing to do with her looks. Bring out the tar and feathers, everyone. Not that she was really a cheerleader anymore either. Only in title.

Sana looked up. Farrah was still giving Sana a long hard stare. Sana went back to looking at the TV.

Oh look, Diane Court, perfect genius, worried she'd done something wrong with Lloyd.

Diane Court would never do anything wrong. She was practically perfect in every particular. Like a Mary Poppins built for young straight male masturbatory fantasies. Fine, her own occasional masturbatory fantasies as well, but she was definitively not who executives had thought about when casting Ione Skye in films.

"Okay. You don't look great. I'm going to call the office and say you're sick."

"Great." *Lock the door on your way out and never come back.*

Sana looked up. Farrah was still standing there, worry coating her face.

"Go." Sana mustered a pathetic cough. "I'll be fine by evening."

But when evening rolled around and Farrah returned home from a day of day shooting—she'd been off night shoots since that fateful evening she'd caught Sana coming back home at one in the morning—Sana was in the exact same position.

"Have you moved?" asked Farrah.

"Sure," said Sana. "I've had to get up and pee."

"Did you eat?"

Sana tilted her head. "Possibly."

She wasn't hungry in any case. Who needed food when you had Lloyd Dobler, driving around, trying to find himself after the loss of Diane Court. Turned out, Diane Court could make a mistake. It was listening to her dirtbag dad. Sana really connected with Diane in that moment.

"You wanna talk about it?"

"Nope." Sana got out her phone to double reinforce her point.

That's when she saw the email notification. Maybe it was Rachel, apologizing. Begging to have Sana come back. Sana wouldn't respond to begging. She didn't want to be begged back.

Not one bit.

But the email wasn't from Rachel at all. It was an application status update from Princeton. Sana clicked on it, her fingers moving beyond her will at the moment. Now was not the time to check this kind of life-altering status update, but Sana couldn't help herself. She was logging in before she'd realized she'd done it. Her password was more muscle memory than thought.

Four days left.

All she had to do was turn in a deposit. The money wasn't even hers, as Rachel had so wonderfully reminded her.

So why did Sana feel a cold pit in the depths of her stomach? Why did the hole that had formed the night before when Rachel told her to get out feel like it was growing larger and larger, threatening to swallow Sana whole?

Sana burrowed deeper under the blankets. Just one more rewatch. She needed one more rewatch of *Say Anything* and she'd finally feel okay again.

26

Like Everybody Else

 Sana

Sana hadn't meant to start crying. She'd reached the end of *But I'm a Cheerleader* and Natasha Lyonne had started cheering and then Clea DuVall decided to stand up to her parents and run away from their horrible nonsense. It was so unreal, so untrue. Nobody stood up like that in real life. They were too scared, too afraid of what the world would think of them. Too busy conforming so they could climb their way to the top. Dadu wasn't going to stand up for her. Mamani wouldn't either. Mom had sold her out, then stood back up for her, but Sana was still upset from the selling out part. And Rachel certainly hadn't stood up with her like that and Rachel was so fearless and bold and mouthy and didn't take crap from anyone but even she was too afraid to be in love.

In love.

That's what Sana was. She was in love and heartbroken and crying over an unrealistically happy ending in a movie. She felt like Elle Woods shouting "liar" at the soap opera in the middle of *Legally Blonde*. If only she had a bunch of chocolate to throw at the screen.

Stupid girls with their stupid artistic vulnerability and their big eyes and crunchy curls and their witty thoughts and brilliant movies. Sana kept crying; it was easier than getting up. She let the movie roll to credits until it rolled into the main menu and Sana selected enter again on the play movie button.

Why not? It was way simpler than finding another movie. This one *spoke* to her. This one knew her. It was a good friend and old friend and even if it was lying at the end, everything else it told was the truth.

Sana checked her phone. It was afternoon again. She had several message notifications from Diesel. And four missed calls. At some point last night she must have fallen asleep. Maybe she'd fallen asleep this morning. She hadn't seen her mom head out. She'd woken up to the sound of the *Say Anything* menu playing on a loop. She got up, peed, changed the movie over, then flopped back down on the couch. She was basically functioning fine at this point. Sure, she wasn't sure when she had last showered and she had been in the same pajamas for over thirty-six hours. They were comfy pajamas. They had polar bears on them. Who would want to take off flannel polar bear pajamas?

Not Sana, that was for sure.

Sana flipped and scrolled through her phone, seeing if she had any messages anywhere. None. Not really. Rachel hadn't suddenly changed her mind. That email still sat in her inbox.

Update: Your Deposit to Princeton

There it was. That bright and shining future she had planned so much for, sacrificed so much for. It was there and waiting and available to her. It was fading away from her. In four days it would be gone.

Sana might have to get up and vomit.

She had spent so much time wanting a thing she ought to, worried that she would never get it, nearly not getting it, that she hadn't thought about what it would mean to have the thing itself. She was the hardworking granddaughter of an immigrant finally allowed into the sacred spaces that lead to big, bright shining opportunities. She was the daughter of a woman who had gotten pregnant accidentally and also too young in the eyes of the world. A woman who was meant to fail and was set up to fail from the very beginning. But Farrah hadn't failed and Dadu hadn't failed and neither had Sana.

Why didn't it feel better?

Why didn't she get the soothing balm of acceptance the way she had always thought she would, the way everyone else seemed to? Sana tossed her phone away. It landed with a moderate-enough-sounding thud that she didn't need to worry about it potentially breaking or cracking.

That's when Farrah walked into the living room, concern in her voice. "Is everything okay?"

"I thought you were at work." Sana didn't look up from the TV.

"I heard a loud noise, is everything okay?" Farrah put her hand on her hips, assessing.

"Yeah, it's fine."

"What was the noise?"

"Probably my phone."

Farrah stared at Sana. Sana didn't look up, but she could feel her mother's gaze through the back of her head. Sana heard steps, then she felt her phone being dropped back into her lap. Farrah had a grim look on her face, but she didn't say anything. She got out her phone and began dialing. Sana couldn't really hear either call she made. Probably for work. During the first one Farrah left a message about call times, and the second one was a tense, short conversation that Sana couldn't make out at all.

Farrah came back into the room. "It's two o'clock now. I'm going into work. I need you to try and get into the shower while I'm gone. Can you do that for me?"

"Sure," said Sana.

Farrah clearly didn't believe her. She perched on the edge of the couch. "What's wrong?"

"I got into Princeton." Sana could hear the monotone quality to her voice.

"Honey. I know about that." The concern in Farrah's was also evident. "I don't understand why you won't put down the deposit. You've been working for that your whole life."

"I have. It's great." Sana paused the movie for a moment, looking over to get Farrah to believe her.

"You sound like you're going to a funeral."

"Mom. Just leave me alone." Sana hit play again.

"I have to go to work," said Farrah regretfully. "But you won't be alone for long, okay?"

"Sure." What did it matter. What did anything matter. She was going to sit here and watch TV until the end of days.

Reluctantly, Farrah got up off the couch. She smoothed her clothes and went out the door. It was about five minutes later when keys jangled in the door and it opened again.

"Mom, seriously, what did you forget?" said Sana from the couch. She looked up for a moment. "Oh, it's you."

Massoud raised an eyebrow. "You been watching this all day?"

"I've interspersed it with *Pakeezah*." *That was a lie.*

"You and that movie, I've never understood."

"Wouldn't expect you to." Sana sniffed.

Massoud reached down and plucked the remote off of the blanket. He turned the TV off.

"I was watching that!"

"I'm sure you were," he said.

"You gonna say why you're here?"

"Your mom called me. Told me she was worried about you. Now I can see why."

"Oh great, now you're worried about me. After all this time I'm supposed to believe you care so much."

"I know you hate to hear this, kid, but you've got me in you whether you want it or not."

"Don't remind me." Sana turned away from him and gave him a great view of her back.

"Spit it out."

"I don't spit. Gross."

"Come on, what's up?"

"I told Mom. Everything is great." Sana was hoping that would be the end of it. That would be the final thing and he would say some platitude about hard work and ambition and then she would be free to watch the movie on her new favorite torture loop. But then she went and betrayed herself. "Still haven't put down my deposit for Princeton. Still don't know if I've gotten into my fellowship in India. I'm in a movie where I play a dumb, beautiful airhead. Oh, and I got dumped."

"Ah." Massoud took a seat on the edge of the couch.

Sana's eye snapped toward him. "You know all about being dumped, then?"

"You don't want what you thought you did, do you?"

Sana gasped. "I hate you."

Massoud raised an eyebrow and said nothing for a long moment. Sana wanted to fight. Wanted to fight him. But the look on Massoud's face—like he understood. Like he knew what she was going through. Knew it exactly, knew it intimately.

Sana gave in. She didn't want to. But she needed to. "It was my dream. My dream for so long. For as long as I can remember it's always been right in front of me. I don't understand why I'm not happy."

"Well, being dumped is always shitty," said Massoud, like he was the wisest of the wise men. "And dreams can change, Sana. Even if ambitions don't."

Sana snorted.

"Look. I gave up on me and your mom. I had to prove I had my life together, prove I could live up to the sacrifices my parents had made. The sacrifices your mother made."

Sana couldn't look away from him now.

"But I lost your mom. I lost you. And I don't blame you for it. I couldn't. I would be twice, maybe even three times as angry at me as you are, if my dad did what I had done. But I threw myself into the one thing I knew I could do, the one path I knew I could follow. I couldn't ask myself any hard questions because I already felt like I was drowning in hard problems. I focused on what I knew I would look good to everyone else. I focused on being impressive." Massoud paused. "But I lost you. I lost something that was so precious. I took it for granted that if I put it down, it would be right back there again when I was ready to pick it up. And it wasn't."

"So." Sana crossed her arms. She didn't want to hear this, wasn't willing to hear this.

"So, I'm here now, kid. I'm showing up and I'm gonna keep showing up even if you never forgive me. I knew you hadn't put down the deposit and I didn't want you to be alone with that. But don't follow in my footsteps on this one. You can listen to that voice inside you. You don't have to keep going because you think you locked yourself into a decision so long ago and now you can't change your mind."

"But I'm not like you. I still want to go to Princeton," Sana said stubbornly. "I still want to be a surgeon."

"Okay. But is there anything else you want more?"

And for once, Sana had been asked a question she honestly didn't know the answer to.

Rachel

Rachel stared at the loop she was editing. She wasn't sure what she was seeing. It went over and over again. Sana, saying her line. It just

271

sounded like garbage at this point. Could have been Latvian or Afrikaans. Didn't matter. Sana's sorrow was evident on her face. It was in her expression, in her eyes, in the slant of her mouth.

Just like Sana's face when she'd seen the movie. When Rachel had dumped her.

Was it dumping if you were never going out in the first place?

During filming, Rachel thought Helen of Troy was an act. Sana, the excellent actress. But it looked the same as Sana's punched-in-the-gut face. Like Sana was a girl who knew bone-deep sadness and wasn't just acting. She was channeling it out. Telling the world in art what she couldn't tell anyone with words.

What was she hiding from?

The easy answer, the obvious answer, was her sexuality. But it wasn't that. Rachel knew Sana well enough. It wasn't anything so simple. Anything so neat and clean that belonged in a movie designed to make straight people cry on behalf of a gay girl. It was beyond any one thing. Sana was hiding because she was a girl. Because she was ambitious. Because there was power and fire inside of her and it only came out through the cracks.

Cracks that Rachel had decided to seal up rather than see.

Note to self: Break up with lead actor after editing a film rather than before.

Death by Sana's perfect face. That's when Rachel's phone had the decency to ring. Hopefully it was Papa, with a story about his latest client.

If only. She didn't recognize the number.

Rachel turned her phone over, clicked the button to make the ringing stop, without actually declining the call. She was going to get back to editing. She was going to figure out how to sculpt this scene—because it was the last one left—without thinking about Sana too much, even though all of the shots revolved around Sana in one way or another. Every shot reminding Rachel of the direction she'd decided to go with her film.

There was so much drama, all across Sana's face. She'd taken a side character and made her tragic, full of depth. She wasn't only the first nonwhite Helen of Troy that Rachel had seen. She was the first empathetic one.

And Rachel had destroyed it. Sacrificed something good, something profound on the altar of getting ahead in her career.

Rachel's phone dinged. A message. No, a *voice message*. Leave it to an old person to leave a message on her answering machine.

Rachel ignored it.

She wouldn't think about the message. She wouldn't think about Sana and her emotional depths. This was a two-dimensional space that Sana had been confined to. It was a flat square of screen. Rachel could sculpt and edit it into the shape she wanted. Rachel was in charge here. She was the god of this world. She wasn't going to be distracted.

She checked her phone again. The message wouldn't properly transcribe. It was every other word, and some of them didn't quite make sense. *Set* was a word. So was *parking structure* and *rhinoceros*. The rhinoceros was clearly a mistranslation. Also, there was a *hey, is Sarah* but Rachel didn't know a Sarah who would currently be calling her. Sarah, in the message transcription, was a girl named Tina's mom. Rachel was filling in the blanks, trying to chart a course through the language, figure out without listening what probably-not-Sarah had been trying to say.

Dammit.

Might as well listen to the message, having wasted so much time trying to decipher the inaccurate transliteration.

Hey. This is Farrah, Sana's mom. I've been working with Ida Begum and I thought you'd be interested in seeing some shoots. Today would be a good day to go onto set. Only four hours of shoots. Call time is four. Don't park on the studio's parking structure; go to the lot on the west end, I can validate the parking there. We're not doing too much green screen today, just a lot of practical shots and

273

some stunts, which I thought you might enjoy watching the process for. I assume
you haven't gotten too much experience with practical stunts. See you at four. Call
if you have an issues parking.

A pit welled up in Rachel's stomach. She did her best to ignore it. She had to finish editing. Had to get this project over the line. But her eyes became unfocused, fuzzy, and she couldn't see what she was looking at anymore. Not her project, not Sana's face. Not even the phone in her hand.

How had Sana not told her mom that they had broken up.

Rachel blinked a few times, trying to get her vision to clear back up. And if a couple of trails of moisture fell down her cheeks while she did so, that wasn't unusual. She often got dry eyes when she was working in the editing bay, and she'd been staring at her screen for hours at this point. She really needed a break. Away from her screen. She checked the time. It was two thirty now. Filming was at a lot in the valley. It would take at least an hour to get there, plus time for parking. If she left right now, she'd be able to make it on time. She'd be able to see a real female director in action with a real budget on a real set.

Rachel had had pride, it was true, but her pride always took a back seat to her ambitions. That she was about to hang out on set with Sana's mom on false pretenses, well, that was something Rachel was going to have to swallow down for the sake of her ambitions.

It was worse than swallowing her pride.

Rachel drove until she was close enough to be able to follow the bright yellow filming signs for the movie. It was easy enough to reach where the security stood. Farrah was waiting for Rachel there.

It should have been easy, to lie to Farrah, or at least slide through by omission, and keep her in the dark for an afternoon for the chance to watch Ida Begum at work.

But once Rachel got a look at Farrah full in the face, she blurted, "I dumped your daughter."

It was the eyes. She had Sana's eyes. Like she'd be exposed one way or another so she better get it out of the way right now.

Farrah didn't smile, but the side of her mouth twitched upward. "I know."

"You *know*?" Rachel was aghast. Had she been invited to set for some sort of public humiliation?

Would she ever in her life not have that be her first thought?

"Then why am I here?"

"Because I thought you'd like to see a woman directing a big-budget production." Farrah walked across the threshold, waving Rachel through, and the security guard let them pass without incident.

"But."

"But what? Don't you want to see a real movie being made?"

"More than anything." Again with the confession. Again with the raw, naked exposed feeling. *What was with the women of this family?*

"So why are you sabotaging yourself?" Keen, observant eyes looked at Rachel for a moment, then darted back to a clipboard. Farrah said something into her mic, then clicked off comms.

"I'm not sabotaging myself."

"Yes, you are. You want me to kick you off of set before you even get on for breaking my daughter's heart. Sure. I could kick your ass for what she's like right now. She's a train wreck who hasn't showered in two days. But sometimes people come into your life and they kick you in the ass and make you take steps to become the best version of yourself. I thought I'd see you for myself."

"You curse" was all Rachel could say in response.

Farrah laughed. "Yeah, me and my kid. We're nothing alike. We're everything alike. Mothers and daughters."

"I wouldn't know," said Rachel, looking down.

Farrah studied her for a moment. Like she was contemplating something. Like she needed to see something in Rachel's face before she came to a decision. "Look."

Rachel looked up, because Farrah would maintain her silence until Rachel did. They stood there, toe to toe and eye to eye in the middle of a set that was bustling all around them.

"You will get shit you don't deserve. Sometimes because you're dating the right person. Other times, because people have suddenly decided you matter. A lot of women were stomped on, and as that starts to shift, you'll get opportunities—ones that didn't exist before—because you are a woman. There are so few women who make it to the top that when someone offers you a chance, a chance with little to no strings attached, you take it. Do you understand?"

"Yes," said Rachel.

Farrah looked sad. Those keen eyes. No wonder Sana looked like she could see your secrets. Farrah had the same assessing look. Like they had had to learn to read people in order to survive. Like they'd had to learn to look into the devil's own soul just to survive.

Farrah nodded. "But come on. Bask in an opportunity you're getting right now. Come and meet Ida."

Rachel felt her eyes basically fall out of her head. Bug out. "Are you kidding?"

"I never kid, kid." And Farrah walked off, with Rachel trailing behind her, hopeful, cautious, and skeptical all at once.

27

Wipe That Face Off Your Head

Rachel

Rachel couldn't believe it, couldn't fathom it. Ida Begum had said hello, asked her sincere questions about what Rachel wanted to do in film. Sure, they had been interrupted a few times. She'd had to make some actual directorial decisions while they were talking. But when her attention had been on Rachel, it had been the full force of it.

Rachel was in awe of that single-minded focus; she knew she wanted to emulate it on her own set, in her own life. Focus on what was important; focus on what was in front of her. Not get distracted by the noise. Ida didn't. If it was important, she turned her attention to it. If not, she let the set handle itself. Ida was in charge, in control, but not controlling.

It was so different than Rachel had been. It was so different than Douga was being.

Rachel had been inspired; she went straight to the Royce campus. Inspired to fix what she had broken. With her film, with Sana. With everything. She was going to go into the lab and she was going to figure this all out. She was going to sit in the editing bay until she had an answer. She wasn't going to move, even if she had to be there all night. As long as she gave her dad a call and let him know, she'd be fine.

She'd get this film project done and she'd figure out how to do it on her own terms.

On the terms she'd promised Sana.

That's when she collided into a force moving directly into her.

Diesel's arms were outstretched. "Dude, are you okay?"

Rachel shook off her disorientation. "What the hell are you talking about?"

"I mean I was standing there the whole time," Diesel said. "Are you okay?"

"Not really, no." Rachel stared.

The whole hallway was behind her and she was worried they were starting to draw a crowd. Nobody could figure out why the water polo god and the film nerd were just hanging out and chatting in the middle of the lockers.

"What's going on? Is it something with you and Sana?"

"Why do you ask that?" Rachel was posturing, and they both knew it.

"There's no way Sana's sick. She never gets sick. She gets injured hanging around you, but never sick," Diesel said.

"So automatically it's my fault?" It was Rachel's fault, but she didn't need to confess that to Diesel of all people.

"Dude." Diesel reached an arm out.

That's when Rachel started pushing. "You have always had it out for me. Always think I'm not good enough. Always think I'm the bad person. Always think the poor scholarship girl is the one who's gonna crush your friend's heart."

Diesel took hold of Rachel's hand. "That's not it at all. Deep breaths. Take a deep breath."

Rachel screamed this one. "Go the hell away."

Diesel went very, very still. So, too, did Rachel.

Diesel was big and tall and strapping and he looked horrified that he'd gotten that reaction—his eyes were wide and his whole face looked taut and slightly pulled back. There was a thread of tension, of fear in him. He clasped his hands together behind his back. He was frozen by shock to his spot, but soon he'd probably flee the sight of Rachel. Run fast and far and away from her just like everyone eventually would.

Rachel began to laugh. She was in the process of scaring away a giant of a boy. She knew she was intimidating. Her role on set had confirmed that for her again and again. But those were people in the arts. This boy was so controlled and athletic and had the looks like he could break most people in two. Then Rachel's laughter went over an edge, changed into something else altogether.

"Oh no. Don't cry, goddammit," said Diesel.

But Rachel couldn't help it. She would have stopped had she any control over the expression of feeling. One minute she had been all energy, all fight. Now she was practically unable to hold herself up. "I screwed up. I screwed up so bad."

Diesel sighed. "Big-time. You screwed up big-time."

Rachel snuffled, collapsed to the floor. "I screwed up hard."

Diesel let go of his two hands that had been still grasped together. Rachel expected Diesel to leave then, to get up and move along with his life. But instead, Diesel sat down, scooted closer next to Rachel, put his arm around her, and cradled Rachel's head to her shoulder.

Rachel could only cry harder. "I cut the film so she looks like a terrible Helen of Troy. The worst. The kind you'd see in a big action movie from the nineties. She's so much better than that. I made her look like that and I went back on our deal and then I was terrified she'd hate me forever."

"You broke her heart before she could break yours."

Rachel nodded. "I did."

"You idiot." There was kindness in Diesel's voice. Real, honest-to-God kindness. "That sounds like something I would do."

"It does?" Rachel sniffed.

Diesel nodded. "It does."

"Does it always have to be this way? Do feelings always clash with ambition?" Rachel took a breath, trying to steady herself.

"God, I hope not. I don't know, but I hope we can have both. Maybe not everything, but at least both." Diesel exhaled. He looked at Rachel. "I hope we can all figure out how to live a good story."

"I have literally never thought that," said Rachel. "And I want to make movies for a living when I grow up."

Diesel laughed at that. "Are you hungry?"

"What?" Rachel startled, looked up.

"Are you hungry? Because I'm starving." Diesel raised his eyebrow into a question.

Rachel really hoped that this wasn't some kind of elaborate joke. "I could eat."

"Then come on, asshole. We're getting Thai food."

Sana

Sana had finally managed to put on some pants.

She hadn't listened to Massoud's pep talk, not really. But for some reason she'd felt like taking off the polar bear pajamas after he'd left. He had tried to coax her into dinner. She had wanted to be alone. But after he left, she'd kind of wished she was around people. So maybe she'd ought to take off the polar bear jammies and put on some real clothes. That had been her line of reasoning, anyway.

Leggings. She hadn't been emotionally ready enough for jeans. But leggings, which weren't really pants, but were soft and cozy and the kinds of non-pant pants you could go out in, those would do for now. After she'd put those on, she figured she might as well put on a T-shirt that didn't smell either. She wasn't quite ready for a shower, but a fresh T-shirt and a fresh swipe of deodorant did wonders for a girl's mind.

And her appetite.

Sana was starving. She walked outside and the sun was going down. One of those majestic but everyday kind of LA sunsets. Pinks streaking across a bright orange sky. It was, truly, the magic hour.

Sana got out her phone. She figured that taking a ride to grab some food constituted an emergency. That's what Mom had always said. *Don't take one of those rides unless it's an emergency.* Sana wasn't sure of the last time she'd eaten. Seemed like an emergency. Even the app button was the same pink color of the sunset. It felt right. She'd get some Thai food at her favorite place. She'd ride through the streets of LA during sunset. The breeze would be pleasant and she'd get some sunlight without it being too harsh, too bright for her mood.

Your driver, Daniel, will be here shortly.

Sana didn't need the friendly text reminder. She was already standing, waiting outside. Soaking in the fading light and breathing in the fresh air.

Her driver pulled up in a silver sedan that wasn't quite new, but it was immaculately clean. She hopped in the back seat.

"Hi there, Sana?"

"Yup," said Sana. "Daniel?"

"You bet," he responded. "Headed to Echo Park?"

"Yup," she said as the car started back in motion again.

"How are you tonight?"

There was something about being in a car with a total stranger that gave Sana the impulse to tell the truth. "Terrible."

"Terrible?" he said. "What's so terrible?"

I just got dumped by the first girl I ever loved seemed like a good answer. But it was more than that. "I don't know what I want."

Daniel laughed. "I hate to break this to you, but nobody knows what they want."

Sana laughed right back. The sound was strange on her throat and foreign to her own ears. A creaky sort of laugh. "So I keep faking it forever until I die?"

"No," he said, his voice serious. "Don't fake it. Just don't make everything mean, well, *everything.*"

"I don't understand."

"I got dumped a while ago," said Daniel. "My wife left me and I had a kid to raise all on my own."

"I'm sorry." Sana didn't know what else to say.

"Thanks, but that's not my point. My point is, I cracked. I drank because I was terrified of what it meant. What it meant to be alone. To be the kind of husband you leave. To be the kind of person left behind. To have to be a single parent, a single dad. I was terrified of all of it. And I ran as far away as I could while staying in the same place. I didn't have much family, but I pushed away my kid. I pushed away my community. I shut it all out."

Sana took a sharp inhale. "How did you stop?"

"Lotta reasons. They say the opposite of addiction is connection. I read it in an article somewhere. Signed up to drive right then. Decided I couldn't drive while I drank and somehow I stuck to that. Not everyone can, you know. I still don't know how I did. And then I talked to people, felt less alone, felt more useful. But I also stopped trying to make everything mean something. Life happens. Symbolism is for poets and artists. For people like my kid—she's gonna be a filmmaker. The rest of us, we can just live, you know? We can just do what needs to be done."

"Yeah," said Sana, her mind in a frenzy. "Sounds nice."

That made Daniel laugh. "It's definitely nicer than the alternative."

They sat in companionable silence the rest of the way to the Thai restaurant.

Sana wish Daniel a good night as she slid out of the back seat and he drove off into the sunset.

A bell rang as Sana walked into the restaurant. The outside was the kind of bright and shining turquoise blue. The walls were white with brown beams interspersed, and brown paneled entryways and doorways. There were old movie posters for *Return of the Jedi* and *Raiders of the Lost Ark* on the walls, but in Thai. The tables were dark wood and the floor was a nice slate tile. The chairs didn't all match but they were made all the same shade. It was the kind of Thai restaurant where ordering a dish with medium spice level still meant Sana needed a tall drink of water and Thai iced tea in order to really enjoy it. Sana recognized the hostess. She was the one who worked most weeknights.

"Your friend just left."

"My friend?" asked Sana, a little bewildered.

"He came in without you. The tall one who looks like Thor from the movies. I was surprised you weren't with him. He came with another girl. Big curly hair. Dodgers hat. They ate your usual: chicken satay, coconut mango salad, tom kha kai soup, lad na, green curry. Same order, same boy, but without you." The hostess's gaze grew watchful. "But now, here you are."

"I was sick," said Sana rather lamely.

The hostess gave her a skeptical look. "Just one?"

"Just one," said Sana.

She sat down, didn't look at the menu. She ordered the usual, even though it was way too much food for one person. Her mom would eat the leftovers. Sana worked her way across the dishes, thinking about what the hell Diesel was doing here having dinner with Rachel Recht.

Sana got out her phone, began a mindless scroll through it. She didn't want to touch her feed right now. Was afraid of what she'd search, what she'd go looking for. Anything attached to Rachel. Anything attached to filming.

Email seemed safe. Seemed like a place she couldn't get into too much trouble.

But Sana forgot she'd been emailing with Rachel, too. She found herself scrolling through message threads. Seeing if there were any signs, any hints, of the changes in the film to come. Any hesitations on Rachel's part that Sana hadn't picked up on.

There was nothing there.

No signs to read. No extra attention Sana could have paid. No more perfect way to have dealt with working with Rachel and falling in love with her and trusting her. Sana couldn't quite tell if she wished there had been or if she wished there hadn't. If she'd wanted to know that the signs had all been there and she'd missed them.

It didn't matter, really, when the result was that she was sitting here eating Thai food alone while her ex-whatever went out with one of her best friends and neither one of them bothered to tell her.

She put her email away. It wasn't doing her any good, looking for a paper trail of evidence against Rachel. Or a paper trail of evidence against Sana's own judgment. It was just breaking her heart even more that Rachel had followed through on so much of what Sana had believed in, but had changed the direction of the film in the eleventh hour.

But Sana caught sight of one of her unread emails. It was from the fellowship foundation. She decided to click it, because she was a masochist and she just wanted to get all of her emotional torture over with in one moment, so she could go back to her delicious curry noodles.

Except she'd gotten in.

It was all there, the *Dear Ms. Khan, We are pleased to inform you* and everything. Sana clicked out of it and then clicked back in, just to be sure. Just to know it didn't change after opening it again.

Nope, there it was. She'd gotten in. She'd gotten in despite—or maybe because of—her interview.

The only problem now was, Sana had to break the news to Dadu. And Mom.

April 28

3 Days Until Deadline

28

Whole New World

—— *Sana* ——

Sana woke up and took a shower the next morning. She got dressed and slicked back her hair into her usual ponytail. She put on a little highlighter on her cheekbones, along her brow bone. She slid gloss along her lips. She looked like herself, like she always looked. The way she'd taught herself to be presentable, honed through years of experience, and subtle input, and online videos. But it didn't feel the same. Didn't carry the weight. It was an aesthetic. The way she liked to look. Maybe one day she'd change it.

I don't have to make everything significant all the time. I can just do what needs to be done.

She could understand that the world was unfair to girls. That her family held her to a higher standard. That people watched her, looking for her to make a mistake that would define her. That was all true. All real.

But she didn't have to believe it. Not anymore.

She headed downstairs. Mom jumped when she saw Sana.

"You startled me," said Farrah.

"Shouldn't I have startled you two days ago?"

"No, you scared the living shit out of me the past two days. You looking normal again startled me, that's all."

"I have to tell you something."

"I'll bet you do," said Mom, taking a sip from her mug of coffee.

"You should sit down."

Mom sat.

"I applied to a medical fellowship. And I got in."

Mom looked startled, her head tilted and her eyes bright. "But that's wonderful!"

"It's in India."

"Oh, Sana," said Mom. "I think you better start at the beginning."

And so Sana told her about her doubts about being a doctor and applying for the fellowship. Told Mom that she had been honest in the interview and that she thought they would disqualify her for it. Sana confessed she hadn't meant to not tell Farrah, but it had become the greatest and worst secret she'd ever kept.

"But you could do a fellowship here?" Mom stared at Sana.

Sana knew what her mom meant. Knew it was the kind of thing people said when they meant to help. Why go somewhere else when you could get something similar here? But it wasn't enough for Sana. Not anymore. "Mom. I want to go."

"Oh." That was all Mom had to say about that. Just *oh*.

But Sana wouldn't be deterred like this. She hadn't taken the time to get her mom to adjust to the idea. She got why she wasn't jumping for joy now. "Also, I need to borrow your car."

"You're joking, right?"

"No," said Sana. Mom had a rental for now. She still hadn't found a new, reliable car to purchase. "I need to borrow the car and drive down to Orange County. I need to talk to Dadu. And I can't do it over the phone."

"Does he know you're coming?"

"No," said Sana. "But I'm willing to wait until he can see me."

Farrah opened her mouth, then closed it.

"I'm sorry, Mom."

"Sorry for what?" Farrah looked wary. She leaned away and her eyebrows came together, forming a line in between them.

"For treating you like you were a failure. I've never thought you were a failure. I always wanted to be like you. I wanted to be like Dadu, too. You both took the nothing you were given and you made so much of yourselves. You did it despite everyone saying you couldn't."

"Baby, don't try to be like me. Don't ever try to be like anyone. Be like yourself. That's enough, trust me. We did that because we had to. We didn't have another choice. You do. I swear to you, you do." Farrah put down her cup of coffee on the counter and she gently grabbed both of Sana's shoulders. "Do you understand?"

Sana sniffed. "Yeah."

"Good. And here." Farrah handed Sana a cup of coffee. "Drink this."

Sana took the cup of coffee out of her mom's hands. It was black and warm and bitter and it soothed and jolted its way through Sana's system.

Farrah went to the counter and grabbed her keys. She put them into Sana's hand. "You are back to school tomorrow, correct?"

"Correct," said Sana. "I'm sorry. I really am. I appreciate this, you know?"

"Yeah, well, remember everything you said to Baba word-for-word because that is the way you show gratitude in this house." Farrah sniffed into her cup of coffee.

Sana leaned over and gave her mom a kiss on the cheek. "Love you."

"Love you, too," said Farrah. "Now go give your Dadu hell for me. It's the least you can do."

Sana laughed, still not quite used to the sensation anymore after a couple days of staring blankly on the couch. She took the keys and she was out the door.

There wasn't any traffic at this time of the day, which was a solid relief. It was miles and miles of highway for a little over ninety minutes until Sana got to the exit she needed. It was a soothing, sunny drive. She gave her name at the gate to the guard the way she and her mother always did, and the man waved her through without incident.

The air was cooler than it had been yesterday, but it wasn't really cold. As she parked and got out of the car, the wind whipped through her ponytail. It was the Santa Anas again. Probably come to tell her she was wreaking havoc on her own life, the way they had warned her before she'd gone into the editing bay four days ago. But Sana wasn't going to be warned off by wind. She would do what she meant to do, what she came here to do, and live with the consequences.

Sana rang the doorbell twice. She was surprised when Mamani opened the door.

"What is this? Don't you have school?"

Sana nodded. "I came to see you."

A smile twitched at Mamani's pursed lips. She didn't like skipping school. But she loved being thought of. "You're here now; let's make you a pot of tea."

"I did also come to talk to Dadu."

"Ah, there it is. I have all you girls and I am second to all of them."

Sana was never sure what to say when Mamani said things like that.

"He's out right now, but he'll be back," said Mamani. "Tea."

"Yes," said Sana. "Definitely tea. Do you need any help?"

Mamani made a tsking noise. She bustled around the kitchen, getting the tea, and getting the right container and the right pot and simmering the leaves in a double boiler for long enough and dropping in the cardamom at the right moment. It always looked like an art, from where Sana stood. From another perspective, Mamani was just throwing it all in as she got it out. But to Sana, it was a dance around the kitchen—a hospitality waltz. Eventually the tea was done and the kitchen was—for the briefest of moments—a little warmer and a little more humid than it had been minutes before.

Mamani carried the tea on a tray into the living room. There was space in the kitchen to drink it but Mamani liked to do things right and proper. She set the tray down on the large coffee table and settled herself into the white couch. She poured the tea out of a glass pot—probably from that fancy French tea store she liked to buy her tea from sometimes—and into the little demitasse cups. Mamani didn't get out the samovar for just two people.

"What are you come to talk to Dadu about?" Mamani handed Sana a cup.

The demitasse rattled against its saucer in Sana's hand. "School."

Mamani reached out to the tray, took the tongs, and dropped two cubes of sugar into her glass she had broken the habit of popping the sugar cubes in her mouth to drink long ago. Instead, she stirred her tea properly—wafting the spoon back and forth in the cup without making a sound. "When I married you grandfather, they told me I would pay. They waited, you know. It was insane to them, the choice I made. To marry for love over duty. They meant well. We were all in a new place, with new rules. They wanted something safe, I think. But still, they waited for me to fail, for your grandfather to fail. But he succeeded in ways they could never imagine. Later, they decided your mother was my failing and my punishment. They said it over and over again, trying to make it true. That was what happened when you let women make those kinds of decisions, they said."

"It's not fair." Sana took a sip of her tea.

Mamani reached out her hand to touch Sana's cheek. "No. But your mother was always a joy to me, just as you are to her, to us all. You are not her scandal. She is not my punishment. Only people who want to control you would say such things. Because they are scared.

Scared of themselves. Too scared to try for what they want. I do not regret my life. Life comes too fast. It can change in a moment. It rolls and crests like a vast ocean. If you want to live as you wish, you *will* be a scandal. But you will also be free. If you wish to be free of criticism, the world will place other bonds on you. That is the great trade-off. The great choice. Scandal comes with freedom. Freedom comes with scandal. They go one hand in the other. You never get them alone."

"Nobody should have to make that choice, Mamani."

Mamani shrugged. It was an old gesture. Handed down through the generations. The shrug of survival. "What should be and what is are two very different things."

"Then believe me. I want to bring them a little closer together. Just a little bit."

When Mamani smiled, it started on the right side of her mouth and spread across to the left. Almost like she resisted the expression on instinct. "You have me in you, too. Not just Dadu's eyes. Nobody ever says you have me in you."

"I know I do," said Sana.

Mamani's smile held. She set her tea down, stood up. "You want cookies? I'm going to get cookies."

Sana got up, embraced Mamani fiercely. Because Mamani only got out cookies on special occasions. Tea was for everyone. Cookies, however, were for brides and new mothers and exceptionally well-behaved children.

And for Sana, when she decided to give Dadu a piece of her mind.

Dadu walked into the house while Sana and Mamani were still embracing. They both quickly jumped back and wiped their eyes with the backs of their hands.

"Guess who came to visit," said Mamani, her voice bright and chipper. She sniffed so lightly Sana barely heard it. "Came to talk to you."

Dadu walked into the room. He held his work bag in one hand and his face had a weary, bone-tired expression. He caught sight of Sana. "Poti."

"Hello, Dadu," said Sana.

Dadu dropped his bag, went around, and clapped a big hand on Sana's shoulder for a moment, then dropped it. "Come. Into my office."

He kept walking, without waiting for another reply. Mamani gave her one of those nods with a little eyebrow motion to hustle Sana out of the room to her grandfather's study. Sana got up and followed him.

It was a bright office, which most people didn't expect. They anticipated heavy wood and dark paneling. Instead the room was open, airy. His chambers at work obviously looked like that, with the dark wood and the leather-bound law volumes. But his office at home had clean, modern lines and elegant furniture. Dadu took a seat behind his desk.

"Sit," he said.

Sana sat. "I'm done, Dadu. I'm done caring about what people think."

"We all have to care what people think, poti."

"No." Sana shook her head. "I care what you think. I care what Mamani thinks. I care what Mama thinks. And I really do care about Rachel's opinion, unfortunately right now."

Here Sana paused, and she watched as Dadu's face formed a grimace that went quickly back to neutral.

Sana went on. "But I am done caring about *people*. A generic people that could judge me at any turn, left, right, and center. And I'm done caring unequivocally what you think. I love you. I respect you. But I can't have you living in my head, judging every decision I make."

"I never wanted that for you."

"But it's what happened, Dadu. It's what happened. I tried so hard to be good. To be a good girl. The daughter you and Mamani did not have. The daughter you wanted. The one who could wipe the slate clean for Mom and make her life easier. The one who grows up and becomes a surgeon and is respectable. The one who is worth the financial investment. But I never made her life easier. And I was never enough, for you or Mamani or for everyone I thought was judging. It was never enough. I was always wondering what people think, wondering what people would say."

Dadu put his head in his hands. "What do you want from me, poti? I did as I knew to be right."

Sana got up. She reached out and put her hand on his shoulder. "I know. I know you did."

When he looked up his eyes were glimmering. Tears. He was holding back tears. "What would you have me do?"

"Something new," said Sana simply.

Dadu took a deep breath. "You have to go to school, poti. You cannot throw your life away. It's my job to prevent that."

She deflated, looked away, toward the door. Maybe coming here had been a mistake. But it was too early to quit. "I've got a deal for you, Dadu."

"A deal?"

"Yes, Dadu. A deal. I go to Princeton next year if you agree to my terms."

"This is not how it works, poti." Dadu's eyebrows furrowed again. "I can send in the deposit."

"You can," said Sana. "And I can not show up to class."

Dadu wiped his hand down his face. "Poti. Please let me put down the deposit."

Sana laughed. "Dadu, I like science. I do. But I want to travel, I want to see the world. There is so much out there right now. So much happening. I want to do something. I want to help. I got into a medical fellowship in Kolkata and I want to go before it's too late and I get on a path and I never get off and then I'm old and suddenly wondering what I did with my life. You chose your path. You chose to make something of yourself in a new and scary place. You say you didn't have a choice, but you did. We always have a choice. You taught me that. Mom taught me that. I want to be able to do that, too."

Dadu shook his head. "I don't like it."

Sana deflated a little. "Then what would you like?"

"No, don't look at me like that. I'm not finished. I don't like it—but I have an idea. You want to take this fellowship? You can. You can work your job in India for the year. Work at that hospital. See if you like it. See if you like the world and see if you like medicine and can treat people who are sick and in need. I can call Nazim Mama and you can stay with them. How would you like that?"

Sana almost sobbed she was so relieved. That's all Sana had ever wanted. Space. Space to think. Space to breathe. Space to travel. "I'd love that, Dadu."

"You would?"

"Of course I would." Sana wrapped her arms around him and gave him the biggest hug she'd ever given anyone. She felt the tears pricking at the backs of her eyes again.

Dadu nodded. "It is your life. I am proud of you, poti. I am proud of the person you have become. I hope you know that."

Sana sniffed. Dadu sniffed. And if either of them cried, well, neither one would have told on the other.

29

Saving Latin

Rachel

Passover was supposed to be a celebration of freedom. The chosen people released from the bonds of slavery. Spared by God and to be finally let go. Kicked out, more like it, was always how Rachel had seen it. And of course, there was the matzo, which everybody complained about but nobody dared not buy. Celebrate freedom, but please eat this bread that tastes like cardboard from one of the special flours, so nobody gets too far above themselves.

Thank God Jeanie always brought matzo ball soup from Factor's for her Passover Seder.

At least, Rachel was thinking that until Jeanie walked up behind her and said, practically shouting into her ear, "Hey, where's that cute girl who was hanging around the diner?"

Jeanie meant Sana. There were no two ways about it.

Rachel grimaced. "How am I supposed to know? She's not Jewish."

"You should have invited her."

Rachel grimaced again. "Probably."

"Oh no. Spill." Jeanie put her hand on her hip and everything.

"I screwed up, Jeanie."

Then Rachel told Jeanie about karaoke and the piercing and the thunderstorm, though not with any real details because *privacy, please*. She told her about the Santa Ana winds and getting into a fight and breaking up before she and Sana had even started anything. She went on and on and Jeanie probably had people to greet and all these duties to perform being the hostess, but Jeanie just stood and listened and nodded and cared and Rachel had never been so relieved in her whole life to tell a whole story from start to finish.

"I messed it all up. I screwed it up before we even had a chance to begin. Maybe I was afraid to ever begin. And now I'll never know. Now it'll be this lingering thing forever."

Jeanie laughed. "I've always loved your sense of melodrama. But let me give you a piece of advice, from my own life and from watching people come in and out of a diner every day for years. The nice thing about life, and not the movies, is that there's no curtains, no *The End*. You can always write your own story. You can always start over and begin again. It doesn't have to make sense or go in a straight line. It happens. You make it happen. And while you don't get a do-over, if you're still alive and stick kickin', you do still have time ahead of you. You never know how much, of course. But time is still ahead of you, no matter how much more you get."

"Thanks, Jeanie," said Rachel.

"Yeah, yeah, you don't believe me. But you will. And when you do, you'll know what I mean."

And then Jeanie was off, yelling at her nephew for putting his elbows on the table like he'd been raised by wolves or something.

Jeanie took over the telling of Passover. She had gotten to the point of the plagues of the lice, which was the part that always turned Rachel's stomach and make her wish that they didn't tell this tale at the dining table. But the table was sacred to the ritual and so she sat listening to the story.

A story handed down, generation to generation. An unbroken and ever-evolving narrative—the lice used to be gnats, after all—carried down generations and across time and around the world. Sometimes Rachel wondered what kind of storyteller she would be if she hadn't been raised in a culture that was so deeply entrenched in narrative and history.

There was a rhythm to it, a finesse. Everybody had their role. Everybody had their place. But of course, it could shift. The fact that Jeanie took over such a central role, rather than any man in the house, was a reminder that the story could change, and the players within them could change, while the central role stayed the same.

Oh. Holy. God.

Rachel shot up. Everyone gave her a look. She was interrupting the Seder. She was breaking a great tradition.

"I'm so, so sorry. So unbelievably sorry." And then, because she couldn't remember which of Jeanie's relatives were actually religious, she tacked on, "I will also later beg forgiveness from God, I promise."

Then she ran from the room.

She had to open up her laptop and look at her film. She had to fix it now. The answer had been in there the whole time—right at the beginning. Fix the opening lines. Have Helen act as the anonymous narrator. Take Douga's notes and cut all her speaking lines while she was on screen until the very last ones. But keep Helen as the voice of the story. Helen as nothing but a face, in the most visual sense. Until those last lines, when the viewer hears that the narrator's voice has been Helen, telling the story the whole time. It had always belonged to her. It had always been her story to tell.

Rachel would have to get this done overnight. She'd have to get in a new file onto the film database before the showcase that Douga had organized. Maybe Douga wouldn't like it. Probably would refuse to show the new file. Rachel would have to go around Douga on this one. See if she could grovel her way into getting Lacey to help her for her screening.

It was a good thing, though, trying to get people to help her in ways they would be reluctant to. After all, Rachel needed to practice her groveling before she talked to Sana. She still wasn't sure how she would get Sana to actually *go* to the screening.

Except Lacey didn't pick up when Rachel called. She'd already tried messaging so the odds of her being screened on this call were high. She wasn't sure what to do. She couldn't fix her edits overnight, set up her room for her screening, and also swap out the versions on Douga's hard drive.

Rachel had one last bid, one last desperate attempt. She started typing on her phone. *Hey I need help*

with what responded Diesel.

Rachel decided to frame this in a way that made it for the most exciting of stories. *Secret mission*

sweeeeeet where to?

Your mission, should you choose to accept it, is to set up all the chairs in the black box theater before my screening tomorrow.

aw man I thought it was gonna be something cool Diesel's disappointment radiated through the message. As though he could frown down at his phone and it would translate all the way across the internet.

You would rather break into Douga's office and swap out versions of the film I'm editing??? Rachel had to stop herself from typing even more question marks.

IS THAT AN OPTION???

Rachel snorted. *Alright, agent of mystery, you wanna pick up a loaded thumb drive tomorrow at 7 am sharp?*

International agent of mystery. Say it again. But with INTERNATIONAL agent of mystery.

DIESEL I NEED YOUR HELP.

I'll wait

*DEAR INTERNATIONAL AGENT OF MYSTERY WILL YOU
MEET ME BEHIND THE TRASH CANS ON THE FAR SIDE OF
CAMPUS*

hell yes I will.

Also I still need help setting up chairs.

fine.

May 1

Deadline

30

You Look Good Wearing My Future

Rachel

Rachel had finished her edits. Somehow she had managed to work through the film and get to a good cut last night. A cut that she could air in public. A final film she was proud of, that took the film where it needed to go. A film that didn't sacrifice art for broad appeal. A film that didn't sacrifice general understanding for the sake of a "capital A for a-hole" kind of Art. She'd passed off the new file to Diesel this morning at seven a.m. sharp. He said he'd get it into the project files in Douga's office. Rachel didn't even want to know how.

He was springy and excited. Probably because she'd promised and delivered on getting him out of his morning English class in order to set up the AV room for tonight. But whatever. She'd done her part, and now he was doing his. The film would be shown in an hour regardless. Maybe it would be an unmitigated disaster. But maybe some disasters were worth trying for.

This one definitely was.

The projector was set up in the middle of the room. The chairs were all lined up in nice, neat rows. Black chairs in a black room. The black box theater was best for screening films. Total darkness except for the light from the projector and the crisp, white screen. The room smelled like paint and freshly cut wood from the last theatrical production that had been done here in early April.

Diesel walked in with two chairs in each arm.

"Don't you think that's too many chairs?" Rachel heard the edge in her voice. It didn't matter how many movies she'd already made, she still got excited when one of her works was going to be aired. Not to mention that she still didn't know if Sana would show.

"Nah," said Diesel. "People can get out of class for a full ninety minutes right at the end of the semester for this. I think you'll be overrun. Even if they only want a nap."

Then Diesel laughed like that was a hilarious joke to tell a filmmaker.

"Thanks, dude." Rachel grabbed a chair out of Diesel's hands and set it down harder than strictly necessary.

"Anytime, Recht." Diesel saluted. It was so embarrassing. "International agent of mystery, at your service."

Rachel half sighed, half snorted. "Thank you so much, for real. I couldn't have done the file swap and all this setup without you."

"Does this mean that I can finally tell people that we're friends?" Diesel looked so hopeful, so earnest, that Rachel had to suppress a laugh.

"Yeah, Diesel. You can tell them."

Diesel grinned. "You ready? It's almost time."

"As ready as I'll ever be." Rachel nodded with as much confidence as she could muster.

God, she hoped Sana showed up.

"Why are you making me go to this again?" Sana was being dragged toward the black box theater by Diesel. At least she'd been able to take off her boot today. Her ankle felt weak, but not injured.

"Because you have to see the finished project," said Diesel.

"That doesn't make sense. I know what the finished product is. It makes me look like a spoiled brat."

Diesel gave one last tug and they were at the door. "Give it a chance."

"Fine," said Sana.

Diesel grabbed a seat off to the side, but right up front.

Great.

The rest of the theater was filling up. Everyone, it seemed, wanted to get out of class early today.

After a couple of minutes Rachel came to the front of the room, dressed in dark jeans, a clean white tee. She held a mic in one hand and had half a smile pulling across her face. It hurt to look at her—she was confident and radiant and in charge of the whole room—but pride wouldn't let Sana look away.

"Hi, everyone," said Rachel. "Thank you so much for being here. I know half of you are trying to get out of class and the other half just really need a nap before finals week starts."

That got a laugh out of the crowd.

"But I've been working on this project for a year. Should have only been six months, but I needed an extension and luckily Douga was more than willing to give me one." This was said with a tip of the head toward the teacher.

Douga nodded back, giving a small hand motion to allow Rachel to proceed.

"As many of you know, I was lost during this project. I couldn't find direction. I got help from one of the most unlikely of places." Rachel's eyes flickered over to Sana. But they went back to the center of the crowd. "But before I get carried away with that, I think you should just watch the film. Roll it, please."

And then the lights in the theater went out and Rachel made it to her seat off to the side and the movie began to play.

Sana tensed as the credits rolled.

And that's when her own voice came in.

Rachel had made her the narrator.

Made her Helen the narrator. It was embarrassing. It was mesmerizing.

It was perfect. No, not perfect. Complicated and messy. *Dynamic.*

Her silent, picture-perfect Helen made sense now. She wasn't a prop for prop's sake. She was Helen as the male gaze had always seen her—every man's Helen. But Sana knew that it was her own voice telling the story, even if the audience didn't know yet. Even if they thought the story was Cassandra's or another one of the Trojan princesses'. Even if they thought Sana's voice was just a nod to the Greek chorus.

It was hers.

Rachel had fixed it.

Rachel had *listened*.

Sana didn't have words for that. A sense of calm washed over her. Sana hadn't made art before. Hadn't felt the need. And maybe she wouldn't make art again. But watching what form her idea had taken—in this final version of the film—that was just like being thrown up into the air. Except, instead of forgetting herself, she felt rooted in what she had done, what she was doing.

And then the moment hit in the film where Sana finally said her first line—despite being seen on screen over and over again throughout the film—and Sana got to hear a couple members of the audience gasp. It wasn't everyone, but still, to get anyone to gasp in a film was something. Satisfaction straightened Sana's spine.

Sana looked over to Douga for a moment. She looked equal parts displeased and proud. Her eyes were narrowed but her mouth ticked up on one side like she'd just told herself a good joke that she couldn't share with anyone else.

The film ended and the lights went back up and Rachel stood at the front of the room like she was ready to give a speech.

But Sana had a question. Her hand shot up. "Excuse me."

Rachel looked flustered for a moment. She fumbled with the mic a bit, but then caught hold of it. "Yes—I mean, I'm taking questions in just a minute."

"I have one now." Sana kept up her hand. "Why did you make Helen of Troy your narrator?"

A smile pulled at Rachel's mouth. "Because someone else had shown me a good vision and I'd been a fool to pass it up the first time."

"I see. So you didn't just change the perspective to Helen because that was better?"

Rachel sighed. "Why do you have to fight me on everything?"

"Why do you have to insist on being wrong all the time?"

"Because if I weren't wrong all the time, I'd never have written a story about you. And then I'd never have run into you on the field and I'd never have broken my camera equipment, never been forced to work with you against my will."

"You're really selling this, by the way." Sana got up and gestured to the crowd in the auditorium.

Everyone was watching the exchange like it was better than theater. Better than movies. Better than streaming.

And maybe it was.

Rachel reached out, grabbed Sana's hands. But Sana didn't snatch them away.

"I always thought I hated you. But it wasn't that. It was just that I love you and I couldn't see it."

Now the audience really did gasp. Sana's jaw hung open.

"Please say something," said Rachel.

"Did you just say you love me?"

Rachel cringed but she didn't back down. "I did."

"Why?"

"I honestly don't know right now. But it's still true."

Sana blinked. "I just went down to Orange County to talk to my grandfather about the future and I told him I wanted to see the world and travel and be a part of what was happening. I want to help people. I'm taking the fellowship."

"Oh," said Rachel, clearly not knowing what to do in front of a room full of so many people.

"Would you . . ." Sana cleared her throat. "Would you be willing to wait? It'll most likely be a year."

"Wait a whole year?" Then Rachel smiled. It started at the right edge of her lips and then curled all the way around to the other side. "Sana Khan, you are awfully full of yourself."

"I know." Sana took a step closer. "I promise not to start a war, if that helps."

"I can't say I'd blame you if you did." Rachel reached out, threaded her fingers through Sana's ponytail.

"Then what do you want?" Sana's breaths were coming in rapidly, but with a lightness that she'd never experienced before. There was no lingering, awful tension. Just hope, threading through her. Just the sensation that the best had yet to come.

"I want you to tell me how you really feel."

"Oh," said Sana. "That's easy. I love you."

Rachel's smile transformed into a grin. It was a real honest-to-God grin. The kind you only saw in old movies, where the driver never looked at the road and only looked at the girl while they were driving. It made Sana breathless, that grin. Made her think anything was possible.

Sana reached out, took Rachel by her free hand. Rachel interlaced her fingers with Sana's, until the hold felt steady and intertwined. It was a little terrifying, not knowing what came next. It was strange to look into the future and only see possibilities and not certainties.

Sana was starting to like it better that way. She'd have to find her own answers. She'd have to make her own endings. Sana tugged on Rachel's hand and leaned into her.

And Sana couldn't have told you what happened after that, because her lips were on Rachel Recht's and she just melted into the moment because the story finally belonged to her and Rachel and nobody else.

Acknowledgments

Years ago, I was listening to Eve's "Let Me Blow Ya Mind" for the first time and I asked why Eve rapped about "sophomore, I ain't scared, one of a kind." I didn't understand the lyrics. I didn't get the sentiment. What I learned was that second albums cause creators and musicians a good deal of stress and frustration. It's called sophomore panic. Or in the book world, book two blues. Annette Sutton was kind enough to explain what sophomore panic was because she's been there to answer many of my questions throughout my life and offer her generous support. Thank you, Annette. You've always been there for an overly curious kid.

But back to the sophomore panic. It didn't make much sense in my childhood. "Just make the next thing," my childhood self would say. I had no idea. When my own sophomore panic hit—it hit hard and it hit furious and luckily I knew it was a real artistic phenomenon. I was humbled, but I was not surprised.

Second books—second albums, second movies, second anything—are like that. You worry if anything can come next, after the sheer amount of work that went into the first book. And I could not have gotten through my second book without the following people guiding me along the way and helping me channel Eve's batshit levels of confidence and swagger.

To my editor, Kat, who has this ability to pull the best books out of me. I've learned so much from working through your edits, and it fills my heart with so much gratitude that I've gotten to work on you with not one but two books. Thank you for everything you've given this book, and thank you for everything you've given and taught me. You are a queen among queens.

To my agent, Lauren, who has believed in every idea I have thrown at her—including when I said I wanted to write an enemies-to-lovers rom-com with a cheerleader and a film nerd, inspired by my love of the Paris Geller and Rory Gilmore ship. You catch every movie reference that I make—even the truly niche ones—and your support means the world. Thank you for helping Sana and Rachel find their home.

To my publicist, Morgan Rath, who has hustled and supported both of my book babies. Thank you for your tireless efforts on behalf of my work. I see what you do and I wish there were a better phrase other than thank you. An enormous thank you goes to the entire team at Feiwel and Friends/Macmillan: Kim Waymer, Jean Feiwel, Alexei Esikoff, Jessica White, and Emily Heddleson.

To everyone who worked on this bananas beautiful cover—Liz Dresner, Michael Frost, and Tanya Frost—y'all gave me a beautiful debut cover and then you topped that gorgeousness with this stunner. I wish I could insert the gif of Lorelai Gilmore singing "Did you ever know you were my hero?" into actual print. Also thank you to the amazing cover models: Yassi Shafaie and Danae Muratore. You are Rachel and Sana come to life.

To my agency siblings, Jodi and Valerie, who read drafts and pieces of drafts at key moments during this process. Thank you for being the agency family I have always dreamed of. Also thanks for having really adorable pets.

To the BV Crew, who were there to put in writing sprints and to talk about frustrations and drafting woes—Maux, Sarah, Zan, Diya, Morgan, and Elissa. Also, thanks as well to most of y'all for punching shit with me and being willing to let me throw a few punches your way. There's nobody I'd rather be hit in the face by, except maybe Laurel.

Shout out to Diya, for letting me pick her brain, re: actual internships that Sana could apply for and for sending me photos of her crying face after she read a draft.

To the LA Electrics—Bree, Bridget, Britta, Dana, Emily, Austin, Farrah, Lisa, Marie, and Maura—thank you for getting me through the wildness that is debut year. To the Electrics I've met through the internet—Somaiya, Ash, Rachel, Tanaz—thanks for letting me slide into the DMs and talk about Victoriana or how cute your pets are. You're all a f*cking delight.

Thank you to Strong Sports Gym for giving me the ability to fight when all felt lost.

And as always, thank you to Steven, who didn't let me quit no matter how much I complained. You're the best cheerleader on planet Earth. Also, you get to read this one as an actual book this time, rather than as a series of panicked Word drafts in your inbox. Grow from love. You still deserve all the maple-glazed donuts that the universe is willing to send your way.

And thank you to the city of Los Angeles, for always being there when I needed you. I hope I never stop driving through your wide boulevards at night, searching.